KNIGH

ACE

KNIGHT'S ACRE

Norah Lofts

DOUBLEDAY & COMPANY, INC.
GARDEN CITY, NEW YORK
1975

Library of Congress Cataloging in Publication Data

Lofts, Norah Robinson, 1904–
    Knight's Acre.

    I. Title.
PZ3.L825Kn3   [PR6023.035]   823'.9'12
ISBN 0-385-03551-9
Library of Congress Catalog Card Number 74–5918

KNIGHT'S ACRE

ONE

WHEN SIR GODFREY TALLBOYS decided to build his house he was thirty-five years old and at the very peak of his career as knight errant. The year 1451, still only eight months old, had been a wonderful one for him. He was not only acknowledged as the premier knight in England, he was for once clear of debt and had a hundred pounds in hand. The Michaelmas and Christmas tournaments were still to come. Now, if ever, he could give his sweet Sybilla the thing she had long craved for—a house of her own.

He was a man of action, not of thought. He lived for the moment, seldom looking backward—and then only to pleasant things—and even less seldom taking thought for tomorrow. But he accepted, as he accepted everything else associated with his way of life, that the day would come when his eyes would lose keenness, his arms their strength and then he would need a place to which to retire, a wall upon which to hang his armour, and some pasture for Arcol, his great horse. However, when he thought of that day, it always seemed far distant: eight, ten years. He would not have considered building when he did had it not been for Sybilla and the children.

Not that she nagged. A sweeter, more amenable woman never lived, but ever since the birth of Henry, who was now six years old, she had been saying that it would be pleasant to have a home of her own. And in the past eighteen months or so she had drawn his attention to a fact which he—unobservant outside his trade—would not have noticed; the Tallboys family was increasingly unwelcome.

She said, cool and tolerant, as was her way:

1

"It is understandable . . ." She listed the places where she and the children stayed while he rode in tournaments or went to take part in one of the recurrent wars between rival nobles, or against the Scots or the Welsh.

At Moyidan in Suffolk which Sir Godfrey's brother James had inherited, being the first-born, there were two children; a girl, sturdy but remarkably lacking in beauty and grace; and a boy weakly of body and dull of mind. No fond father and mother could help contrasting their offspring with Henry, big and handsome and precocious, and Richard, a bare year younger and so forward that he might almost have been Henry's twin. And look at Margaret, an angel child, so very pretty, three years old; and John, now a year old, again big, handsome, and forward.

Sybilla well understood why they were no longer warmly welcomed at Moyidan.

At Beauclaire, where Godfrey's pretty sister Alys ruled as Lady Astallon, there was less cause for that kind of envy. Lady Astallon had produced a son, handsome and lively, and a daughter, very pretty. But Beauclaire was a huge and complicated place and Lady Astallon had waiting ladies who took sides when Henry and Richard squabbled, as they did interminably.

The third family house—that of Godfrey's second brother, who like many second sons had gone into the Church—was at Bywater, where William Tallboys was Bishop, a most estimable man, given to good works, immensely hospitable. But he kept such a bad table, and children, growing and active, needed food. In her cool, reasonable way Sybilla had said, "We cannot stay with William again. The boys were hungry all the time, and when I went into the kitchen that sloven who calls herself housekeeper ordered me away, most rudely."

It was plain, even to Sir Godfrey, that a house of her own was Sybilla's necessity as well as her right.

"I will ride to Intake tomorrow and put the building in hand," he said.

The choice of place was obvious. Sir Godfrey was not, like many younger sons, a landless knight. In this, as in so many other ways, he had been singularly fortunate.

"It need not be a large house. Or grand," Sybilla said. She

knew that when he had money he was inclined to be free with it. "We shall not be able to afford a large household. A hall to live in, a kitchen, and four bedchambers will be enough."

He knew many women who would have wished to choose their own site, give their own orders to the builder, but that was not her way.

In the morning she rose early to see him off, as she always did, even when his errand was peaceful and his absence to be brief. As his horse's feet rang hollow on the drawbridge—they were spending the summer at Beauclaire—she called after him: "My love, let it not be damp."

Intake was rather less than five miles from the family manor at Moyidan and when, on the second day, Sir Godfrey arrived just as dinner was being served, his brother Sir James and his wife Emma groaned inwardly, thinking that he had ridden ahead and that somewhere behind him on the road was a wagon bringing Sybilla and her brood, and behind them his squire, Eustace, and that great horse Arcol who must have corn every day.

Their obvious relief when he said that he was alone, showed even Sir Godfrey that Sybilla had not been imagining the lack of warmth in recent welcomes; and when they heard that his purpose was to choose a site and build a house they became positively joyful. What a wise decision! Children needed a settled home. Sybilla would relish a place of her own.

"The harvest will be in by the week's end if the weather holds," Sir James said. "I will lend you six or seven of my fellows to help with the building."

The institution of serfdom was dying out, but the lord of the manor of Moyidan still had some tenants who paid for their strips of land in the great open fields by tending his as well, and by doing at all times anything they were told.

"That would be kind. And what builder would you commend?"

"Hobson of Baildon," James said without hesitation. "He made an excellent job of our new barn. I'll send a boy in to tell him to meet you there, first thing tomorrow morning."

Anything to speed on the work. Let the house be finished by Christmas!

3

Intake lay, shaped like a dish, embraced on one side by the river Wren and on three by Layer Wood. It was not a manor—it never had been; it was, as its name implied, intake land, snatched from the forest. Sir Godfrey's great-grandfather had had a surplus of serfs at Moyidan, some of them a bit discontented, and one day he had told them that any man who liked to go and hew himself a field, build himself a hovel, was free to go and do so. They could live rent free for five years; after that they would pay ten shillings a year.

A number of men had taken advantage of this offer. The strongest and most determined had survived. Intake now consisted of eight small enclosed farms, each tenant still paying ten shillings a year. Much less in purchasing power than it had been in the old man's time, but fixed in some obscure legal way. And in any case, four pounds a year was spending money for a family who ate at other people's tables and slept in other people's beds. And though Sir Godfrey was careless, inclined to lend and to spend, Sybilla was thrifty and very clever at refurbishing old gowns and headdresses, so that she was always abreast of the latest fashion at small cost.

On this hot August morning—the weather was holding—Master Hobson was waiting; his rather sorry-looking horse tied to a tree. He was a prosperous man and could well have afforded a better mount, but he was cautious; if you *looked* prosperous, people thought they had been overcharged. He kept a good table, had money saved, and his wife had the silk gown of every respectable woman's ambition, but it was never worn outside her own house.

He greeted Sir Godfrey with happy servility. This would be a good job, and the money was certain. Before he dismounted Sir Godfrey looked out over his village, seeing, in his single-minded way, nothing but potential sites. There seemed to be unoccupied land near the river, but he remembered Sybilla's last words and turned his attention to a space that lay between the edge of the village common and the fringe of the wood. It had been a farm once and was now covered with light, secondary growth, self-sown saplings, brambles, bracken, and gay wildflowers. The ruins of the original clod-built farmhouse could still be seen. A good spot, he thought, well away from the river. The oak tree would be a bit of a drawback.

4

It stood almost in the centre of the site, Layer Wood's last outpost. It had been a well-grown tree when the Normans landed at Hastings, and by the time the first settlers came to Intake it offered more of an obstacle than they could tackle.

Master Hobson looked about with an experienced, calculating eye. The ruined farmhouse would make a shelter for his workmen and save the building of the lodge which was the rule when they were employed beyond walking distance of their homes. He could also see a use for the huge tree.

He gave no sign of satisfaction. It was a sound rule to make any job sound as difficult as possible.

"Take a bit of clearing, sir." He sounded gloomy.

Sir Godfrey looked rather helpless. He was out of his depths. If the wood had been full of Welsh archers, or the undergrowth crawling with Scottish reivers, he would have known what to do; but the decision of whether to build to the left or to the right of the great tree was a difficult one. The site seemed to demand that the house should be in the centre, and this was impossible because of the tree. Not that it mattered; there was plenty of room on either side.

The builder, now applying another sound rule, became helpful.

"We could use that tree, sir. Centre the house round it, like. Spare planting a king post. Good branches, too. Left and right. Beams."

"You couldn't have a tree growing in the middle of a house."

"It wouldn't be *growing*. Not with its top lopped and all the bark off, and its roots under the floor."

Sir Godfrey tried, and failed, to visualise this, and said dubiously, "I suppose you know best. But . . ." There was a word he wanted, it eluded him for a second or two as words so often did; a word used of men as well as of wood. "Seasoned! I thought timber had to be seasoned."

"Thass right, sir. For planking, panelling and such, anything likely to *warp*. Not a thing this size." Hobson regarded the tree with covert approval; the time it would save; not only as a king pin, but with the staircase, if Sir Godfrey wanted—as so many people did these days—to have his house on two floors. The inner side of the staircase could be fixed into the great trunk for at least half the way.

5

Aloud he said, "It'd take a bit of contriving. But it could be done. Now, what size of place was you thinking of, sir?"

"Not large. A hall, a kitchen, and four sleeping chambers." That was what Sybilla had told him. But he had been thinking. Sybilla had been so patient, had waited so long, the place should be worthy of her. He said recklessly, "And a solar, and a still room. And a stool room."

Sybilla deserved a solar, a place to which a lady could withdraw from the hurly-burly of life in the hall; she deserved a still room too, for often enough he had embraced her and said, "You smell very sweet," and she had said, "I have been helping in the still room." The stool room was definitely an extravagance.

In most castles human needs were catered for by places called garderobes, so called because the smell of them was supposed to deter moths, so that furs and woollen clothes hung in them were protected. There was a stone seat—very cold in winter—and a hole; the excreta made a dark, slimy track down the outside wall to end in the moat. In summer not too unsightly, for ferns and other plants took shallow root and flourished.

However, at Beauclaire more civilised custom had taken over; copper pots set in velvet-covered stools.

Why should Sybilla be less comfortable in her own house than she had been in Beauclaire?

Master Hobson approved the order which meant building an extra room; the principle he deplored. Outside the house was the place for *that;* at some distance from the house, screened by a few bushes and emptied not less than once a month. Still, grand gentleman had their own ways.

"Now, as to the outside. In what style?"

"I had thought . . . something like the new part of Moyidan."

It was new in that it had been added, by his enterprising great-grandfather, to the haunch of the cold, draughty castle. But it had already been old when Sir Godfrey knew it, his home, from which at nine years of age he had been torn away and sent to join the pages at Beauclaire. He would now have denied, and believed it, that he had ever been homesick, or felt ill-done-by. Those first wretched weeks had been the be-

6

ginning of his very successful career; page, squire, knight. But something in him remembered, not the bad, because he had a happy nature, the good; and amongst the good was the face of his birthplace.

"Half timbered," Master Hobson said. "With pargetting?"

An unfamiliar word.

"What is that?"

"A way of working plaster, sir. Very pretty."

It was an art and Master Hobson's son-in-law was an expert at it. Pargetting had become the fashion as timber became harder and harder to obtain, and the width of plaster between the outer beams widened. Master Hobson did not much like his son-in-law, a sour, scornful young man. A rebel, too. But he was a good plasterer, where plain work was concerned, and his other fancy stuff, the pargetting, was much admired.

For Sybilla the best! Sir Godfrey agreed to the pargetting. Then, most crucial of all, there was the question of time.

"When can it be ready?"

Master Hobson had another rule; faced with a downright question, say "Ahh." Long drawn out, giving you time to think.

"Ahh. A bit hard to say, sir. Dependent on the weather. You can't plaster in a frost. Better leave that. But we'll waste no time. Of that you may be sure, sir."

Never give a positive date. If you did, and exceeded it by so little as a day, all you had was complaints; and if luck and weather and all else favoured you and the job was done before the given time, customers expected a bit off the price.

"I'll get along now, sir, and draw up a bit of a plan. And let you have it—at Moyidan, sir?"

"No need," Sir Godfrey said. He was back on his own ground. He had laid out camps in his time. "We can settle it now."

He took up a twig and with a sure, steady hand drew in the dust under the old oak. Hall and solar at the front. Kitchen just behind the hall—he and Sybilla had spent such a long time in places where food grew cold between cooking place and table. Behind the solar the still room. Neat and foursquare. Upstairs the same.

Then he drew an oblong which completed but did not enclose the shape made by the house with its two back-jutting wings. Stables tended to attract flies.

"And the stables here," he said.

"Very clear, sir," Master Hobson said.

The most vital thing—the price—had not yet been mentioned.

"And what would be the cost?" Sir Godfrey asked.

"Aah." The hesitation was perfunctory, for there again Master Hobson knew the rules. Where a price was concerned it was simple—extract the last possible penny.

"Solar, still room, stool room *and* stables," he said thoughtfully, carefully naming the extras. "A bit hard to say, sir, and a bit dependent on the weather. I'd say—a bit of a guess, sir, and I could be wronging myself—a hundred and ten. Pounds."

He waited for the expostulations. They did not come. Sir Godfrey said, "Yes. I could manage that." He would have won ten pounds in prize money, or their worth in prizes, by the time the building was completed.

"Oh, one thing I forgot to mention. My brother of Moyidan has promised to lend six or seven men to speed the work."

A curious expression came into Master Hobson's shrewd little eyes.

"Aah. I'm taking it they'd be craftsmen, sir."

Sir Godfrey looked puzzled. Hobson went on:

"Guild members? Carpenters? Masons?" He knew the answer to that!

"Why no. Just ordinary men. As soon as the harvest is in."

"They might be useful, clearing the ground and so forth. Fetching and carrying. But they couldn't build, sir, not less they'd done their prentice time and joined the guild. None of my men'd work along unskilled chaps."

And why indeed should they? Craftsmen spent from eight to twelve years as apprentices, unpaid and often overworked; then they qualified as journeymen, paid by the day; finally, if they were good enough, they were taken into the guild of their particular trade and sworn to observe its standards and its rules and regulations. And how would *you* like it, Hobson thought, if you was called on to play about in a tournament with a lot of chaps straight from the plough tail?

"I see. I didn't realise," Sir Godfrey said. There were millions

8

of things in the world about him that he did not realise. He was single-minded, unobservant, illiterate and all his life had been part of a system designed to make him exactly what he was—a first-class fighting machine.

"Thass how it is, sir," the builder said, and waited politely for the word of dismissal.

"That'll be all, then. And try to have it done by Christmas . . ."

Making no promises, Master Hobson mounted his old nag and plodded away.

Sir Godfrey stood for a moment and looked out over the little village, this time with a more seeing eye. Smoke rose from the smoke holes of the little low houses, and the fields were lively; men, women, and children scything, stooking, gleaning. On this bright day the river looked like half a silver necklace. In the woods behind him doves called softly.

He indulged in a rare, far-forward-looking thought. Quiet old age in his own solid house. He thought: I could be happy here . . .

"The man is a rogue! One hundred and ten pounds! And you agreed! Didn't you realise that he meant ninety and expected you to beat him down?" Exasperation rendered Sir James almost incoherent. He cursed his gout which had prevented him riding to Intake and putting some sense into Hobson. He blamed himself for not asking the builder to come here, in the first place.

The fact was that, in all concerned with ordinary living, Godfrey was a witless fool. Charming, of course, everybody liked him, but he had no sense. Like a child in a world of men, and like a child, headstrong and stubborn. Look at his marriage!

Look at his marriage, indeed.

For a poor knight—but famous, handsome, popular, and well connected—a good marriage had seemed to be a matter of course. There were hundreds of heiresses in England; so many families seemed to have lost the trick of breeding boys, the great Earl of Warwick had only two daughters. And Godfrey moved in the right circles. For years all the family, except unworldly William, had been finding and displaying likely

9

young women. Godfrey had remained single until he was twenty-eight and then gone and fallen in love with a sixteen-year-old orphan without a penny. The family grieved over such reckless improvidence, and one member of it never forgave him. That was his sister Mary, the clever, dominating Abbess of Lamarsh, who had had charge of Sybilla Fitzherbert since she was orphaned at the age of two. The Abbess had seen in the girl some quality, seldom apparent to others, and had convinced herself that if only the girl could be persuaded, or forced into the right mould, she would make a splendid successor to herself. Sybilla Fitzherbert was very clever; she could learn anything—reading, writing, needlework, domestic skills, work in the infirmary. She would, when the time came, be fit to govern. All she lacked was a sense of vocation; and the very frankness with which she denied having any simply added to the Abbess' certainty that here was a young woman of unusual promise. God would recognise it . . .

All ruined! A whole edifice of hope and endeavour brought crashing down because that stupid Godfrey looked in to pay his respects to his sister and saw Sybilla. It was enough to make angels weep.

Apart from the Abbess, and a few disappointed ladies, everybody soon accepted this most unfortunate marriage, and most people liked Sybilla, modest, tactful, helpful, so devoted to her husband that she constituted no threat where other men were concerned.

Sybilla's attitude towards Sir Godfrey was tinged with a kind of adoration. He had come to her rescue; he was her saviour and if she lived to be sixty she knew that she could not possibly express her gratitude to him. When she thought of the cold cloister, of the essentially lonely life that every nun lived while seeming to be part of a community, she was so grateful that the idea of criticising anything he said or did, any arrangement he made, or failed to make, was utterly unthinkable. She was no fool and the Abbess' training had already shaped her judgement; there were times when she saw Godfrey Tallboys as feckless, extravagant, easily imposed upon, unobservant, and insensitive, but such clearsighted moments made no difference: she loved even his faults. And one of the reasons

10

why she ruled her two naughty boys so badly was that they were his, and so like him as he must have been before the discipline of life tamed him to some extent. To Henry, to Richard would come all too soon the cuffs and the beatings, the rules and the rebukes; but they would come from other hands and from other voices.

At Moyidan, Sir James said, trying to make the best of a bad job: "Well, my summer gout ends next month." He suffered two kinds; one in hot weather—June to September—one in cold—November to March. "And I will ride over to Intake and see what Hobson is about. Builders have a bad habit nowadays of getting one job under way and then taking on another, playing put and take. But I assure you, Godfrey, if I find any slackness, I'll light a fire under Master Hobson. A hundred and ten pounds! Have you got it?" The question was an afterthought.

"A hundred. I thought that might be enough. I've never built a house before," Godfrey said. That was the kind of thing that was so endearing about him, a kind of downright simplicity.

"But I'll get some more. There is talk of a war on the Welsh border. It might pay better than tourneys. Would you be so kind, James, as to take charge of this?" He tumbled his money out. He had had a vague idea that a hundred pounds would build a house and partly furnish it. Apparently he had been wrong.

Sir James said that he would gladly take charge of the money and pay Hobson in stages. And he would see that the house was ready by Christmas. It would be, if he had anything to do with it.

And Emma, no less eager to see Sybilla in her own house for Christmas, said, "I am sure, Godfrey, that I can help with the furnishing. I will look to it."

"That is extremely kind," Sir Godfrey said. He rode happily back to Beauclaire to report the success of his mission.

11

TWO

IN NO TIME AT ALL, it seemed, she was seeing him off again, this time to war. Such partings were always heart-wrenching, but she had learned self-control in the convent and from experience the need for keeping a cheerful face and manner. Once, soon after their marriage, he had gone to fight on the Scottish border and she had cried and cried. He had been greatly distressed and said, "Sweetheart, you knew when you married me that I was not a shoemaker plying his trade at home." He had also explained to her that for a knight who knew his business, who was well armoured and well mounted, the risk of death in battle was small. "Plainly, a knight is worth more alive than dead. Think of the ransom!"

So now as he was about to leave—this time for Wales—she reminded herself that his armour was good, Arcol, his warhorse, an exceptional animal, so extremely well trained that his price had kept them poor for two years. He was also lucky in his squire, a distant Tallboys cousin and completely devoted. Any hardships of the campaign would be mitigated for Godfrey by Eustace, who could shove and kick with the best, and was not above a little cheating at times.

Godfrey himself was in high spirits, certain of returning much enriched. There would be loot and ransom money. "All these Welsh chieftains call themselves princes; and any I take will pay a prince's ransom," he said. "Then we can furnish our house fittingly."

One thing worried him; the house might be completed while he was still away. "In which case you would be advised to remain here until my return. Or, if you wish to move, with borrowed furnishings, you will have Walter."

12

"Oh yes," she said, "I have Walter."

Walter was God's gift to an impoverished young couple. Five years earlier when they were in Dover, about to move on to Richborough, he had approached Godfrey and said that he wished to be their servingman. Godfrey had explained that, useful as such a man might be, they were in no position to afford one. Walter said:

"I'm not looking for a wage. I have a pension of fourpence a week. If needs be I can provide my own provender."

To such an unlikely tale the natural, sadly human reaction was suspicion. The man could be a serf running away from his manor, or a criminal; and a peripatetic yet respectable, family like that of the Tallboys would provide perfect cover. And neither Walter's appearance nor his manner offered much assurance. His clothes were noticeably neat and of good quality, but his face was scarred in such a way that it wore a perpetual sneer, and his manner was offhand, almost arrogant.

Yet everything he said about himself proved, on inquiry, to be true. He was a freeman born—his name was Freeman. A younger son with no hope of inheritance, he had gone, as an archer, to the French wars with Lord Bowdegrave of Abhurst, and when Lord Bowdegrave was unhorsed stood over him; hence the scar, hence the pension.

Why such a man, of independent means and markedly unservile nature, should wish to serve them remained a mystery. Sybilla had a rather romantic explanation; Godfrey had done so well in the Dover Tournament, any old soldier, looking for a new master, and with pay no object, might well have fastened upon him. Godfrey, very modest over most things, said that old soldiers liked to be on the move. Most of those now tramping, hobbling, limping about the roads of England would have fared better, he said, had they stayed in one place where they had relatives or friends. But the habit of movement was so ingrained . . .

So Walter joined them and not only served them well but saw that others did. In the vast, ill-organised households of the time, there was a system of "vails," presents given to servants. Those unable or unwilling to give substantial vails were remembered and when they came again, ill served. Servants, from high to low, were in connivance and a bad vail meant, next time, inferior accommodation and neglectful service at table. Walter would not accept what Sybilla had taken for granted and Godfrey never noticed. "This will not do for my lady." And there was something about him, his size, his assurance, his sneer that made other servants give way. Nor was he an easy target for retaliation; more often than not, with his family installed and everybody properly intimidated, he would take himself off to eat, drink, sleep at the most convenient inn.

In other ways he served Sybilla and Godfrey well. He had the sharpest eye for a bargain ever known. His expression was, "I happened on it." His happenings were always timely and ranged from a roll of blue-green silk, slightly scorched by a fire which had put a mercer out of business, to a mount for Eustace, a four-year-old horse in tiptop condition which he had happened on in Winchester. And paid, he said, knacker's price for.

That bargain could hardly be accepted without question, horse stealing being a capital offence.

"Like I say," Walter said. "There's this man, leading a horse and howling like a baby. I asked what ailed him and he said his master was just dead and had left orders for the horse to be destroyed. And he'd looked after it since it was foaled and couldn't bear to take it in to the knacker's yard, but must, dead men's wishes being law. So then . . ." Walter hesitated a second. "Well, I said I was the knacker—at least his nephew, come to help him. I reckoned the real one might be known by sight. The fellow was only too glad to take the hoof-and-hide money and spare himself a nasty job. So I took the halter. You can tell a knacker's by the smell. We went in, waited a bit, and came out."

Inquiries corroborated this fantastic tale. A rich old wool merchant had just died, leaving all his money to the Church and ordering his horse to be destroyed.

With his usual courtesy Sir Godfrey apologised to Walter for seeming, even for a moment, to doubt his word. Walter said:

"I've been thinking. It'd be worth-while for somebody to nip along and ask about the harness. There might be a bargain there. It'd likely be better than yours."

After that Walter's bargains were accepted unquestioningly. So were his loyalty, devotion, and ability. Sir Godfrey, riding

14

off to join Lord Malvern's punitive expedition, knew that he was leaving Sybilla in safe hands.

Sir James kept his word. In his gout-free autumn, September and October, he rode to Intake almost every other day, acting and sounding like a dog dealing with a flock of laggard sheep. He started the campaign with the most acrimonious reproaches about overcharging and did not withdraw them when he realised that the price included solar, still room, and stool room, though he and Emma exchanged some sharp comments upon this latest proof of Godfrey's stupidity and extravagance. Master Hobson accepted the rebukes in the proper respectful manner, but took leave to point out that things had altered a bit since he last did a job for Sir James. Apprentices now demanded meat three times a week and day worker's wages had risen by a ha'penny a week; in fact, if bad weather set in and this job wasn't completed by Christmas, he'd be out of pocket.

Sir James went on nagging; why this, why that, why the other thing? If on any visit he did not see Master Hobson's ancient grey mare tethered in her usual place, he would bark, "Where's your master?" and proceed to track the rascal down. On one memorable occasion he found the builder measuring up and preparing to give an estimate for another job. His rage so frightened the would-be client that he withdrew his order.

Sir James did not accept as easily as Sir Godfrey had done the explanation for the comparative uselessness of the men he had lent. They had cleared the ground, done a lot of work on the digging of foundations, they carried stuff, but they were not, in their master's opinion, fully occupied.

"God's blood!" he exploded, one day early in October, "they could do the stables and outbuildings. No skill needed there. Set them to work, man! Make use of them!" In another, craftier, calmer mood he asked, "Is there a guild of well diggers, Hobson?" Master Hobson was obliged to confess that if such a thing existed he had never heard of it. "Then set my fellows to work on a well."

The harassing tactics were effective; the house grew apace. It acquired its name. All those early settlers, suddenly emancipated, frenziedly trying to clear land and make a living on a subsistence level had been very conscious of the word *acre*.

15

Most of the little farms, though now wider than an acre, were known by the names of their makers. Robin's Acre, Martin's Acre, Will's Acre. It was inevitable that Sir Godfrey's growing house should be known as Knight's Acre.

Coming up, echoing from an ever farther past was something which nobody now, in the middle of the fifteenth century, was fully prepared to admit to, a superstition older than memory. Nothing to do with the cheerful custom of putting a green bough on the highest point of a new building, with a bit of ribbon maybe, and somebody saying, "God Bless This House." Nothing to do with the equally cheerful custom of spilling a little wine or ale on the newly set doorstep in order to make sure that plenty would be the rule here. Old customs died hard and they died patchily. Master Hobson, a bit of a sceptic, was fully prepared to fix a bough, spill a drop of ale, because, like almost everyone else who had come in close contact with him, he had liked Sir Godfrey.

About the other ritual Master Hobson was not so sure. And when he was not sure he said to himself, "Aah . . ." and waited. Wait; see how things went, see how the men felt.

Early in November, Sir James's winter gout set in, exacerbating his temper but not preventing him from doing his duty, though he reduced his visits to two in a week. On a day when early mist gave way to a curious and beautiful luminosity, he arrived at Intake. The grey mare was not there, and to his critical eye the thatching seemed to have made little progress since his last visit. At the front of the house there was a young man on a ladder, doing something very peculiar. The space between the upright beams had been plastered for at least a fortnight, well ahead of the onset of frost; yet this young man had a bucket of plaster slung from the rung of the ladder. He dipped into it, spread it on the space between two of the upper windows, smoothed and pressed it with his hands and then applied to it what looked like a thick wooden dish. He wiped around the dish very carefully, flicking bits of exuding plaster away, and waited, and then withdrew the dish, surveying what was revealed with smug satisfaction.

Sir James shouted, "Hi, there! You fellow! What do you think you're doing?"

The young man looked down and said mildly:

16

"Pargetting, sir." Despite the mildness there was something cocksure about his manner, about that brief downward glance and then back to his work, that was infuriating.

"Come down off that ladder."

The young man obeyed, not with alacrity but with a kind of weary patience—what now? As soon as he was on the ground he studied the inside of the dish-like thing, took an oily rag from his apron pocket and began to rub. Altogether too much!

"Stand up when you speak to me. Take your cap off! Where's your master?"

"Dead, sir."

For a moment rage gave way to another emotion. Younger than me, and in good health!

"Hobson. Dead? How? He was here on Monday."

"Master Hobson is not my master. I served my time with Master Turner. Then I set up on my own."

"Where's Hobson?"

"Gone to Marshmere to complain. The thatchers found straw mixed with the reeds."

Reasonable; indeed praiseworthy. But anger must be vented.

"Now, what's this pargetting?"

"As you see, sir." He looked up, drawing Sir James's gaze to the three completed panels.

The design was based on the family badge. A hare, up on its hind legs, defying some invisible enemy, in defence of a little leveret, crouched low behind her.

The badge fitted exactly the family motto: "I defend my own," for the hare, though usually a timid animal, had been known to fly at the nose of a bullock in defence of its young.

The silver gilt light of the morning brought out the shape and contours of this white-on-white decoration, revealing a beauty which Sir James was not in a mood to appreciate.

"A lot of nonsense," he said. "You can stop it at once and find a job of work."

Something sparked in the young man's eyes, but he remained civil.

"Pargetting *is* work, sir."

The mould, cut into solid beechwood, had taken five days to complete. Allowed more time he would have carved the motto, too, and the date. But Hobson, pressed by Sir James, in turn

17

pressed his son-in-law, and apart from the hare and the leveret, both most lifelike in their postures of defiance and terror, all he had added was what looked like some blades of grass, just in front of the hare's hind feet. The intertwined grass blades were in fact his signature, his initials— His name was Walter Weaver.

"Sir Godfrey ordered pargetting," the young man said, seeing that no word of appreciation was forthcoming.

Sir James thought: He would! The young fool!

"You tell Hobson I cancelled that order. Find yourself something useful to do."

The pressure of the stirrup increased the pain in his gout-swollen foot; the delay in the thatching increased the risk that Sybilla and her horrible children would be at Moyidan for Christmas—they'd been at Beauclaire for a full six months—and he simply could not wait to tell Emma about his latest proof of Godfrey's wicked extravagance: so, contrary to custom, he did not ride round to the back of the house to see how the stables were going up or the well going down. He turned his horse and rode home.

He was no sooner out of sight around the little flint church which his great-grandmother had built and endowed—being a pious woman and fearful that a five-mile walk from Intake to Moyidan was too much for the young, the old, or men who had laboured for six days—than William Weaver, more often known as William Pargetter, resumed work.

He was, as his father-in-law knew, a sour-tempered, scornful young rebel, far less appreciative than he should have been of his profound good fortune in marrying Barbara Hobson, with her generous dowry which had enabled him to go into business on his own, and her chestful of household linen which many a lady might envy. All he cared for was his work—good work. Even his grudging father-in-law admitted that and found him a job whenever he could. He was not really the right husband for Barbara, too much engrossed in his work—"Chippings all over the place," too little grateful for good meals. "He does not care whether his supper is hot or cold."

In Sir James's presence he controlled himself, having no wish to offend, or to do or say anything which would be det-

18

rimental to his father-in-law—the only outlet, so far, for his beautiful work.

So he had restrained himself, spoken civilly, but at some cost. Find yourself something useful to do. I cancelled that order. Tremulous, despising himself for allowing somebody so wooden-headed as Sir James to upset him so, William Weaver, the pargetter, set about moving his ladder into the next space between the windows. But, upset by anger and the need to control it, he forgot that before the ladder was shifted the bucket of plaster should be removed.

The ladder moved, lurched, and the bucket of plaster tilted.

Master Hobson, coming back from Marshmere where he had dealt with the cheating reed supplier more harshly than anybody had ever dealt with him, was sorry, but not altogether sorry . . . He had never much liked his son-in-law, while admitting his skill.

And William Weaver's death, though not in the old ritual way a sacrifice to ensure luck on the house, was opportune. Master Hobson had been planning to bring a stray cat or dog, and damn what his son-in-law might have to say about superstition. Now the house had been given its sacrifice. It would stand firm and prosper.

THREE

THE LADY EMMA, though she had not had a convent upbringing, had mastered the arts of reading and writing and had twice written to Sybilla reporting upon the progress of the building: *It will be done by Christmas.* Neither letter contained an invitation for the family to spend the festive season at Moyidan and Sybilla could read, between what was said and what was left unsaid, that she and the children were expected to remain at Beauclaire for Christmas and then move.

Emma's third letter arrived on the 20th of December; the house was ready and furnished with most essentials. Emma also had kept her word and listed the articles which Sybilla did not need to bring or buy.

Sybilla had no intention of moving before Christmas. The festival was always observed in great style at Beauclaire, and this year Henry, almost seven, and Richard, hard on six, would be able to participate—something to remember—and in the roisterings, with the Lord of Misrule in charge, their rowdy behaviour would give no offence.

It was with a certain innocent pride that she imparted to her sister-in-law the news that the house was ready. Lady Astallon's reaction was astounding, the more so because she was a woman who never seemed to be aware of anything. She appeared to go through life like a beautiful somnambulist. She had been the beauty of the family, had made a grand marriage, was adored by her husband—and by a number of other men who seemed to be content to worship at the shrine of her icy loveliness with no more reward than an inattentive attention and a remote smile now and again. Sybilla had expected her to say, "Indeed. I am happy for you, my dear."

Lady Astallon, suddenly sharp and practical, said, "My dear, I think you should go at once. Snow always falls immediately after Christmas. I will see that a wagon is ordered for you. And tell Dame Margery to give you anything in the way of stores that you may require. What about beds?"

The Abbess herself could not have spoken more briskly or sensibly. It was the first time that the slightest resemblance between the two sisters had evidenced itself.

Dame Margery, who from the still room actually ruled much of Beauclaire, had a soft spot for Sybilla who, before the children came—and later, when the boys were small and manageable—had often lent a hand with the making of potpourri and such delicate work as candying violets and rose petals.

"You see to the packing of your own gear, my lady," she said. "I'll see to it that you have stores for a month. I'll make sure you have a good horse and wagon, too."

Fond as she was of Lady Tallboys, Dame Margery would be glad to see the back of those two terrible little boys who had once stolen into the still room and drunk an incredible amount of raspberry cordial in the making. They had been first drunk and then sick; in the first state they had been destructive and in the second disgusting.

The wagon and the horse, selected by Dame Margery's distant but powerful finger, were both good, and the wagon was loaded before sunset that day. Lady Astallon, without stirring, had been active too. Emma at Moyidan had provided *two* beds; she added another and some good blankets.

The hitch came over the question of who was to drive the wagon to Suffolk and bring it back.

Nobody actually *said* he would not go, setting out on a journey that would take at least three days—and three back—which would mean missing all the merry preliminaries, the bringing in of the Yule Log, the cutting of holly, ivy and mistletoe, the election of some humble person, servant or clown, to be Lord of Misrule whose most fantastic orders must be obeyed. Nobody refused to go to Suffolk, but everybody was ready with a reason why he should not be the one. Beauclaire like all overgrown establishments was riddled with favouritism, with corruption. In the end Lady Tallboys was to be driven to her new home by a boy, a near idiot who owed his place in the

21

household to the fact that he was related to one of the under-cooks, and could pluck a fowl.

He could be trusted to return without the horse and wagon. All the servants at Beauclaire wished to protect their master from any depredation but their own, so from some hidden place a rickety wagon was pulled and the load transferred. When, at first light, Sybilla emerged into the courtyard, the half-wit was hitching the wagon to a decrepit old horse. Walter, who had preceded her by a few minutes, carrying down her clothes chest and her lute, was raging. The boy was an idiot, there was some mistake; if the lady would just go back inside for a minute he'd see it set right.

"There was no mistake, Walter. If it takes us a mile I shall be content."

A glance at her face enlightened him. He placed the chest and the lute in the wagon and helped Sybilla in. The well-stuffed feather mattress made a comfortable seat, and the framework of the bed—one of the low, truckle kind—covered with a blanket made something to lean against. Walter tucked the other blankets around Sybilla, the baby and the little girl who, strictly speaking, was no longer a baby, but who acted like one.

"Up you get, Master Richard. I'll just get my own box . . ." He had it somewhere handy, for he was back in a minute with the old arrow box which contained all he owned. "And we're not taking that numbskull. So much dead weight. If they want this contraption back they can send for it. Now, Master Henry, you can sit alongside me. To start with," he added, knowing the boys well, "you'll take turns."

He looked at the horse and thought: Hit it and it'll fall over! So he clucked to it, it leaned against the collar, the wheels creaked and they were off.

It was still very early in the morning, the sky in the east rose-flushed.

The insult of this shameful equipage stung for a little in Sybilla's heart but was soon assuaged. Perhaps not deliberate, simply a matter of muddle and servants' cunning. The Abbess has taught her that in certain situations a dignified acceptance was preferable to futile protest. Besides she was going home. To the first place which after more than twenty-three years of

22

living, and almost eight of married life, she would be able to call her own, her very own.

Presently Henry said, "I want to drive."

"Then want'll be your master."

Henry grabbed the reins and Walter said, "Do that again and you'll go in the back."

"I'm not going to ride with children!"

Richard wriggled forward and from behind took his brother's arm in a known, painful grip. "Don't you call me *children*." Henry twisted round and retaliated with another hold, a bending down of the fourth finger.

Walter said, "Whoa," and glad of a respite, the old horse stopped. "You want to fight, get down and do it in the road." They tumbled out willingly enough. Walter clucked to the horse and said, "A bit of a run'll do them no harm, my lady. I'll keep them in sight."

He had more to think about than two naughty, squabbling boys. The horse must be guided, for the mud in the road had frozen into high sharp ridges, and there were water-filled potholes, crusted with ice. He was also on the lookout for some place where the horse, perhaps the wagon, too, might be exchanged.

He had travelled this road before on his way to Moyidan or Bywater, but he had not realised how lonely this stretch of it was; only one inn, so far, at a crossroads, near a gibbet, and that as miserable a place as any peasant's hovel. It had some tumbledown stables, but no horses.

Behind the wagon, their breath like smoke on the frosty air, the boys would stop to pummel each other or roll each other over; then they would run to overtake the slow, creaking wagon. Their faces were like poppies, Sybilla thought. She had no anxiety about them; they never inflicted real damage on each other. Just as a fight could break out for the flimsiest reason— or for no reason at all—so it always seemed to stop short of actual malice. And here there was nobody to exclaim, or feign alarm, to say, "Those boys are at it again," or urge her to rule them more strictly.

At last Walter found what he thought to be a suitable halting place. There was water in a little stream by the road, a clump of beech trees.

23

"I'd reckon it's nearly dinnertime, my lady. Do us all good to stretch our legs a bit." Walter had an inborn tact and courtesy. When she came back from among the beech trees he had covered the sweating, steaming horse with a rug, and was offering it water from his hat—an archer's hat made of stiff felt and leather-lined.

The boys came charging up, a truce declared, for exercise had worked off their surplus energy and they were hungry.

Dame Margery—God bless her—had thought of everything. At the top of one hamper was a bowl of delicious brawn, pork pieces in firm jelly, a long loaf of bread; a stoppered jug of mild ale and two horn cups. As Sybilla prepared to cut the brawn, to the top of which white fat had risen, Walter said, "I could do with some of that grease. For the wheels." With his own knife he scooped up a handful, and went around, pushing the grease, half melted from the heat of his hand, into the dry axles.

Nobody had ever talked to Walter in abstract terms about resignation to unalterable circumstance, but life had taught him that in order to survive a man must make do with what he had. And he had been thinking about the horse.

Why at Beauclaire, where everything was in abundance and waste the rule, should there have been in the stables such a thing of hide and bones available at just the right moment? Just as somebody had provided for human needs, so somebody else had provided for the horse; a bag of oats. Holding his slab of bread and brawn in one hand, offering the horse oats from his hat with the other—December days were short and there was no time to waste—Walter hit on the truth. This horse was so old that its teeth were worn down; it could not munch. In the midst of plenty, with nobody noticing, it had been slowly starving.

He went round to the back of the wagon where the mood engendered by freedom, by eating in the open air had taken over.

"Can I have the rest of that loaf, my lady?"

Crumbled and soaked, it was the nearest thing to the bran mash which kept ailing or overexhausted horses on their feet.

By sundown they reached a village and an inn which Walter remembered as a stopping place for dinner on former, swifter journeys. He threw himself into the business of compensating for the shabby wagon by being as demanding as he could. Lady Tallboys must have a fire in her chamber and a roast fowl for her supper: Did The Three Pigeons stock no wine? then Lady Tallboys's supper ale must be mulled; the shoes of the young masters must be dried and cleaned. Henry and Richard had amused themselves by jumping on ice-covered puddles.

In the morning Walter looked anxiously at the sky, less clear than on the previous day. Snow was his dread. He imagined that two thirds of a loaf of bread and two bran mashes had done something for the horse, but not to the extent of rendering it capable of contending with snow-clogged roads. In fact snow, though threatening for the next three days, did not begin to fall until midday of Christmas Eve when they were within a mile of their destination.

It was through a veil of snow that Sybilla first saw Knight's Acre.

She knew its position, for once or twice in the early days of her marriage she had ridden with Godfrey to look at what he called his little estate, but she had had no clear mental picture of what the house would look like. He had no talent for describing things, and having said that it would be rather like the new part of Moyidan, though smaller of course, he had exhausted his powers; he had not mentioned the solar, the still room, or the stool room because he wished them to come as a surprise to her; and he had not mentioned the pargetting because he was still uncertain what it meant.

It was rather bigger than she had imagined and had more windows; two to one side of the door, one on the other, and five above. It looked solid and strong against its background of leafless trees. It also looked entirely unwelcoming. This, she quickly realised, was because nobody was in it, and just as this was the first time she had ever looked on a building and been able to think: Mine! so it was the first time that she had ever approached a place, at this time of afternoon, in such weather, without seeing a glow of light from fire or candle.

She was aware suddenly of a decline in spirit. It went farther and deeper than the mere lack of welcome which the blank-eyed house presented; she thought: If Dame Margery did not think to put in candles, we shall have no light; and, abruptly,

25

that this was typical of the lighthearted, unprepared way in which this whole thing had been undertaken. Insufficient forethought. She had said that it would be pleasant to have a house of their own, Godfrey had ordered it; and here it was.

She had been too much surprised by Alys's behaviour, too busy concealing her surprise and in making ready to go that she had not thought about candles.

Nor had she thought about what owning a house involved—with the only *certain* income four pounds a year. Taxes!

It would all have been different if there had been a glow from those windows. But Sir James and his lady had discussed the question of providing servants and decided against it. They did not expect Sybilla to travel before Twelfth Night; servants chosen by other people were never satisfactory; Intake, though not a manor, must have a certain feeling of obligation—and young people to spare; and Sybilla had Walter.

"Here we are, my lady, and just in time. It's thickening," Walter said. He helped her down, John sound asleep in her arms, and Margaret clutching at her skirt. The boys ran about painstakingly scooping up enough snow to make snowballs with which to pelt each other.

Master Hobson might be a rogue, but he was an honest rogue, what he built he built and the new house had a good solid door; oak, two inches thick and on the outside an iron ring which lifted the latch within and could also serve as knocker. The door had no lock, though it could be bolted from within. Walter threw open the door and stood aside. Sybilla stepped in.

Darker than out-of-doors, and almost as cold. The smell of fresh plaster, the smell of lack of use sharply called to mind the convent parlour.

Outside Walter shouted to the boys, "Gather wood and take it in." He edged himself through the doorway, her chest under one arm, the lute and the blankets clasped in the other.

"Get a fire going, it'll all be different, my lady," he said and hurried out again. Next time he came in he was carrying the hampers that Dame Margery had provided. The baby was awake now and Sybilla put him down on the floor where he began to crawl about vigorously.

26

Dame Margery had visualised a new house lacking Christmas provender; she had visualised some makeshift dinners on the road, but she had not foreseen an unlighted house. There were no candles.

The boys ran in and out bringing wood of all kinds, the debris of building. The competition between them had now focussed upon who could find and carry most. Sybilla heard the snow-muffled clop of the old horse's hoofs as Walter led it around the house. Next time he entered he came in from the kitchen, his hands full of straw and thin wood shavings. He knelt on the hearth, worked flint and tinder vigorously and abruptly the room sprang to life.

My first fire on my own hearth, Sybilla thought, but joy refused to come at call. Walter chose the driest and slimmest pieces of wood and placed them tent-like over the first flames.

"We have no candles, Walter."

"I'll get my box. I've got one and a half. And a lantern."

He went out to the front where he had left the wagon and returned with the old arrow box.

Thrift rather than generosity had governed Emma's giving. There was a table, old and battered and unsteady because it had one leg badly worm-eaten; there was a backless bench, capable of holding four people, and a three-legged milking stool. Nothing more, and the lack of furniture made the place seem larger than it was; voices and footsteps sounded hollow.

Instead of the interest and curiosity which would have been natural in the circumstances, Sybilla felt a disinclination to move about, a temptation to remain near the bright-burning fire. Such weakness must not be pandered to.

"I'll take the foodstuff into the kitchen," Walter said.

"I'll bring a light. Boys, see that John and Margaret do not get too near to the fire."

Walter was bilingual, his two brands of English, foul and decent, being as far apart as any of Babel's tongues. He never confused them. In foul he had been communicating with himself ever since he saw how the lady had been fobbed off at Beauclaire; to see how she had been treated here—and not by servants, by her own kin—rendered even foul inadequate.

27

In the decent, from which he never varied in her presence, he said, "It's a good kitchen, my lady." It was a good kitchen, with a wide hearth, and a bread oven in the wall. It contained a table, bigger and more solid than the one in the hall; it looked as though at some time it had been used as a carpenter's bench. Laid out on it were such items as Emma had thought essential and which could be easily spared. It was the kind of collection which anyone, living poorly, and suddenly inheriting a fully furnished house, might be expected to throw out from his own humble abode.

"We'll get this straightened out in the morning," Walter said, eyeing the rusty spit; the pewter candlestick, so bent that no candle could live in it for long, the pile of platters, wooden, potsherd, battered pewter.

Alongside this the contents of the hampers looked munificent. There was even a game pie with what was called a raised crust, patterned and highly glazed.

"We'll eat this for supper," Sybilla said, "and then the children must go to bed. All else can wait until morning."

Upstairs there were two beds, akin to the one brought from Beauclaire, a frame and a mattress, no more. Bleak. But adequate. And what right had she to expect anything to gladden the eye and say, "Welcome"?

Walter carried up the clothes chest and placed it in the room which contained the larger of the two beds; and then, for the first time in all the years he had travelled with them, she gave a thought to his sleeping arrangements.

"The children will share this bed with me," she said, "and the boys will sleep next door. That leaves two empty rooms, and the bed we brought with us. Make yourself comfortable, Walter."

"I've found myself a place, my lady."

His old-soldier's eye had spotted it as he led the horse to the stable. Slightly to one side, the remains of the original farmhouse, used, and patchily repaired by the carpenters, masons, and casual labourers who had worked here. Watertight, windproof; what more could a man ask? There was even a bed of bracken upon which Walter Freeman, who had standards of his own, did not hesitate to lie. Bracken did not harbour lice as hay and straw and flock and feather did.

When Walter had gone to his own place—wherever that might be—Sybilla experienced something new: loneliness. She had spent years at Lamarsh, where even if voices were muted and footfalls soft, they were there. Then Godfrey had whisked her into places where voices were louder and gayer, and footsteps rang. Here with the boys, rolled together like puppies in one room, and the two babies fitted like spoons together in the bed she was about to share, there was a ringing silence, an emptiness, a feeling of isolation.

I should have bargained for this when I said I should like a house of my own. I am under my own roof, my children are sleeping peacefully. I should be thankful. God, I do thank you . . . She managed two Our Fathers and two Hail Marys before she slept.

FOUR

FATHER AMBROSE was the first person in Intake to be aware of the arrival. The snow had ceased during the night and, looking out into a glittering white world, he spied the hump of the snow-covered wagon which obscured his usual view of Knight's Acre's front door. He called briskly for his heavy boots—so well greased as to be waterproof—and wrapped himself in the shawl which was his winter wear . . .

"And not even a fire to welcome you, my lady. Had I but known . . ."

His kind heart was genuinely grieved to think of anyone arriving at an unlit, unheated house in the middle of a snow-storm—and on Christmas Day, too; but he was also concerned for a missed opportunity for ingratiating himself with the lady who was to be his most important parishioner. He had been very much excited about the building of the house. Ladies were usually pious and charitable; they did embroidery; altar cloths and copes; they could usually be relied upon to set a good example, which God knew Intake could do with. Had he been warned he would have seen to it that the fire was lighted, have been there himself to offer words of welcome. He hastened to repair the situation.

"You will need servants, my lady. I think I can put my hand on the very couple. Both named Wade, a woman and her nephew. They have both known service in great houses, but are temporarily out of employment."

God had called him to what at first sight seemed a sinecure but which had turned out to be hard labour in a very stony field. In the period before Sir Godfrey's great-grandmother built and endowed the little church the people of Intake seemed to have lost the habit and in some cases, even the outward forms of piety. The founders of the village had, after all, been an unruly lot, men whose master at Moyidan had been glad to be rid of. And while Intake had had no priest, and during the encumbency of Father Ambrose's immediate predecessor, who was lax in such matters, there had been a good deal of inbreeding which had hardened the mould. Father Ambrose had never succeeded in breaking it, though he never relaxed his efforts. Just before Christmas he always made a round of the farms, reminding everybody of the seasonal obligations. They knew it was Christmas; they were boiling bag puddings and chopping mincemeat; the young children had dragged in the festive greenery—ivy, holly, mistletoe, and they seemed to resent the reminder.

In the house at Wade's Acre—once a single room of clods, and now a substantial place with six rooms—he noticed that Bessie and Jacky were back. He had said, "Home for Christmas?" and the unacknowledged head of the family, an old woman of incredible age, had muttered sourly, "Back for good, by the look of it."

The two were misfits. The inbreeding against which Father Ambrose had set his face, twenty-five years ago—yes, a quarter century; how time sped!—had curious results. Most of the Wades were strong and sensible and very hard workers, far from witless; but the woman, Bessie, nearing forty and very fat, the boy Jacky, fifteen and thin as a rail, were, to put it at its kindliest, simple. The woman was said to be a good cook, but undependable, the boy willing enough but forgetful.

Father Ambrose felt it unnecessary to mention this, or the catalogue of jobs found and quickly lost, to Sybilla. Neither of the pair had ever been employed in Intake—for who was there to employ them? And perhaps in far places, Baildon, Clevely, Muchanger, they had suffered from that debilitating ailment, homesickness, and had lost jobs because they wanted to lose them. Here, within easy reach of their relatives, and under his own eye, they might well do better. Without hesitation he recommended them to Sybilla.

She felt better this morning; everything seemed better. She was faintly ashamed of her overnight feelings of which nothing remained except a kind of caution, the feeling that this was rather a big house to be sustained on such slender resources.

She was not without money. The Intake tenants paid their rent twice a year, at Michaelmas and on Lady Day; two pounds. And at a Michaelmas tourney, Godfrey had won a silver-gilt cup which Walter had sold, happening upon a buyer who wanted a cup as a christening present and had not quibbled at paying ten shillings for a thing which on an open market would have brought no more than eight.

Godfrey had left it all with her; he was taking service under Lord Malvern's standard; he was well provided for, and hoped to come home rich. But something about that looming bulk, the reach of the roof, the widths of the hearths, and the extra rooms which had indeed surprised her, had made an impression that remained, even in this blue and white morning, and she said cautiously that she could not afford *expensive* servants. Like everybody else who knew the family, Father Ambrose had assumed that Sir Godfrey was well-to-do and Sybilla's remark roused surprise and disappointment; however, he assured her that Bessie Wade would probably be content with three shillings a year, Jacky with eighteenpence, "And their keep, of course," he added. "I will walk across to Wade's Acre and arrange it at once."

In the doorway he looked about at the waste of hard-trodden, wood-littered ground on which the new house stood, and another dream revived. "I expect your ladyship will be making a garden." Ladies cared about such things, farm wives did not; he visualised the altar decked with roses and lilies. The only flowers it now knew were occasional offerings from young children, primroses, oxslips, wild daffodils, and bluebells, all gathered much too short and damaged by hot little hands.

"I shall hope to—in time," Sybilla said. She also looked at the unpromising ground and once again felt the weight of the task she had undertaken. As she had slept in other people's beds and eaten at their tables, so she had enjoyed their gardens, their roses and lilies and gilly flowers, their lavender and rosemary. Would this waste ever flower?

Self-pity was not an actual *sin,* but it showed weakness of character. She braced herself. Here is the house I wanted and asked for and here in due time will my garden be . . .

Walter looked at the cleared land before and around the house with a different eye. Fourth son of a yeoman farmer and as much the victim as Sir Godfrey of the Norman institution of primogeniture, he had always been land-hungry. Now here it was, enough even for a land-hungry man; acres of it. Sir James's men, fearful of seeming idle, had cleared the ground well. Walter could see that, even under the covering of snow.

This year it would be hit or miss; no autumn-sown seed, lying there waiting. It would mean spring ploughing and spring sowing; but he'd manage.

Because he must.

He knew far more about Sir Godfrey's finances than either Sir Godfrey or the lady knew about *his*. Four pounds a year and some price money soon earned, soon spent, did not, in Walter's view represent security. A place of this size should, must, be self-supporting. And would be, if he had anything to do with it.

Walter bitterly resented the twelve wasted days of Christmas; all very well for the rich, playing the fool and guzzling. And the poor, blind, stupid, copied their betters. Everything stopped for Christmas and it was twelve days before Walter could really get to work. What could be done in the interval he did. He coddled the old horse which responded gallantly, he bullied the Wades, who, if they had ever as the lady said been in service before, showed no signs of any training. A great fat slob of a woman, a flibbertigibbet boy. The lady, as always, had listened to soft talk—this time from the priest, and Walter distrusted priests, and monks, and friars; even the one Bishop he had encountered, William of Bywater, who literally starved himself and his guests in order to support a Lying-in Hospital for fallen women and a Foundlings' Home for the children who were the product of the falls.

In Walter's opinion, William, Bishop of Bywater, should have fed his guests better, and as soon as he heard that the lady, his brother's wife, was about to move in, should have sent wall hangings, some chairs, a settle with cushions.

The lady would have such things in time, because Walter would obtain them for her; in the meantime, first things first . . .

33

The men of Intake no more liked Walter than the servants in great houses had done. He had an unpleasant manner and they could not, as they said, "place" him. He was only a servingman, but his manner was brusque and lordly and they thought his speech affected. It was not Suffolk. Bessie and Jacky Wade reported unfavourably on him, too. He'd threatened Bessie with the sack unless her cooking improved, he'd given Jacky a clip on the ear. Such behaviour from a master would not have been worth remarking, coming from a fellow servant it bred resentment.

Dislike of him took the form of refusing any of the mutual aid usual in a small, isolated community. Nobody was prepared to *lend* him a plough; he could *hire* one and it'd be a farthing a day.

From afar they watched his first ploughing with malicious curiosity. Ploughing with a horse; what ignorance! Some of them were interested enough to inspect his furrows, certain of finding many crooked ones, dog's legs. Ploughing was an art and straightness of ridges was closely related to evenness of planting and ease in reaping. There were no dog's legs in Walter's field; in the last of the daylight the furrows lay straight and sure, washed with a faint mauvish light on one side, deep brown on the other. Such a skilled performance—and comparatively quickly done, since a horse moved faster than an ox—was not endearing, and when Walter went the round again, this time offering to buy seed corn, nobody had any to sell.

Walter made the first of his raids upon Baildon.

What sort of fist would he make of the sowing? Disappointingly good. He had the rhythm of it; striding along and matching the throws to his paces. Walter, with a stern father and even sterner elder brothers, had been well trained. As he sowed the boys followed, dragging branches like rakes, to cover the seeds.

With two fields ploughed and sown, he turned his attention to making a garden; the house would need peas and beans, carrots, onions, cabbages. He made small spades for Henry and Richard, so that they could help with the digging. "And he's nigh as strict with them as he is with us," Bessie said.

A household also needed livestock of its own. Sharp-eyed in the market, Walter found a bargain, a cow with two defective teats. It took longer to find a sow going cheap, but his luck served him again; an elderly sow, in pig; she was a known good breeder, but savage-tempered. Her owner had recently died, his widow was afraid of the beast, and in fact the sow was offered for sale immobilised in a fishing net. Everybody knew what that meant!

"And the net thrown in," Walter said gleefully. "Handy for catching pigeons."

Pigeons mattered.

Dame Margery had not envisaged a household with no resources, no pork or beef salted down in casks, no sides of bacon in the smoke hole. She had merely seen that, leaving so suddenly, on the brink of Christmas, Lady Tallboys needed the festive season's trimmings. She had packed the game pie, and that delicacy, a sugar-cured ham, cooked and garnished. Once they were consumed, the household had been dependent upon what could be bought from the grasping villagers, snared, trapped, or shot in Layer Wood.

Walter had not even been able to indulge in ritual swapping. When you kill your pig, let me have a half, or a quarter and when I kill mine, you shall have the same. Presently he would be able to do so.

Once he had shot a deer and Sybilla, glad enough of the meat, had been rather dubious about the law.

"There are so many rules about venery, Walter. We may have no rights in Layer Wood."

"It was on our field, my lady."

"I am not sure that that justifies . . . I seem to remember . . ." The convent at Lamarsh had included amongst its properties a belt of forest, and the Abbess had been very meticulous about her rights.

"Never mind, Walter. Just this once. I will ask Sir James when I see him. He will know. Meanwhile, roast venison! Can you fletch it, Walter?"

"I should hope so, my lady."

When I see him, Walter thought, dealing expertly with the deer's carcass—once, in a forgotten siege in a forgotten place, he had flayed what remained of a dead horse. To himself, in foul language of an extreme sort, Walter denounced Sir James of Moyidan. Not a . . . visit, yet! . . . his gout! Could he . . .

not have come in a . . . wagon? . . . well ashamed to show his . . . face, to look at the . . . stuff he had allowed his . . . wife to send . . . her and him and all connected with them.

It was over the deer's carcass that Walter found a fault in the house. It had no smoke hole, that wide chimney in which meat could be hung, with a slow-burning fire of turf or sawdust burning below. But he improvised. The hearth cold, he set a stool amongst the ashes and reached up as far as he could and drove in a nail. Anything hung on it would be beyond the scorch of a flame. The whole process might take longer than usual. In his home, with a proper smoke hole, a ham and a side of bacon took about a month to be cured; here with the smoke anything but steady, reckon six weeks.

"Walter," Henry said, "why don't you *shoot* pigeons?"
"Because there'd be nothing left. Just a smear. I've sent an arrow through a four-inch door. Ask yourself what a pigeon'd look like."
To Walter, as to everyone else, the boys had been almost indistinguishable, handsome, noisy, badly behaved. But since the move had been made Walter, somewhat surprising himself, had taken a fancy to Henry because, given a job, Henry would stick at it till he dropped. Henry was the stuff out of which men were made. About Richard, Walter was not so sure. Always wanting to be treated as an equal, but not prepared to measure up. Henry, Walter had concluded, was teachable in a way that Richard was not.
Now that the boys spent so long doing things with Walter the house was reasonably peaceful for long hours at a time. Sybilla tended the two young children, John just beginning to totter about and Margaret, soon to be four, still very childish. Reaching back to her time in the kitchen at Lamarsh, Sybilla resurrected her domestic knowledge and tried to teach Bessie, who was incapable of remembering anything from one day to another and seemed not to care. Really, Sybilla sometimes thought impatiently, it would be quicker and cheaper to do things myself!
Whatever she was about, so long as daylight lasted, she was listening. For a hoof beat; a knock on the door.

36

Godfrey could not write, but he knew that Sybilla could read, and over the years she had received brief, stilted letters from him, written by another. More usual was the verbal message. The invisible lines of communication covered the country, a web woven by knights on the move, foot soldiers, pedlars, cattle-dealers, wool-buyers. Anybody would carry a letter or a message because it was the rule that in the main payment was made by the recipient.

Nobody came to Intake except an old woman hawking fish; and presently, as soon as his winter gout receded, James of Moyidan. He was still a little lame and hobbled in and sank down thankfully on the comfortable high-backed, cushioned settle and said that he was glad to see, and he was sure Emma would be glad to hear, that Sybilla was so well installed. As he looked around it struck him that nothing he saw was familiar, but Moyidan was a big place. He had left the furnishing of Knight's Acre to Emma, and, as usual, Emma had done well.

It was Walter who had furnished the hall and made it fit to live in.

From the first Walter had been forming his scheme, letting it wait until more essential things were done; but when Sybilla said that she was not certain about her rights to the deer in Layer Wood, he thought: Oh! And what about those two young oaks? He had adjusted his programme. Slightly sooner than he would have done had he not felt the pressure of time, Walter sought out a man who made furniture to order and proposed a reasonable deal. Two standing oaks in exchange for a table, cushioned settle, a cupboard, four bedposts.

Oak was becoming scarce, especially in a neighbourhood within easy distance of the sea. Ship builders grabbed all the oak.

"What girth?"

"One I can just put my arms round. The other a bit larger."

A trick somewhere. The old man who made beautiful things, but who shuffled and mumbled and blinked and left all dealings to his son, said:

"Very well, I will send my son out to look at the standing timber, tomorrow."

Walter assumed his most disagreeable expression. He said:

"Take it or leave it. I want the things *now*."

37

"For Lady Tallboys?"

"I told you, didn't I? Lady Tallboys."

"Moyidan?"

"Knight's Acre."

A reliable name.

"Very well. The difficulty is, I have no cupboard."

God forgive him the lie! Pushed into a corner, shrouded in sailcloth was the most beautiful thing he had ever made. Years ago, a thing made for the joy of making, without any thought of selling. A thing of his own. Long ago, when he was an outdoor working carpenter, mending broken floor boards at Muchanger, he had seen what was called a court cupboard, or livery cupboard. A beautiful thing. For the sheer joy of making, in snatched minutes from ordinary day-by-day work, the carpenter had made such a cupboard. The doors that enclosed its lower compartment were carved in the linenfold pattern; its two upper, open shelves were carved with oak leaves and acorns. And into the arch, above the upper shelf, he had set his sign: *J Woodey maid me 1440.*

He had intended the cupboard to be a gift for his wife and she had rejected it. "Take all day to dust," she said; not meaning to be cruel, simply sensible.

"So what would you call this?" the scarred man said, twitching at the canvas that had so long covered the masterpiece and the dream.

"Well . . . Yes, it is a cupboard. But not for sale."

"Belong to somebody?"

"Well, yes, in a manner of speaking."

"Who?" Walter was relentless. It was a beautiful thing, the kind of thing the lady should possess, and there was something shifty about the man's manner. People in illegal possession of things for sale sometimes wore that look, and they were easy prey.

"Well . . . me." The admission was made with reluctance.

"Then you can sell it." A course of action frequently urged on the old artist, by his wife, by his son; and doggedly resisted.

"I don't want to. I didn't make it for sale."

"Then the deal's off. I'll offer the oak to somebody willing to do business."

Sweating, the old man thought of how his son would scold.

38

He'd hear somebody boasting about *his* bargain; two standing oaks!

"I never thought of selling it. I got fond of it. I spent a lot of time on it . . ."

Walter knew the signs of submission.

"It'll have a good home with Lady Tallboys," he said, speaking as though of a pet animal.

And that is more than it would here, when he was gone; his son would sell to the first bidder.

"Well . . ."

"Right then. Now for a table and a settle."

Sybilla was delighted, but dismayed at the thought of the price such good things must have cost.

"Not a penny, my lady. A straight swap for a couple of trees."

Whose trees?

So now, when James had finished admiring the things which Emma had not provided, Sybilla, without mentioning either the shot deer or the swapped trees, asked an artless question about Godfrey's rights in Layer Wood.

"Difficult to say. For one thing there were never any fixed boundaries. All the manors, Clevely, Muchanger, Nettleton, and half a dozen more meet somewhere in the wood. I'll get Emma to look it up. There's a document somewhere, granting the Intake people a right to take pigs in at acorn time and to gather dead wood for fuel. Not to cut trees—once their houses were built; or to take game."

"Strictly speaking, then the wood around here is still yours—part of Moyidan." How unfair that one man should have inherited so much, his brother so little.

"Strictly speaking, yes. But between brothers . . . When Godfrey comes home if he and friends want to hunt, or you need a tree for any purpose, I shouldn't go to law about it." He gave her one of his infrequent smiles. He was making a concession, with—he thought—good grace, but it was a concession nonetheless, and he hoped she was aware of it.

She was. She said, "Thank you, James. That is very generous of you." She gave him not a smile exactly, but a look which reminded him that in the past, once the monetary disappointment of Godfrey, so poor, marrying a girl equally poor had been accepted, he had been inclined to think, from time to time, that in fact Godfrey hadn't done so badly for himself. Sybilla had always been welcome at Moyidan until she came with those two great healthy boys, a girl who bade fair to be pretty, and then a third son.

What a court cupboard should have, and this one lacked, was a display of silver. Drinking cups, bowls for salt.

No man of his generation had won more silver cups than Sir Godfrey had—a drinking cup, either with or without some coins inside—was the universally acknowledged prize. The Tallboys family had never kept one for much longer than a fortnight though Sybilla had expressed a wish that each child should have one, a thing for everyday use and also a memento of his father's prowess. Something had always cropped up to render sale imperative and Godfrey had always said, in his lighthearted way, "Time enough."

Tournament prizes were in fact growing less valuable. In this, as in everything else, fashion worked downward and King Henry VI was not a good patron for tourneys. He was scholarly—even monkish—far more interested in founding a school at Eton, a college at Cambridge . . . Some people said he was slightly mad.

And Godfrey Tallboys was almost equally unworldly. Some contests in the lists were run under the rule that any knight unhorsed forfeited his horse—in some cases even his armour, to the one who had struck him down. Of this rule Godfrey had never taken advantage: "Bad enough to be so shamed, without being stripped."

Once she had made a mild protest, saying had things been reversed, *he* would have been stripped; and he had laughed and said, "Time enough to think about that when it happens. And God pity anybody who takes Arcol. He'd soon learn that he'd got the wrong cat by the tail."

She did not argue; there was something about his eyes, very blue—not that the colour was worthy of notice because blue eyes of varying shades were commonplace—but his had the candour of a child's. Transparent, concealing nothing. It was sometimes a little difficult to associate that mild, candid look with the precise ferocity with which he fought, or with the innocent pleasure with which he received adulation—the shouts and cheers, the flung flowers . . . and ribbon bows and bits of lace from headdresses. Sybilla had sat in the space reserved for ladies at more tourneys than she could count, knowing that she was envied.

Walter owned a silver cup, won in an archery competition. A silly prize, he'd thought at the time, to offer to men who would far rather have had its worth in money; but over the years he had grown attached to it, often used it for drinking and kept it well-polished with fine wood ash and spit.

He thought it would look well upon the cupboard and smuggled it into the hall at a time when Sybilla was not there. Another surprise for her! But . . . It was worse than nothing. He'd always known it was a little cup, but not *so* little. On the beautiful, massive cupboard it looked trumpery and silly. He put it back in his pocket.

It was just possible, he reflected, that this time Sir Godfrey would come home with a sackful of loot; possible, but not likely; he wasn't very good at acquiring things, and even worse at keeping them. Wales was a long way from Knight's Acre and somewhere along the road the silly (foul word) would be accosted by starving widows with multitudes of children, by old broken-down knights gone wrong in the head; and he'd get into a card game, or a dice game with some (foul word) swindling rogues. Walter liked Sir Godfrey and at times admired him, but he had no respect for his acumen or even his good sense.

Sybilla's next visitor was William, Bishop of Bywater. Once again at the sound of hoofs, the momentary halt of the heart, the running to the window.

William had remembered the amiable custom of bringing a gift to a new house and fortunately had the very thing to hand, so that the poor Magdalens and the foundlings need not be deprived. It was a wall hanging which some well-meaning parishioner had bequeathed him—possibly because she had heard that on taking up his appointment he had sold all those that his predecessor had acquired. A well-meant gesture, but the tapestry was far too secular to be hung on his walls. It depicted some very lightly clad women, one indeed so lightly

41

clad as to be wearing almost nothing, bowed over a casket from which some strange thing was emerging, a kind of winged serpent.

As he had guessed, Sybilla was delighted with it—he had always thought her, with her pretty headdresses and fashionable clothes, curiously worldly for a convent-bred girl—still mourned by Mary, over at Lamarsh. ("What you do not realise," Mary had once said to him, "is that Sybilla had an almost infinite capacity for adjustment. Soft as dough on the outside, iron at heart. I shall never now find such another.")

He asked about Godfrey; agreed that no news was good news; explained why he had not come before. His was, except for those in the extreme North perhaps, the widest diocese in England and he was conscientious about the visitations which he must regularly make to all the abbeys, priories, convents within this wide area. He loathed these visitations. One day he dined in princely splendour with the Abbot of Baildon—and no fault to be found there; next day he was at Clevely where a few old women, good women, lived in extreme poverty, in a decaying house—nobody's fault. And even at Lamarsh, which was typical of many, nothing much to put a finger on; the women, not nuns, who walked about with little dogs in their sleeves were merely being temporarily accommodated; this one a widow, his sister Mary explained, quite brokenhearted, the little sleeve dog her only solace; and this one . . . an orphan, an heiress who had taken a dislike to the man whom her guardian wished her to marry.

In a way William, Bishop of Bywater, was as single-minded and superficial as his brother Godfrey or his brother James. He was happy to see Sybilla comfortably established and well served.

(Out in the kitchen Walter had said to Jacky, "This is the first time my lady has ever had a guest at her table. You make a mess of serving and I'll foul word break your foul word neck." It was a remarkable fact, one which Walter had long ago observed; decent could be misunderstood, foul was universal.)

On his good horse—the one luxury he allowed himself, because time mattered—William Tallboys trotted away content that he had no cause to worry about Sybilla, well housed, well served.

42

FIVE

HORSE HOOFS AGAIN. And a very splendid young man, quite dazzling in the March sunshine. News at last!

"Lady Tallboys?" And well might he ask for she had come straight from the kitchen, from the latest, hopeless attempt to instruct Bessie in the making and baking of bread.

Hastily she pulled down her sleeves, rolled up above the elbows; and was glad that—great as the temptation was to discard such an inconvenient thing—she was wearing her headdress, six months ago the latest fashion. Godfrey, when he came, must not find her like a farm wife.

"At your service, my lady. I bring a message from Sir Godfrey."

"God bless you . . ."

"Sir Simon. Simon Randall. I am on way home to Cressacre and it was only a short detour."

"Is he well?"

"In most excellent health, I assure you. Disappointed about the war—as indeed we all were."

Not that it mattered to him, with all Cressacre behind him. He had only gone to the war for the sake of excitement and to please Lord Malvern who was both his uncle and his godfather—and, a knight should be truthful, if to nobody else, at least to himself, to escape for a season his masterful mother's matrimonial schemes.

Gently, but firmly, Sybilla broke Margaret's clutch on her skirt. "Darling, go and play with John . . . Yes, Sir Simon?" She knew that this was an occasion that called for wine, and she had none.

"Sir Godfrey asked me to tell you that he is bound for Winchester—the Easter tourney there; the war being so unprofitable."

Unprofitable indeed! The Welsh fought like devils and any place, hard-taken, offered just about as much loot as this place would, and men who called themselves princes could only offer for ransom some lean-barrelled, long-legged sheep, wild in the hills. Covertly he looked around. What a poor place! Not at all the background he had imagined for Sir Godfrey Tallboys. The lady was a surprise to him too; so very young to be the mother of four.

She apologised for having no wine, no saffron cake to offer. "We have but recently moved in." She managed to imply that as soon as the move was really complete wine and cake would be plentiful, silver would shine on the cupboard shelves, and the one, rather narrow wall hanging be joined by a multitude of others. She had pride and dignity as well as a kind of look which he found attractive, something tranquil and delicate. He found himself wondering how Sir Godfrey could bring himself to absent himself for so long. Easily answered: money. He repeated in his mind the wish he had expressed upon parting with Sir Godfrey—that he would be victor ludorum in the Winchester lists.

He set himself to entertain her, picking out the lighter episodes of the campaign against the Welsh and not mentioning the hardships or the dangers. They laughed together over the difficulties of telling one Welsh name from another. Time went quickly. Once she excused herself and rose, "I must see to the bread. My kitchen wench is not to be relied upon, yet." She went out, leaving the door ajar and presently the sweet, appetising scent of fresh baked bread came through.

Outside Walter looked at the sun and said, "Dinnertime." He and the boys had been planting peas and beans in what would one day be the kitchen garden. "There may be company. I heard a horse. Wash your hands before you go in. And mind you behave yourselves." He had given them the same instructions before they went to greet their Uncle James, their Uncle William; boring times. Both men, meaning well, had commented upon how they had grown. "It'd be funny if we hadn't," Henry said afterwards to Walter.

Now he said, "Oh Walter, must we? Couldn't we fetch our dinner and come and eat it with you?"

"You know the answer to that! When I want you in my place, I'll ask you."

He didn't want them or anybody else in the place he had made his own. He was having a little trouble with Bessie whose attitude towards him had recently undergone a most unwelcome change, from sullen resentment to fawning devotion. It was not the first time this had happened and he judged himself capable of deterring unwanted attentions, such as offers to mend or wash his hose; but the more stupid people were, the more thick-skinned they were. Even a snub like, "You want to wash anything, wash yourself!" bounced off Bessie's dull mind just as Sybilla's culinary instructions did.

"Boys, this is Sir Simon Randall who has kindly brought us news of your father. Sir Simon, this is Henry. And Richard."

She had managed to instil some rudiments of manners and both boys bowed. After that they stared. Sir Simon was indeed something to look at, for after the filth and mud and sweat of a campaign, however brief, finery was imperative. He wore on this day the latest in men's fashions, the particoloured outfit. One half of his tunic was the colour of turquoise, the other cherry-red; hose the same, the turquoise leg under the cherry of the tunic and vice versa; even his shoes were half and half. The cap which lay beside him on the settle was turquoise, with a cherry coloured feather and an ornament of ruby stones. On one finger he wore another, single, large ruby.

To this very elegant young person Sybilla could offer only a very humble meal, some cold boiled belly pork which Walter had happened upon; but he ate with apparent enjoyment and —judging that she had had a hand in it—praised the bread.

The two boys, he thought, were handsome little fellows—as was to be expected, considering their parentage—and he was disposed to like them, for the same consideration. He did not mind their staring, any new fashion was designed to attract attention; nor did he resent their ill-concealed amusement. Rustics, and some not so rustic, reacted in a similar way. It was when, the sharpest edge taken from their hunger, they began to quarrel for some obscure reason and, checked by their mother, resorted to kicking each other under the table, that he felt that they were out of hand. He was pleased to hear that Henry was presently bound for Beauclaire. He had himself been a page in his uncle's household, and if Beauclaire was anything like that, Henry Tallboys would soon be brought to heel.

For the rest he only noticed that the baby of the family, his chin almost level with the table, fed himself with energy and neatness, once his meat had been chopped, whereas the little girl, some bit older and larger, had to be fed, coaxed, and persuaded to eat.

The time came to leave.

At the end he hit upon something he could do for her.

"You will be making a garden, Lady Tallboys?"

"I hope so—in time."

"My mother *grows* roses—I mean, not that roses grow for her, she propagates them. She has found a way of grafting a real rose onto a good wild briar. I am sure that it would give her great pleasure to send you a few of her trees."

And so it would. If only it could be concealed from his mother that at last, at last, he had seen a woman whom he would willingly marry, and could not.

Up to a point, in falling in love with Sybilla, Sir Simon was conforming to pattern. Every young man was supposed to cherish a hopeless passion for the unattainable one; active to do her any small service, to beg a favour to wear in the lists and if he had any talent make verses, make tunes in her honour. And then from the impossible to turn to the possible and marry as advantageously as he could.

Not for me, Sir Simon thought.

The Easter Tournament at Winchester, Sybilla knew, began on Easter Monday and lasted three days. Any minute now, she thought. But he did not come and there was no message.

She told herself that perhaps Winchester had proved unprofitable too, and that Godfrey had accepted another invitation, another challenge.

And then, on a beautiful early May morning, with Layer Wood full of bluebells and cuckoos, he came home.

As always, at the slightest unusual sound she ran to the window and saw, nearing the house, a flat cart, drawn by the horse that Walter had saved, and driven by an only-just-recognisable Eustace. Arcol, wearing only a halter, was attached to the back of the cart.

Godfrey was dead! Brought home for burial.

There was a second or two of blackness. Then dizzy, sick, supporting herself by clutching at the wall, she made her way to the door, which stood open.

"It is all right," Eustace called. "Only an accident . . ."

Unaware that she was crying, she ran to the cart.

What kind of accident could reduce a man in the prime of life to skeleton, all skin and bones, with sunken, senseless eyes? And the boy looked little better—except that he was in his right mind. Godfrey seemed not to know her. She said, "My dear! My darling!" and he seemed not to hear.

Stiffly, moving like an old man, Eustace climbed down.

"He took a fall, my lady. He made light of it and we set out for home . . . Then the fever set in. People thought we carried the plague . . ." As he said that, he attempted to laugh and produced a woeful, hooting noise. He was near the breaking point, but sensible enough, when she had shouted for Walter and Walter had come, to say, "It is his knee. Mind his knee. That is where it started."

Walter took charge.

One thing about mean, truckle beds they were light and easily moved. On the one brought from Beauclaire and never yet used here, Sir Godfrey was placed, and carried into his home.

She knew a dozen febrifuges, but she had nothing to hand; not even sage or mint from which to make an infusion. Walter said all that was needed was cold water, inside, outside, and he would deal with it.

Father Ambrose, seeing the cart, had come along, and asked what was afoot, and told, plodded down to the village to Robinson's wife, a woman for whom he had, in his deepest heart, both a dislike and suspicion; but she made good brews.

Eustace made his last effort. "I must see to Arcol; nobody else . . ." And that was true; Arcol, besides being an excep-

47

tionally valuable horse was an exceptionally difficult one. Then Arcol stabled and Sir Godfrey in good hands, the boy who had not had a sound night's rest for a fortnight, lay down on the settle and slept for two nights and a day.

By that time Sir Godfrey was himself—or almost himself again; allowing for the accident and the fever. Either Walter's cold-water cure or the rather sinister black brew which Father Ambrose had brought from the village had been effective. Behind those frightening, fever-blanked eyes, there was Godfrey.

But not as he had been.

Almost the first thing he said to her was, "I was unhorsed; by a beardless boy!"

Eustace, waking from a long, restorative sleep, explained and elaborated. It was true. For the first time in his whole career, Sir Godfrey had been unhorsed and had hurt his knee —his right knee. A mere bruise, he said: and, since they were now almost without funds, they had set out for home. By evening the knee was discoloured and swollen and very stiff and in the morning he had had the utmost difficulty in mounting. Next day the fever struck.

With any kind of open wound, or after loss of blood, fever was expected, but for a bruise . . . ?

"I found a doctor, my lady, and he said dark swellings and fever were signs of plague. He held a pomander to his nose and did not even wait for payment. Sir Godfrey was in his right mind then, and said it was not plague. And he said he wanted, above all things, to get home. So I bought the cart . . ."

So Eustace had bought the cart. He did not dwell much upon the nightmare days and night that had followed, with Sir Godfrey out of his mind; hurting his injured knee by tossing about, and whimpering like a child; attempting to stand up and hurting himself more, screaming like a trapped hare; mistaking Eustace for an enemy and trying to grapple with him. People at inns and at private houses, people who passed or met them in the road all shared the doctor's opinion, summer being the time for plague. Luckily the weather was warm and camping out no hardship.

"At the worst, my lady, I was obliged to tie him down to save him from injuring himself more. And then some people thought I was taking a lunatic to Bedlam!" This time the boy managed a proper laugh; for he had done what he had set

48

out to do—and his beloved master was home, and back in his senses.

"You have been wonderful, Eustace. I shall pray God to reward you." She turned upon him that look of gratitude which seldom failed to reach the mark. "I have always felt that whatever happened, Godfrey was safe with you."

Embarrassed, the boy muttered, "It was nothing . . . It was the least . . ." But privately he thought he had done rather well. A few acts of larceny which he had been forced to commit did not trouble his conscience.

Walter examined the knee. His hands were enormous, but they had a delicate touch. He listened as his fingers probed around the swelling and the fading bruise. "Nothing much, Sir Godfrey," he said hearteningly.

"Only enough to lame me for life." An invalid could be excused his peevishness.

Privately Walter said to Sybilla, "Something's splintered there. I could hear it grate."

"Oh dear! Ought we"—she faltered over the dreaded word —"a surgeon?" An operation performed by a barber-surgeon was the last resort of the desperate. She was relieved when Walter said:

"Best leave it alone. It might work out. If not, I'll see to it."

Day by day, almost hour by hour, she became increasingly aware that Godfrey ailed more than an injured knee. He was silent for long stretches and when he did speak it was always to say something either petulant or melancholy.

He needed nourishment, so Walter killed one of the six recently acquired fowls, and she made chicken broth in the way she had learned at Lamarsh.

"We can't afford fowl now," Godfrey said. "I suppose you realise that we are ruined."

"Not quite. The rents were paid on Lady Day, and I have spent very little. You mustn't worry about such things. You must just think about getting better."

"I shall never be better. In any case, I was unhorsed. By a beardless boy! Who'd want me now?"

He always came back to that. One day she said, with feigned lightness, "Beardless boys have to start on somebody. You did yourself."

49

He gave her a glance of something that looked dangerously near hatred.

Godfrey took no joy in the children—of whom he had always been so proud and fond. He didn't want them near his bed—they might jar him—though in fact even the boys were awed at first and simply stood and stared. He couldn't bear their noise, and when one of their fights broke out in his presence, he shouted at them in a frightening way. Formerly their antics had amused him and he had called them his two young fighting cocks. Once he said a very cruel thing about his angelically pretty daughter: "There's something about her that reminds me of James's Richard." The remark had just enough of truth in it to be shocking.

But worst of all were the moments when, alone with her, he broke down and wept, using the old endearments, but in the wrong fashion. "Sweeting, you got a bad bargain when you married me. Darling, I wish I'd been killed. You'd be better off without me."

Fever, she told herself, often left an aftermath of melancholy. Perhaps company would cheer him. She suggested that Eustace should ride to Moyidan, and to Bywater and tell his brothers that he was home.

"They'd gloat. I used to poke fun at James and his gout . . . And William would talk about the will of God . . ."

He'd always had a sweet, sunny nature. But then he had always been healthy, happy, and successful . . . And that is no way to think of the man you love! No! Think rather that he always gave his whole mind, his whole self, to the thing of the moment, and now for him, poor darling, the moment had narrowed down to pain and a sense of failure. And to that he was devoting all his single-mindedness.

Walter was right. One morning through the now naturally coloured skin of the knee, a tiny protrusion showed itself, white and sharp. It had made its way so gradually that no blood had come with it. Walter greeted the needle-like thing with enthusiasm; it proved what he knew, left alone and not messed about with, the body had a way of healing itself.

"You'll be up and about in no time."

"And lame for life."

50

"But, sir, that does not follow. I once knew a man . . ."

"Spare me your memories, Walter. I have my own. And bitter they are. Unhorsed by a beardless boy."

The bit of bone, pointed like a needle, and no thicker than a bodkin, did work its way out, leaving, Sir Godfrey said, his knee weakened.

The melancholy did not recede.

He who had never looked far ahead, now made plans for a desolate future.

"We must let Eustace go. I had the best horse, the best squire; but Eustace must go and take service with some able man, and get his knighthood."

That was just and sensible; but when Godfrey suggested giving Eustace Arcol and his armour as a parting present, she was bound to protest.

"Arcol would be an embarrassment and an expense to a mere squire, dearest. And your armour would never fit him. Give him the other horse and I will write, recommending him, in the warmest terms."

It was perhaps too early to say that one day he would need his horse and his mail again; but one day she must.

So Walter drove nails into the wall and hung up the armour, and Arcol went out to pasture on the village common, tethered beside a donkey to whom he took an inordinate fancy.

Godfrey remained sunk in gloom, a gloom which deepened at the sound of a would-be cheering word.

James and William eventually heard of his homecoming and paid brotherly visits.

James said, "You have my true sympathy. I know what it is like to be lame."

"But not ruined and done for. Old and finished at thirty-six!"

"You'll be better. Able to ride again."

"With dotards and beardless boys!"

William did, inevitably, mention resignation to God's will, and suggested that Godfrey should be thankful that he had not sustained worse injury. "After all," he said mildly, "you might have broken your neck."

"I wish I had! I wish to God I had. Then your infinite charity could extend to my widow and orphans."

Both brothers missed the real nub of his misery—a career ended without dignity, almost in ridicule. As for the circumstances, both for various reasons, ignored them. James did not wish to feel responsible, and William saw nothing much wrong. Godfrey had a house, two fields under cultivation and a third waiting; hens clucked and pecked about in his yard; there was a sty full of pigs, a cow soon to drop a calf . . .

Only Sybilla, who had loved the man he had been and still loved what he had become, saw the truth. Her mental similes were homely—let a garment go unmended and the hole would widen; let a crumb of mould stay on a cheese or a loaf and it would grow and take over; the same with rust; one speck, a patch, a collapse.

He still limped, the injured knee weak and, from disuse, stiff; health restored, temper still uncertain. The worst things —the moods of weeping and self-reproaches—had become fewer; the gloomy silences had prolonged themselves. And the situation threatened to harden. By mid-August, he could climb the stairs and share her bed. To no purpose.

She had had no training in the arts of seduction and was not, in truth, a hot-blooded, passionate woman. Fourteen years in a convent had tempered her. Always, from the first moment of real marriage, she had sought rather to please than to be pleased, and during his absences she had missed his cheerful talk, his smile, his laughter rather than . . . Well, what? Like Walter, she knew another language. And for its most used word . . . that she could do without, except that the lack of it indicated something badly wrong.

The old Abbess had said of apparently unassailable situations: "We must work around. Nobody is completely invulnerable." She had been speaking of some complicated rights about a mill and Sybilla had forgotten all but the general principle. "Work around."

So, how could one work around a man who had a weak, somewhat stiff knee and a broken spirit?

Work around.

SIX

SYBILLA SAID, "We must make some decision about Arcol. He is growing fat on grass and becoming extremely unruly."

"And what is there to decide about that?" This was the kind of thing he was more and more inclined to say these days, and had she been a crying woman she would often have hurried away to shed a few tears when he sounded so sour and so hostile. "I would have given him to Eustace, but I have no intention of selling him."

Eustace, with many expressions of regret, had gone off to Lord Bowdegrave at Abhurst. His regret was genuine enough, he admired Sir Godfrey and in the fashionable way imagined himself to be in love with Sybilla, but his overriding emotion was excitement and the anticipation of a bright future natural to his youth. Arcol did not like Walter and always behaved awkwardly when being tethered out in the morning and brought in at night. Walter said, "Let Jacky try! Arcol's very fond of one donkey!" Really it had come to something when, with Godfrey in the house, she could be pleased with and smile at such a simple joke.

The suggestion was to Jacky's simple mind the last straw. He had always been scared of Walter, he was terrified of the master who had even less patience with clumsiness or forgetfulness, and now the idea that he should go near that great rearing, iron-shod, tooth-flashing beast filled him with panic, and he fled.

"Good riddance to bad rubbish," Walter said: and Sybilla thought: He wasn't much good, and his going has saved me eighteenpence a year.

She had known that Godfrey would not wish to sell Arcol. She was working round.

"He is in need of exercise—and grooming."

"I daresay I could groom him. I shall never ride him again."

"Why not?"

"I could never mount him."

"Then I must." That, at least, penetrated the surly gloom.

"You! My dear, don't talk nonsense. A woman on a war-horse."

"It has been done. That French girl, Joan of Arc, rode a warhorse."

"Yes. And wore hose like a man, and was burned for a witch."

"I shall borrow Henry's hose and ride Arcol round and round the fallow field. And if that makes me a witch, then a witch I must be."

Sir Godfrey knew his wife. The iron core was seldom much in evidence, but it was there. That afternoon he brought Arcol in from the Common himself, and, reverting to the days when he had been a squire, spent two hours grooming him until the amber-coloured hide shone like satin, mane and tail, a shade darker, like spun silk.

Next day he said he would harness Arcol and try to mount; if he succeeded he would ride to Moyidan.

"That would be wonderful," Sybilla said. "Those dark red apples will be ripe. Ask Emma for a bagful. And ask her, too, if her Richard has outgrown any clothes. Henry grows so fast."

Arcol was, as Sybilla had said, growing fat and flabby on his grass diet; even when Sir Godfrey had given him the ritual punch to make him breathe out while the girth was buckled, it had to be fastened three holes farther along.

Then came the mounting. Clumsy and slow, a climbing into the saddle rather than springing—an old man's performance. But it was accomplished.

It was a morning in late August, sunny and warm, but just touched with a hint of a change of season to come. Going out to see him off Sybilla saw for the first time that there was a touch of silver in Godfrey's bright fawn-coloured hair. Four

54

months of pain and misery had aged him by five years. But at least, she thought modestly, I have got him into the saddle again, and from that who knows what may result? At Baildon and at Bury St. Edmund's and Thetford there were tournaments, not of the very first class, but not to be entirely despised. She turned back into the empty house. Harvest was in full swing; Walter was scything; the two boys were gathering the severed stalks and binding them into sheaves, as Walter had shown them, the competitiveness between them put to useful purpose. And behind the boys Bessie was stooking, five sheaves to a stook. She had volunteered for the job and it was obvious that she was more useful in the field than in the kitchen.

Outside the kitchen door Margaret and John were playing.

Resolutely Sybilla ignored the truth that now it was less a matter of Margaret looking after John, than of John looking after Margaret. Almost as soon as he could stand steadily on his feet, the little boy, as precocious as his brothers, had taken charge.

There was bread to make, and a rabbit pie. Rabbits were at their best when the corn was being cut.

Thump thump on the front door. Father Ambrose! He called almost every day. The only road out of Intake ran past his church and his house, he had indubitably seen Godfrey ride past and had come to say how glad he was to see such an improvement.

It took a certain amount of resolution in order not to regard Father Ambrose as a rather silly old man. One must remember that he had brought the black brew. But he had, since then, shown a lack of tact, telling Godfrey that he should come to church as soon as he could walk, even with support, saying what a pity it was that he did not read, a book could offer so much consolation.

Once Godfrey, the new Godfrey, had said, "Keep him away from me. Tell him I'm dead!"

However, when she opened the door it was not Father Ambrose who stood there. It was a Dominican friar. A Black friar.

Lamarsh had been a Franciscan house, and all Sybilla's training there had been, despite an underlying personal strict-

55

ness, liberal. After all, St. Francis had preached to the birds and called his donkey "Brother."

The Dominicans were different, more concerned with organisation, with politics; and the very word "black" when applied to them had significance, for their garb was in fact not wholly black; it was black over white; the blackness referred more to their general temper, their strictness, their assiduity in sniffing out and hounding down heretics.

In fact when Sybilla first saw the Dominican her heart gave a little jolt and she thought: Walter! Not that Walter had ever been known to express any heretical sentiments, but he had resolutely refused to go to church, even at Easter. Father Ambrose had tried persuasion, Sybilla had added her word. Walter had remained obdurate. It occurred to Sybilla that the priest might have sought some support from the Order known to be stern in principle and in argument unbeatable.

She made her curtsey and said, "Good morning."

"Good morning. I am Father Andreas. I wish to speak with Sir Godfrey Tallboys."

"He is from home at the moment. He will not be back until evening."

She was aware of his giving her that remote, slightly disparaging look which most celibates turned upon women. In fact he was wondering about her status. Sir Godfrey had been reported to him as being hard on forty. Daughter? Young sister?

Behind him, in the space where the garden was yet to be, stood a mouse-coloured mule, very sleek and lively looking.

"If you would care to wait," she said, and gritted her teeth a little. With Godfrey out for the day and everybody in the field, she had planned to carry out a makeshift meal of bread and cheese. "I am Lady Tallboys," she added as though to confirm her right to invite him in.

If possible his scrutiny became even more impersonal and at the same time more intense. Men were uxorious. Would a man married to this very young, very comely little creature . . . ?

He said, "I thank you, no. I have another errand. I will come back. At Vespers."

He mounted the mule and rode away. She stood for a moment in the doorway, staring after him, and then turned back to busy herself with the bread and the rabbit pie.

In the field, handing Walter his portion and a cup of water, cold from the well, she said, "Walter, a Dominican, Father Andreas, came this morning and is coming back later. To see Sir Godfrey. It could be about your refusal to go to Mass."

"Could be," Walter agreed.

"It worries me a little, Walter."

"It shouldn't," he said. "I know what you're thinking, my lady. About the churchgoing. So far as I know there's no law about it. I'm no Lollard. I never said anything *against* the Church. I simply stay away."

"I know. But *why,* Walter? I never understood why."

"Too much of it when I was young." For the first time he lifted the curtain and gave her a brief glimpse into the past. "My old granny," he said, "very religious. Church every day; she was past being useful and I was too young to be. So she'd haul me along . . . Once—it was a dry year—she prayed for rain. So did I; little boy doing what I was told. *Not a drop fell.*"

Sybilla knew all the arguments about unanswered prayers, but this was not the time or place for them. She knew about Lollardry, too, a movement fully as much political as religious. Lollard had been persecuted years ago, less because they had protested against certain Church practices—such as selling beforehand a pardon for an offence one intended to commit—than because they had advocated freedom to all serfs . . .

Sir Godfrey had had what should have been a happy day. James and Emma welcomed him warmly and James, in the middle of his summer gout which this year had encroached into his eyelids, was pitiable, even by the standards of a knight with a weak knee. Emma had most graciously taken Sybilla's request for a few of Richard's outgrown clothes . . . for Moyidan's Richard had grown, too; upwards, not outwards. Weedy. And why did one use that word, weeds being the toughest things on earth?

He rode back through the rather hazy sunlight of a late August afternoon. He rode slowly, for a heavy warhorse like Arcol was not bred for speed. Arcol and all like him were made for short charges—the length of a tourney ground, the length of the distance between two opposing forces. Arcol had two speeds, full charge and idle along.

On one side of Sir Godfrey's saddle as he rode home through the lingering sunset was a bag of the dark red apples which Sybilla had asked for, and on the other a bag of Richard's outgrown clothes. A successful errand. I have mounted again, I have ridden, I am healed. Not enough; the inner wound still bled, quietly leaching away, day by day, all confidence and joy.

In the stable at Knight's Acre, with everything done that a good squire would do, Sir Godfrey leaned for a moment against the great amber-gleaming shoulder. "Arcol, old boy, we're done for, you and I."

Carrying the bags he limped in, by the kitchen door and Sybilla, nodding towards the hall, said, "There is a Dominican, Father Andreas, waiting to see you."

No Christian denied the possibility of miracles; the blind man healed, the dead man restored to life; but unlike Walter's old granny few reasonable people expected to see a miracle performed, under their very eyes, except perhaps at shrines like Walsingham and such places. Yet one seemed to have happened here.

When Godfrey entered the kitchen he was limping badly and his shoulders sagged in the new way they had, his face was gloomy and his voice flat. "Emma sent what you wanted," he said, putting the two bags on the table, and Sybilla thought: Alas, the outing has done him no good! When she told him about the caller waiting within he had shown no interest, simply limped on wearily towards the door of the hall.

She waited. She could hear the voices but not the words. It was suppertime, the children, Bessie and Walter came in, waiting to be fed.

She cut the pie, sparingly, aware of the obligations of hospitality towards a stranger under her roof at mealtime. Soon she must go in and extend the invitation to supper. She chose the three less battered of the ill-matched platters, three of the least shabby of the horn cups and then, as an afterthought, went into the larder and drew a jug of wine from the small cask which she had asked Walter to buy in Baildon so that she could offer sops-in-wine to an invalid with no appetite.

That done, she straightened her headdress and went towards the door into the hall.

"I shall be there!" Godfrey's ordinary voice, strong and ringing.

The outer door thudded as she opened the inner one. Godfrey turned from it and came the length of the hall to meet her. He hardly limped at all. He greeted her as he was accustomed to, after any absence, lifting her from her feet. "Darling, I have such news!"

And in fact it was as though he had been away for three months and had now returned. Over her shoulder he saw the cups and the jug ready and said, in his own voice, "How did you know?"

"Know what?"

"That we had cause for celebration."

"Tell me."

He told her. One must not question or carp at a thing which had in an hour restored him. And Dominicans, whatever else they were, were not liars, in fact they dealt with the truth, even when it was unpalatable. Yet it was a fantastic story.

As usual he told it badly and had to be helped out with questions, but soon she had a gist of it.

In the South of Spain, a part known as Andalucia, there was a nobleman, the Count of Escalona, vastly, vastly rich, who wished to give a tournament of the utmost magnificence with such prizes as had never been heard of; the first the equivalent of a thousand English pounds. (Disloyal to think: But you were unhorsed at Winchester!) And not prizes only; pay of a kind, five hundred pounds to every man who presented himself; and all expenses paid.

Surely too good to be true. Was that why, secretly, her heart doubted and her mind resisted, and aloud her tongue questioned? Why English knights; had he none of his own, so great and rich a lord? A simple answer: English knights were known to be the best in the world.

Why a Dominican as his errand boy? Another simple answer: the Count of Escalona was a patron; the Order owed him much and wished to make some return; besides, he needed somebody who knew England and spoke English.

And that emphasised the foreignness of the whole affair. It entailed a voyage on the sea! Is that what I fear?

William's abode at Bywater, called a palace because a Bishop resided there, though it was far from palatial, stood a little above the port of Bywater, and Sybilla remembered the sea—her first glimpse of it—so huge, and the ships so tiny. Yes, that might lie at the back of her resistance to this thing.

She asked: When?

"We sail on St. Michael's Day. An omen for good."

"It leaves only a short time to prepare."

"If I exercise Arcol every day . . ." He looked at the armour on the wall. "That needs a good going over, too . . ."

As from a distance she observed that he was no more really aware of this change than he had been of the other. He would not deliberately have become surly, melancholy, bad-tempered and despairing, unloving. In the same way he seemed to be unaware of this change for the better, lameness ignored, appetite restored, cheerfulness in the ascendant.

A weathercock nature? No! No! Simply a man as trained and conditioned as Arcol.

And for that I should be thankful; a less single-minded man would never have married *me!* He'd have listened, been dissuaded—and I should now be at Lamarsh!

Now—and here was the irony—she had regained him, only to lose him again.

It was being *wanted* that had worked the cure. If he told her once he told her a dozen times about the little book which Father Andreas carried, a book in which were written the names of those worthy of invitation. Again and again he said, "And I thought I was done for. Arcol, too."

He was confident—as he always had been—of coming home safe and sound; and this time with certain money. Knight's Acre would be transformed; there would be proper servants, proper beds; there would be new gowns for Sybilla, a dowry for Margaret, now his "pretty little dear." And when Henry went off to Beauclaire he would go not as a poor relation. Richard, too, in time. And John. He no longer minded their noise, thought their quarrels amusing.

60

Sybilla kept her head. Could they, she asked, hope to get Eustace back?

No, he said gaily, it would be unfair to the boy. A knighthood bestowed by a Spanish Count, however rich and grand, might not be valid in England.

"And I need no squire. I have not forgotten the tricks."

Happily, happily he hauled down his armour and polished it, whistling as he worked. And she stitched away, repairing the faded or frayed work on the emblem, the hare at bay, on his blue mantle.

There were so few days, and each one shorter than the one before. But they were happy days, followed by happy nights, for, remanned, he was again her lover.

Exercising Arcol he rode to Moyidan and she had the slight hope that James might call this a wild-goose chase and suggest life at home with little affrays at Baildon, Bury St. Edmund's, Thetford, and such places. And James, very level-headed and clearsighted, might even spot the flaw—she was sure it existed, though she could not put her finger on it. But James regarded the whole thing as wonderful; five hundred pounds, win or lose, with the possibility of double that amount.

And what about William, so unworldly? Would he not speak out about being too much involved with money, of a man's first duty being to his wife and children, and how dangerous the sea was? William, of all people, knew how dangerous . . .

But William failed her too. He had—as she had—seen a man soured and prepared to sit down and rot, and now restored, eager and happy. Godfrey, not far from the brink of despair, that ultimate sin, had been snatched back, just in time; and although the sea did claim some victims, roughly four out of five ships that put out from Bywater did come back.

No support anywhere.

The old Abbess had said, "In the end you must be prepared to be alone with God."

She prayed often—not for some direct intervention, but for the courage, the strength, the cunning that would enable her to deter him from this venture without casting him back into gloom. When he spoke of what he would do with his money she said they had all they *needed;* that people could be happy without curtained beds and silver drinking cups. "After all, darling, we have always been poor and we have always been happy."

"Not always. Not lately. Not until Father Andreas came. I used to sit and think . . . Thinking was something I'd never had time for." He gave her his old, sweet smile, but then added with sudden violence, "You cannot know how I *hated* being poor and useless."

Although the physical signs of age had disappeared, he was older in himself, his prolonged boyhood outgrown at last.

She fell back on feminine wiles, how lonely she would be, how helpless she sometimes felt when the boys were unmanageable. His reception of such remarks was sensible, but all wrong; how about asking one of Eustace's sisters to come and live with her; how about buying a palfry and riding over to visit Emma sometimes? As for the boys, he would speak to Walter and give him leave to chastise them when necessary. In any case Henry would be going to Beauclaire . . .

On the verge of tears she said sharply, "I don't mean that kind of loneliness! I mean being without you."

"But, sweetheart, you have been without me often. This is unlike you. Why are you *against* this?"

"I don't know. I only know that I am." Now the time had come to speak frankly. "I know that you are happy about it, but I am not. I never have been, from the start . . . From the very start, when I opened the door to the Black Friar. There must be a trick. No man could be so rich and so crazy . . . Godfrey, don't go. I beg and beseech you, *don't* go."

He ended all that with a simple statement: "I gave my word."

"There's one thing, my lady," said Walter—the only one who seemed to understand—"Sir Godfrey won't drown."

"How *can* you be so sure?"

"I got him a caul. That Bessie knew where to lay her hands on one."

It was an old, and prevalent superstition. A baby born with a caul—a bit of membrane over its head—would never

62

drown; what was more, the caul in itself could convey its protective powers to anyone who possessed it.

Bessie, so anxious to please Walter, had dragged up this tale and offered to procure this emblem of magic, and Walter, insufficiently impressed, had said that he supposed it could do no harm. In a place like Bywater there was a ready sale for such things, and even in Baildon a caul was easily disposed of. No genuine one was available, but Granny Wade was equal to the occasion: a pig's bladder, shrivelled and darkened by exposure to smoke and torn about a bit, would deceive anybody.

"That was kind of you, Walter. But—there are other dangers."

Like Sir Godfrey, Walter thought that this was unlike the lady; in all the time he had known her she had been as brave, in her own way, as Sir Godfrey in his, never fretting, never crying.

"Is it foreigners you're thinking about? Can't speak of Spain, never having been there, but I know the French. Well, this'd surprise you, but they're just people. We were led to believe they had tails, and they thought the same thing about us . . . First prisoner we ever took, we stripped him, just to make sure . . ."

Maybe that wasn't quite the thing to say. He fell back on safer ground. "As for danger, my lady; after all you could stay at home and choke to death on a fishbone."

So the last, precious days ran away. The last Mass together; the last meal; the last night. Early morning of St. Michael's Eve. Misty, everything swimming in a blue haze. He had to make an early start because Arcol, with brief charges and longer amblings, would take almost all day to cover the twenty miles to Bywater; and everything—men, horses, and gear— were supposed to be on the quayside at Bywater by late afternoon, so that the ship could sail on the morning's outgoing tide.

He had no send-off from the village which was not a manor. From all that he represented, Intake had long ago broken away; the old feudal sense of belonging severed when Sir

Godfrey's great-grandfather had said to their great-grandfathers, "Go make what you can of it," and trees had been felled, the first acres turned by the plough. Not one of them had ever seen a tournament—which was a practice for war; they had never been threatened by any enemy worse than those that threatened any rural community, a bad harvest, animals sickening, drought when rain was needed and rain when dry weather was essential. Sir Godfrey meant nothing to them; a landlord who could not even—and God be thanked—raise their rents.

Sybilla did not shed a tear at parting. They embraced; she said, "God keep you. You take my heart with you."

"And I leave mine with you."

Rounding the corner of the little church, he turned in the saddle and raised his hand in a final salute. He had not realised how small she was, or how small she seemed standing there between those two great boys.

SEVEN

LATE FOR THE TRYSTING PLACE. And Arcol to blame. Arcol
had tolerated a bag of apples, a bag of outgrown clothes; but
the leather bag of armour was heavier and noisier; everytime
he obeyed the word "Charge," the thing, whatever it was,
clanked and bumped, so in the end he refused to charge at
all and simply went forward at his other, plodding pace. So,
despite his early start, Sir Godfrey was late.

But he was there. Fifty, Father Andreas thought. Not easy
to gather. The English were very insular and in the main
curiously content with what they had, unseduceable. The company he had gathered divided itself rather sharply into young
men, attracted as much by the adventure as the money, and
men a little older than he would have chosen had choice been
free. Sir Godfrey did not know it but he had been low on the
list of desirability.

Riding in he saw several familiar faces—an old friend and
rival, Sir Stephen Flowerdew, as well as Sir Ralph Overton
and Sir Thomas Drury. Greeting and being greeted by them
gave him a sense of homecoming, and of excitement, and
also the comforting assurance that this was not quite such
a fantastic adventure as Sybilla had made it seem. Ralph
Overton was a much-travelled man and shrewd as a lawyer,
not one to undertake anything with a possibility of trickery in
it.

Now, an unfamiliar face. A very young man, so brilliantly
clad as to dazzle the eye. He bared his head and bowed in a
most respectful manner and when Godfrey had returned his
greeting, wondering who? wondering where? said in the rather

affected way fashionable nowadays amongst the young, "Now my happiness is complete. No squire, Sir Godfrey? Here! Gilbert, take Sir Godfrey's gear and stow it with mine."

Raised, in that masterful, authoritative way, the voice at least was remembered. The voice that had said at Winchester: "Take him up gently. No, of course I shall not take his horse!"

Lord Robert Barbury. The beardless boy!

Bywater was a busy port but almost entirely devoted to commerce; fifty knights, with their horses and other belongings was a sight to see. Embarkations and disembarkations during the French wars had been at the Cinque Ports: Romney, Hythe, Sandwich, Hastings, and Dover. Everyone who could spare time now stood about to watch the colourful show, which included the biggest hound anyone had ever seen. As big as a donkey. But the most entertaining performance was given by Arcol. Word went round quickly: There's a mad horse!

Arcol's nerves had already been strained by the clatter of the armour bag; he did not like the smooth, slippery stones of Bywater's jetty; he refused absolutely to be coaxed or compelled to step onto the little gangway which connected *The Four Fleeces* with the jetty. The whole thing frightened him and he knew just what to do when he was frightened. Even blindfolded he was resistant and dangerous.

Sweating and breathless, Sir Godfrey said, "I'll try him again in the morning," and led the horse, now meek as a lamb, to the stables at the rear of the inn, Welcome to Mariners.

"If he continues to be awkward," Father Andreas said, meaning well, "I am sure that the Count of Escalona can provide you with a mount."

But the relationship between a knight and his horse—or in the case of a rich man, his horses—was a thing not easily assessed. They were one. The Count of Escalona had been aware of that when he made an order for fifty knights, their mail and their horses. It had taken Sir Godfrey long hours to become one with Arcol when his first destrier had failed.

He said, "Without Arcol I cannot go." His happy mood, so many old friends, such cordial greetings, had clouded when he recognised Lord Robert. Weeks and weeks in the company of one who, courteous and civil as he was, would always be a reminder . . . There were two ships, but the order, "Stow his gear by mine," meant close contact.

Once a bad mood began, it grew and darkened. A year ago, without a thought, except that he had a noble in his pouch, he would have gone gaily to join the crowd who were merrymaking in the inn. He'd joined such gatherings hundreds of times, often when he had nothing to pay with, but confident that when somebody said, "Toss for the reckoning," the dice or the coin would favour him. In the unlikely event of its not doing so, well, one could always borrow . . .

But broken confidence was less easily healed than a broken knee. He had a good gold piece—Sybilla had insisted upon his taking it: "Darling, you never know what might happen." But he was not going to risk it in frivolity. And he had a perfect excuse; he must go and take leave of his brother.

As he toiled up the incline to William's so-called palace, melancholy deepened.

He thought he had done with it, done with it on the night when Father Andreas had talked to him—but here it was again, as persistent as an unwanted dog, or the three-day fever which haunted the marshes. And a meal of William's unidentifiable meat did nothing to cheer him.

"William, if anything should happen to me, have a care to Sybilla and the children . . ." Never in his whole carefree life had he said such a thing, never before had he looked ahead to an untoward happening.

"But naturally," William said. He had noted the difference in mood. None of the elation Godfrey had shown on the visit when he announced that he was off to Spain. It was the parting, he assumed. Godfrey never looked all round a subject; he probably had not realised until yesterday that what he had called a golden opportunity, such a chance as came to few, would involve parting from his family for a long period. William set himself to be cheerful—there was the voyage, of course, but on the sea, if anywhere, a man was in God's hands. He knew *The Four Fleeces,* knew she was a sound ship, and Captain Briggs a skilled, experienced seaman. And once ashore—well, going to a tournament was not like going to war.

Godfrey kept saying, "I know. I know." But without looking much happier. "The terms were, five hundred pounds to any man who presented himself . . . I've been thinking, if I get there and become entitled . . . And then anything should happen to me. Somebody would see that Sybilla got the money, no doubt. But it is a large sum—and she has never had much." Completely unlike himself.

"James and I between us would see that it was well handled . . . And now, I think, your last evening, a glass of wine."

William's wine was as bad as his meat and did little to lift a heavy mood.

Arcol was no more amenable in the morning; a near ton of frenzied, fighting horse. The companion ship, *Mary Clare,* loosed her ropes; clear water showed between her hull and the jetty, and still Arcol would not go aboard. Captain Briggs was dancing with impatience and cursing, Father Andreas, more controlled but equally concerned about the tide, said, "Sir Godfrey, you must leave him." Amongst the spectators was the old fishwife, loading her donkey's panniers. Inspiration visited Sir Godfrey; he called, "Good mother, may I borrow your donkey for a moment?"

The little donkey, well schooled in obedience, trotted along the jetty and onto the gangway, down into the hold. And Arcol followed the familiar, the loved donkey shape and smell.

"Cast off!" Captain Briggs yelled.

The old woman lifted her skirts, showing skinny shanks and large flat feet, and ran along the jetty. "My donkey! My donkey!" The watchers laughed and shouted.

Feeling something almost like physical pain, Sir Godfrey put his hand to his pouch. A whole noble, six shillings and eightpence, for an old donkey worth a shilling at most.

Then coins rattled on the stones. Screams and imprecations changed to blessings, "God bless you, gentlemen all. God bless you."

Turning to see who had forestalled him, Sir Godfrey found himself face to face with Lord Robert.

He said with no marked gratitude, "Thank you, my lord. I must reimburse you." He held out his coin. No great perception was needed to see that it was his only one; full pouches clink when handled.

"I was afraid she would have a fit—or curse the whole outfit. Could we defer the payment? I flung her all my small change."

"I shall remember that I am in your debt, my lord. And for the second time. You could have claimed my horse that day."

The boy laughed. "And who would want Arcol?"

It was meant tactfully, a joke to explain a gesture, but Sir Godfrey seemed to take it amiss and did not smile. Lord Robert said:

"I wonder how many horses you have taken, Sir Godfrey, fighting under similar rules."

"One. But the fellow was a bad knight and a bad opponent. I reckoned it would be to everybody's advantage to have him on foot for a bit."

"In any case, my unhorsing you was pure accident. I know and you know that we could meet again, a thousand times, and you would win."

"That may be put to the proof in Escalona, my lord."

Stiff, unfriendly, denying absolutely his reputation as not only the best knight, but the most courteous, the most merry. Until the Easter Tournament at Winchester Lord Robert had never seen Sir Godfrey Tallboys, but he had heard of him, even in his native Yorkshire which, though part of England, was so far away as to be almost a different country. For a man who had an almost legendary quality the boy had developed a kind of hero worship. How sad, he now thought, that that purely accidental happening should have had this effect.

A sailor coiling rope said, "So now we have a donkey aboard as well as a priest! Sure bad luck."

Even more than most men in a superstitious age, seamen were superstitious. Bishop William had said that on the sea if anywhere, men were in God's hands; it cut both ways; on the sea if anywhere, men were in the hands of blind chance, or the Devil. Priests were bad cargo; so were donkeys and corpses—the last worst of all. In fact, dead men—soldiers killed abroad who had relatives rich and important enough to

69

want them brought home to be buried with their fathers—were often shipped in the most ignominious fashion, crammed into barrels, rolled up in tapestries. Captain Briggs himself, an enlightened man in his way, had been a bit sorry when Father Andreas chose to travel on his ship and not on the *Mary Clare*. And he had suffered a moment's indecision about the donkey, sail with it or wait while it was taken off. The sailor's remark, chiming with his own unacknowledged feelings, provoked him. He administered a clout on the ear. "Lay off that. Talk of bad luck invites it." Privately he determined to get rid of the donkey. That proved to be impossible; the little animal shared Arcol's narrow space between the bulkhead and the buffering wall of straw bales, and the only person allowed near was Sir Godfrey himself. And he, tactfully approached—"Your horse would have more room and be more comfortable, sir"—said that the donkey might well be needed again.

No bad luck was immediately apparent; a brisk following wind sent *The Four Fleeces* skimming down the Channel. The way the ship handled, though, was a constant reminder to her master that her cargo was lighter than usual; knights and horses were great consumers of space in proportion to their weight. In the Bay of Biscay *The Four Fleeces* would bounce about like a walnut shell. Knights and horses were also extremely demanding; but Captain Briggs had struck such a bargain with the Dominican, who seemed to have unlimited money, that it made the whole thing worth while. Half the charter money was already paid and safe with the captain's wife in Bywater, the other half was to be paid in Seville. Not only that, Father Andreas had guaranteed a return cargo, a full cargo of real sherry wine, a thing practically unheard of.

The price agreed included food for men and horses; and there again some profit might be made, with management and cunning, meticulous though Father Andreas had been about details; fresh bread every other day, fresh meat twice a week. Captain Briggs had carried a few passengers before but they had either provided for themselves or eaten whatever was available; now he carried sheep, pigs, calves, fowls; all closely penned and all—by the sound of them—ill-contented. But the Bay of Biscay, even at its best, was a great curber of appetites. He derived a sour amusement from the thought of a pig killing and a pig roasting with *The Four Fleeces* attempting somersaults . . .

But at the end of it all with God's blessing and a modicum of luck—peace. Just this one immensely profitable voyage—a chance that came to few men—and he'd sell out and retire. Not as many old sailors did to a place within sight and sound of the sea; he wanted no more of it. A little house in that part of Baildon called Saltgate; on winter nights the shutters closed —he did not aspire to the luxury of glazed windows—a blazing hearth and let the wind blow where it liked. His son should be apprenticed to an easier and safer trade . . .

"It occurs to me," Sir Ralph Overton said, "that God, if He is up there, must often have a good laugh."

The older knights had naturally gravitated to one another, finding out and becoming tolerant of the little physical habits, mental quirks which had not been noticeable in larger, looser gatherings, but on shipboard did obtrude.

Sir Ralph was terribly, boringly given to extraordinary statements, near blasphemous; or, as an alternative, sentences beginning, "When I was in Calais . . . Rome . . . Pamplona . . ."

On this, the last peaceful evening they were to know for a while, Sir Stephen Flowerdew, orthodox to the core, said with some irritation:

"What do you mean? If He is up there. We know He is. And why should He laugh?"

"At us, my dear man. All rushing about and busying ourselves. And all playing Blindman's Buff. Whereas He knows. Why we are here, for example."

"I know why I am here. I have four daughters; the eldest needs some dower now, the others, presently."

"Oh, that," Sir Ralph said, dismissing an excellent reason with a shrug. "By the same token, I am here because my sister, rich as she is, refused to allow me a penny, or pay another debt. She called me a wastrel."

Sir Godfrey made his contribution. "I have a wife and four children, and but a small estate."

"And you could ask every man and get a reason. But not

71

the one God knows. I sometimes myself hazard a guess." He said the last words in his irritating, half-mysterious manner. Neither of his hearers encouraged him by a question. "You see, when I was in Pamplona—my first visit, as a very young man—Escalona was there." That at least was new and interesting, and he had their attention. Indeed Sir Thomas Drury, conscientiously exercising his wolfhound, halted and said, "What's that? Did you so. What's he like?"

"A very strange fellow. Not mad, but given to fits of madness. He fell in love with Princess Blanche of Pamplona, a mere child. Asked for her hand, in fact, and took the refusal so badly that her father asked him to withdraw and never set foot in Navarre again. She's Crown Princess of Castile now."

"Interesting," Sir Stephen said. "But no concern of ours."

"That is what you think. I ask myself whether we may not find ourselves engaged, not in a tourney—but in a rebellion. All this"—he waved a hand in a comprehensive gesture which included *Mary Clare* somewhere out of sight, left behind on the first day—"seems to me rather a high price to pay for a tournament, even for so rich a man."

Sybilla had said almost the same thing. And now Sir Thomas, fondling the wolfhound's head, asked a question that she had asked:

"Then why the Dominican?"

"John of Castile is unpopular with them—indeed with all the Church. He is an open blasphemer, and dabbles in alchemy."

"If you are right it would put us in a very grievous position," Sir Stephen said; orthodoxy told him that Kings were Kings, God's anointed. On the other hand—those four sweet girls! "Not that we owe any allegiance to the King of Castile."

"Why should you think such things?" Sir Godfrey remembered feeling relief at seeing Sir Ralph on Bywater quay, so knowledgeable, so shrewd.

"I only said that I asked myself. Well, we shall see when we get there."

Then came the time when it seemed likely that they might not get there. The Bay of Biscay, dangerous at any time, was a giant cauldron, stirred by the autumn westerlies. All but the most hardened seamen were prostrate, and even they went about green-faced and reeling; even Captain Briggs abandoned his idea of a mocking pig-killing.

Above deck it was like being in a plague-stricken camp under constant rain; below it was an Inferno.

("You will need three men accustomed to stable work," Father Andreas had said. "All knights will not have squires —and in fact I have discouraged them.")

The hold had been most thoughtfully prepared for a cargo of horses; bags of chaff and bales of straw, held by nets and steadied by ropes, separated the horses from one another, and in ordinary conditions prevented too much lurching about. The place had been kept much cleaner than any stable because odours tend to rise and nobody wanted to live, to eat and sleep in the odour of horse dung and urine; droppings were removed almost as soon as they fell, and complete swilling down twice a day was the rule.

Lord Robert had again offered Gilbert's services to Sir Godfrey but Arcol would not tolerate him, so Sir Godfrey did his own feeding, grooming, and cleaning. He did the feeding, doggedly, even at the worst, feeding and watering other horses, too. Cleaning was impossible, and though horses were physically unable to be sick, when frightened they staled frequently. The few hardy men still active joked about the smell —it was that which kept them on their feet, they said. But the evening came when Sir Godfrey found himself single-handed, wading over ankle-deep in filth which swilled about from side to side and from end to end as the ship rolled and pitched.

He had succeeded in watering six horses when he was aware of the sound of vomiting. He turned and there, at the foot of the ladder, was Lord Robert. When he straightened up his pallor was almost phosphorescent in the gloom. "Better now," he said, wiping his mouth on his velvet sleeve. "Able to . . . lend a hand."

During the earlier, pleasanter part of the voyage Lord Robert had been one of the younger men who did not observe, more or less, the gap between the young and the older. Second son of the extremely wealthy Earl of Thorsdale, he had come aboard well provided with his own wine and every kind of delicacy in the way of food; and often enough he would break away from the rather sycophantic group by which he was always surrounded and invite Sir Godfrey and his cronies: "Do us the favour of joining us." Or he would join them. "May I sit with you? I find Sir Ralph's tales so entrancing." Entrancing, but now and again somewhat questionable, and the boy did not listen with the apathy or full acceptance of the others. Immensely courteous, always, he would sometimes say, "But Sir Ralph, I always understood . . ." He was, what? between eighteen and nineteen, with a girlish complexion, extremely long eyelashes and the fashionable long hair, chestnut coloured and curly; he appeared to have brought a lot of clothes—all most unsuitable; he was, in fact, a type which older, harder men tended to despise. But he was extremely well informed, and once Sir Ralph, corrected twice in an hour—and with wine in him—showed irritation. "My lord, you are so well informed. Were you intended for the Church?"

"No. What I know I owe entirely to my grandmother. A most remarkable woman. German by birth and a woman of the people."

What an admission to make!

"Her father made stained glass and she travelled with him acting as assistant—so many processes being secret. She spoke four languages and was fluent in all. Her father died, somewhat suddenly and she was stranded. Rescued by my grandfather. In return she made his fortune. She knew coal when she saw it and recognised its possibilities."

That was strictly true and no more than her due. Coal was a fuel that gave, weight for weight, bulk for bulk, more heat than any other, logs or turf. And under the thin skin of the sheep-nibbled, rabbit-gnawed surface of Lord Thorsdale's many acres, it lay there, just waiting to be scooped out. People were slow to change, but coal was making its way; smiths and armourers and bakers had begun to use it because it gave a more equable heat; and there were cities, London, Norwich, Lynn where year by year the distance between the hearths where wood burned and the trees from which the wood was brought increased, every mile adding to the cost of every log. The coal, just under the surface, easily hacked out, easily transportable, by sea—it was known as sea coal—was becoming increasingly popular.

As a rule, Sir Godfrey, whenever possible, avoided Lord

Robert, the living reminder of something he preferred to forget, but on this terrible evening, in this hideous place, he felt differently, glad of that helping hand, and after a while respectful of the resolute temper the boy displayed. He was sick three or four times before every horse was watered and fed, but he kept on, tottering and slopping about, and from time to time essaying a mild joke.

They worked alone for the next two days, and by then the term "beardless boy" had completely lost its sting; for this was no ordinary boy. Sir Godfrey developed for him a feeling which he thought was paternal.

The Four Fleeces, battered, filthy and stinking, staggered in to Mondeneno, a small, sheltered place on Spain's north coast. It was comparatively sophisticated for a place of its size; seaborne pilgrims to the shrine of St. James of Compostella used it—chiefly in summer—and it was accustomed to and equipped for the reception of ships which the Bay of Biscay had battered; many of them in far worse case than *The Four Fleeces.* It boasted three taverns, two acknowledged brothels, a Dominican house, several men skilled in ship repairs and even more men skilled in the making of fake relics.

The ship was to be cleared. Arcol, last in, was first out, led by the donkey and giving no trouble at all. In this sheltered corner pasture was available even at this late time of the year. Men and horses, cleansed and freed, were disposed to enjoy this respite for the four days which Captain Briggs deemed necessary.

Lord Robert, now on such terms with Sir Godfrey as he had despaired of, settling a sky-blue tunic, tricked with silver over hose the colour of ripe mulberries, said, "Sir Godfrey, you intend to sample the wares?"

"No." In the past, a time infinitely remote, when he was this boy's age he had taken a sample or two and found them . . . well, disappointing to say the least. Nothing to it in fact until he met Sybilla.

The boy said, blushing his ready blush:

"If it is a question of cost . . . I could accommodate you, Sir Godfrey, without the slightest inconvenience to myself."

"I could buy myself a harlot for half an hour, if I wanted one," Sir Godfrey said harshly. "I am a married man."

"But . . . but so are many others . . ."

"And I have something to do. Run along, enjoy yourself. And keep an eye on your purse."

A whore in Westminster had made away with his once when he was about this boy's age.

"My wife," Sir Godfrey said to Father Andreas, having finally tracked him down, "can read. I cannot write. But I would like to send her a letter."

"I will write it for you, Sir Godfrey. With great pleasure."

Father Andreas was capable of changing his mind. This man, not amongst the most eligible, nearing forty and lame, had seemed at the end of a long and disappointing recruiting campaign rather like the scrapings of the barrel. But, much less lame, much less old, he had kept his word, shown sound good sense about the donkey; never missed Mass and recently when almost everybody else lay about, wishing to die, had kept active. And now, when all the others had gone off to eat and drink and fornicate—let's not mince words—he was here wanting a letter to be written for his wife. A man in a thousand, ten thousand.

"Yes," Father Andreas said, dipping the quill's point.

"Tell her, please, that I am safe and well and that the worst is over now." He changed his rather tentative dictating voice to ordinary speech. "Captain Briggs said so—fairly plain sailing from here."

"That is the general experience. Yes?" Pen poised, the single word asking the question: What next?

"Tell her I am well—no, I said that before . . . Say that I hope she is well. And all the children. And Walter." He paused and the quill squeaked.

"And that is all, Sir Godfrey?"

It was not; but he realised that the man wielding the pen was a man vowed to celibacy. How to put it?

"Would you write that I regret the waste of time . . . in the summer . . . when we were together. She will understand."

Father Andreas thought that he understood, too.

"Sir Godfrey, can you sign it?"

76

"Oh yes, I can write my name."

He wrote it, bearing down so hard, as people unaccustomed to writing did, that the nib of the quill splayed out and the ink sprayed.

"Could you so arrange it that the next ship to put in here, bound for England, could take it? I was told that there was traffic . . ."

"There is. Even in winter. Rest assured. One of my Order will be watchful. No, no, Sir Godfrey, there will be no charge."

Soft footed and saying little, Father Andreas had been observant. Sir Godfrey never gambled, had brought no extra provisions of his own, and when asked to share others' either excused himself or partook most abstemiously. Plainly a poor man. A man who had behaved most admirably during the difficult days.

Father Andreas took out the little black book in which every knight's name was listed and against Sir Godfrey's he made a cryptic little mark. Then he looked at the letter and thought about how far it must travel, of the many hands needed to get it to its destination. It should be made worthwhile. He took up his pen again and above the signature wrote: Your loving husband and faithful knight.

They spent the four days while the ship was repaired and cleansed in exercising the horses and practising their skills against one another. To the boy whom he now looked upon as a son, Sir Godfrey said, "Your eye is clean out, Lord Robert. And will be if you go a-whoring."

It was a generally accepted belief that sexual exercise detracted from performance; and certainly some of the most redoubtable knights in the world were vowed to celibacy.

"I shall have time to recover before we reach Escalona," Lord Robert said.

Also generally accepted was the convention that whereas women of one's own kind must never be discussed, prostitutes could be talked about freely. Sir Thomas Drury could remark that the girl who had fallen to his lot was very young, very small, very dark, and very expert.

"In all probability a Moor," Sir Ralph said, always ready to air his knowledge. He informed his somewhat indifferent audi-

77

ence of all he knew about the Moors; how they had overrun and held the whole of Spain until the Re-Conquest, when the Castilians had won it back, city by city, province by province, until only the southeastern corner remained in their hands. "Escalona," he said, "was the last area to be retaken. The present Count's grandfather took it and thus gained his title— and his wealth. Escalona said that his grandfather would have gone farther, but for the mountains. As it is, when we reach Escalona we shall be on the very edge of Christendom."

"And the Moors are kin to the Turks," said Lord Robert who had unobtrusively joined the group.

Nobody much relished the mention of the Turks, who had overrun much of western Asia and were now threatening Constantinople, the centre of the Byzantine Empire. And Sir Ralph, when he was talking, did not welcome interjections. "You could, I suppose, say kin to. Much as all Infidels would call English, Scots, and Irish akin. They look on Christendom as one, and we look on Islam as one . . ."

So with water casks filled, with fresh onions, some very bad wine and some very good dried grapes, with every man and every horse in good health—no mean achievement—*The Four Fleeces* made her way, out of the sea, into the mouth of the Great River, the Guadalquivir, where there was nothing to fight but the current. Easy now.

Father Andreas said, "To the right—you call it to starboard —there is a landing stage and a tower. Put in there. Then go on to Seville."

EIGHT

ONE BRIGHT OCTOBER MORNING a gaily painted cart arrived,
bearing the gifts which Sir Simon Randall had promised; six
well-grown rose trees, young bushes of lavender, rosemary,
and southernwood, many other plants in baskets and bundles,
all labelled: HERE BE LILY BULBS . . . ROOTS OF COLUMBINE.
Lady Randall loved her plants and was anxious that they
should be treated properly in their new home, so she had sent
the cart in charge of an experienced gardener who proceeded
to instruct Walter. Walter hated being told what to do and the
Cressacre man resented the lack of hospitality in this place—
no cakes or ale. They managed to quarrel in the time it took
to unload and for Sybilla to write an appreciative letter. She also
wished to be civil and send some small gift in return, and she
had it handy, for amongst the things which Dame Margery
had packed was a sizeable bag of potpourri. It should have
been opened and its contents stood about in wide-mouthed
bowls, but at Knight's Acre every bowl was needed for a more
utilitarian purpose; so all the sweetness was still sealed within
the waxed cloth bag. Sybilla wrote that she had helped to
make this potpourri from flowers and shrubs grown at Beauclaire, and that next year, thanks to her Ladyship's great
kindness, she hoped to make her own from her own garden.
(That was another thing the Abbess had taught her—the
turning of a pretty phrase.)

One thing the Cressacre man had said was that the roses
should be planted at once and that they liked muck. Walter
was slightly torn between his farmer's commonsense—there
was more to do in October than plant roses; and other things

79

than roses liked muck—and his wish that the lady should have everything suitable. Sentiment won and having ascertained where Sybilla wished her roses to be, he fetched manure in pails—when he had time he must make a barrow—took his spade and told Henry and Richard to bring the miniature ones which he had made for them.

They all set to work in the mellow autumn afternoon. Walter did the real work, breaking the soil and leaving the boys to widen and deepen the hole. John stamped about, fell into a hole, fell over something, picked himself up with invincible good humour, and Margaret kept, as always, within reach of Sybilla.

Sybilla was holding the fourth rose tree straight while Walter stamped its carefully spread roots down to the muck it would thrive upon, when the quarrel between Henry and Richard broke out, unexpectedly because it was usually allowed to lapse when they were fully employed, and more violent than ever before. Ordinarily they punched and kicked, this afternoon they were armed, hacking away at each other with their small spades, using them like battleaxes. Sybilla cried, "Boys! Stop it!" Walter took action. He strode over, seized each by the scruff of the neck and pulled them apart, holding them at arm's length, kicking and struggling, and then threw Henry to the left, Richard to the right and said, "That's enough of that!" Sybilla was finishing the stamping in from which Walter had been disturbed and he said, "Leave it, my lady; you'll foul your shoes," when the incredible happened. Both boys, yelling, and still armed with their spades, closed in on Walter.

Sybilla said, "Let go, Margaret," and shook off the clutching hand. She took Henry, nearest to her, about the waist and when he struck out at her wrested the spade from him. Walter with only Richard to deal with did much the same. It was all over in a few seconds. She said, "You are very naughty, naughty boys. You will go to bed at once and have no supper." Nor comfort for the wounds they had inflicted on each other.

They slouched off, defeated, but just at the doorway before which next year roses should bloom, they put their arms one around the other; comrades in distress. Margaret stood rigid with fright and must be reassured and John pulled out from the muck-filled hole over which his brothers had quarrelled . . . and Walter was bleeding.

"It's nothing, my lady," he said, dabbing at the gashes. "These should be got in. There'll be frost tonight."

"I do apologise," Sybilla said. "And so shall they, or go without breakfast. Also—I don't know, Walter, whether Sir Godfrey told you—he did tell me. You have leave to chastise them."

Walter had his own ideas about that. Boys should be hammered. But a clout on the ear, a kick on the backside, three or four cuts with a stick or a strap, administered at the time of the offence, or because somebody was in a bad temper differed somehow from a formal flogging performed at a later date. That savoured too much of the army, or of the law.

"I've been thinking about this, my lady. They get worse, not better. Apart they're all right, but together they're more than anybody can handle."

"It will not be for much longer. Henry goes to Beauclaire at Easter."

That meant five months to get through. And for Walter it was in the wrong order. Of the two boys he preferred Henry, nicer natured than Richard who was sly, and inclined to be cheeky.

In the evening Walter gave his mind to finding some method of driving a wedge between the two, something that would give him a hold over Henry and put Richard down a peg or two. How about making Henry a bow of the right size, and teaching him to use it?

Sybilla was also thinking, and the result of her thought was a letter to Alys at Astallon, asking could Henry possibly go to Beauclaire at Christmas instead of Easter. She wrote it unwillingly for, though she always acted with impartiality and loved both boys, Henry was her favourite too. He more closely resembled his father, both in looks and in nature; he had the same extremely candid blue eyes, the same lack of guile.

Lady Astallon seemed to share Walter's opinion, one of the boys would be tolerable while together they were unbearable. And of course poor Sybilla, left alone for so long, was finding them difficult to manage. One of the Beauclaire ladies wrote

81

a cordial letter; Henry would be welcome for Christmas; and if he could be got to Chelmsford by December 12, he would be met there.

"But, Mother, I don't want to go. I want to stay here, with you—and Walter."

Hundreds of boys in the same situation had doubtless said the same thing. She set out to coax and persuade, using the Christmas festivities as a lure.

"You have no idea of the merrymaking, darling. Last year we missed it altogether and the year before you were too young. This time . . ."

"Why do I have to go?"

Sybilla explained the custom which she and everybody else accepted as they accepted night following day. Boys of good family left home, joined other households, became pages, squires, and knights.

"But I don't want to be a knight. I want to be a bowman, like Walter."

She realised that he had no conception of what knighthood meant.

Because I must have a house of my own! Had I stayed at Beauclaire, Henry would by now have been admitted to one end of the Ladies' Gallery; seen knights in full panoply going into action. As it was, the only knight he knew was an irritable lame man, then a man preoccupied with preparations, and then riding off in plain, serviceable clothes.

In fact Henry knew more about knights than his mother guessed. Wittingly or unwittingly, during the archery lessons and the talk about archers, Walter had imparted his own opinion of knights, which was not high. They wore armour which was not as impervious to an iron-tipped, six-foot shaft, as they liked to think; and once they were unhorsed was a positive disadvantage. "Once they're down they're as helpless as beetles on their backs. Can't even *run,"* Walter said. The longbow had proved its superiority again and again. It was the weapon of the future. Archers were capable of swift, secret movements, they could operate anywhere where there was a foothold and a bit of elbow room. And they were cheap: look at what a horse needed in the way of food to keep it going and the time needed for the feeding and the watering.

Bowmen could eat as they moved, sleep in their clothes, get up and be ready at a moment's notice, whereas it took the handiest squire at least ten minutes to get a knight into armour.

Bit by bit, mainly in the way of stories, all this information had seeped into the boy's impressionable mind.

Sybilla said, "You will think differently, Henry, when you know more." She was tempted to make a class-conscious statement about the low status of archers, but refrained out of loyalty to Walter. The best thing to do, she decided, was to go quietly ahead with her preparations, ignore Henry's protests and his glum looks and assume that all would be well.

Then one cold, snow-threatening evening, Henry's place at the supper table was empty.

"Where is Henry, Richard?"

Richard hunched his shoulders in a sophisticated, unchildlike shrug.

"With Walter, I should say. Playing with bows and arrows."

The scorn was cover for envy. Walter's scheme had worked well. Henry was secretly pleased to have his eleven months' seniority established in a way which Richard could not possibly challenge. Richard was mortified and humiliated by being excluded. The exclusion was total: "No, Master Richard, you're too young," or "Maybe this time next year, if you behave yourself." And for the first time Henry was unwilling to share either the tricks or the tools of the trade. "It's a kind of secret, Richard."

"Run across and fetch him," Sybilla said. She had noticed Henry's increased attachment to Walter during the last few weeks and was secretly, perhaps unworthily, glad that it would soon end. Walter was wonderful, clever, faithful, loyal; and she had never heard him use a bad word, or even a coarse expression. But, after all, Henry was Godfrey's son, not his . . .

John could now feed himself, competently if not neatly; Margaret still needed urging and helping, her attitude towards food as remote as her attitude towards most things. Sybilla served, chopped, and spooned the children's portions, while her own and Richard's and Henry's kept warm on the hearth.

Richard rushed in, panting, fresh-faced, bright-eyed from the cold.

"He isn't there and Walter says he hasn't seen him since milking time."

That meant since dusk, which came early in the first week of December.

A kind of panic seized her. She remembered Henry saying "I will not go to Beauclaire." She remembered that Godfrey was stubborn, that she was stubborn.

"Help Margaret to finish; keep John away from the fire. Your supper is there," she said, and ran out. The wind was bitter.

Walter said, "If he's where I reckon, he's all right."

"Where? Where?"

"Where he'll take no harm, my lady. He'll come home when he's hungry."

That was the voice of experience. Walter had made two ineffectual attempts to escape when he was young and being hammered. And fond of Henry as he was, he was not worried about him. Whatever the outcome of this escapade, whether her ladyship won, or the boy did, a night's sleeping rough and a meal or two missed would do no harm.

"Do you know where he is?"

"I could make a good guess. But he won't come out for the asking. You know what sent him into hiding?"

"Beauclaire? Then please, Walter, find him and fetch him at once. It is so cold . . . Tell him he needn't go."

"Better think for a minute, my lady. It's giving him his head."

It was only fair to warn her, even though the turn of events pleased him.

"Never mind that, Walter. This is no time to argue about such things." That from Lady Tallboys was curt speaking.

The place of which Walter had instantly thought was in the wood, under a half-uprooted beech tree, almost a cave, in which a vixen had had her lair. Henry had remarked upon it, saying in the soldier-to-soldier fashion that now existed between them that it would make a good hiding place.

"That'd depend what you were hiding *from.* Anybody with a lance or a dog'd have you nailed. Give me the open every time."

84

Now, striding along the path he knew so well that he hardly needed the dim light of the lantern, Walter thought in foul language what a fool he'd look if the boy wasn't there. He began to shout "Harry" while he was still some way away. No answer, but then anybody hiding would be a fool to give his whereabouts away. And the boy was no fool.

He stooped at the mouth of the cave and saw the faint light reflected from Henry's eyes. With the roughness of relief he said:

"Come on, out of there."

Henry said in the bitter voice of one betrayed by a friend:

"I might have known. Well, you can stand and shout till you're black in the face. I've got my arrows and I'll use one like you used yours at Vernay. So don't reach in."

"I don't need to. I've got a message from the lady, your mother. She's changed her mind."

"About sending me away? Oh, Walter . . ." His voice shook with relief. Then suspicion came. "Or is it a trick to get me out? Will you swear on your word of honour?"

It was strange, Walter reflected, how the terms of chivalry came so easily. He said gruffly:

"Did I ever tell you a lie? Honest men give their word and I give you mine. Now then, out of there."

The boy had bested his mother. Somebody must now take over control.

Smelling very strongly of foxes, Henry crawled out. Walter had a small quiver of the heart at the sight of the bow. But he acted coldly, giving such short answers that finally Henry said, "Are you very angry with me, Walter?"

"You expect me to be pleased? Dragged out from my fire and my supper. And your mother half worried to death."

"I'm very sorry, Walter. But it was the only way."

"Left to me," Walter said, thumping the lesson home, "you could have stayed there till hunger brought you out."

"I'd sooner starve than go to Beauclaire."

"Don't talk silly rot. You don't know what hunger is, leave alone starvation. You've never missed a meal in your life."

"Supper I have."

"And made up for it next day. Now, listen to me. You go in and tell the lady, your mother, that you're truly sorry. *And mean it*. Moreover, you don't go telling Richard where you've been, or why. You know how he copies everything you do."

"What can I tell him, Walter?" Very meek now.

"You just say, 'I can't tell you,' or 'mind your own business!' See? This is between us, the lady, your mother, you and me."

Already, rather cloudily, Walter saw the next step.

A few days later, when Sybilla said, "Richard, Henry does not wish to go to Beauclaire, silly boy that he is; would you like to go instead?" Richard was not merely willing but eager. The wedge between the brothers which Walter had inserted had been driven home by Henry's behaviour. There was some mystery, some secret about which Henry would not talk, even when they were in bed together, the time when, in the past, all differences had been made up. Richard whose knowledge of the world was small, visualised Beauclaire as a place where he would not be Henry's young brother and kept out of things. He had also overheard some of Sybilla's coaxings.

So Walter had his way. He had not deliberately manoeuvred Henry's escapade, though he had prepared the way for it by his stories—Henry had heard how bowmen could live off the land, and given two bits of dry wood to rub together make a fire. Sending Richard to Beauclaire in Henry's place had been Walter's idea entirely. After all, he asked, what was the difference between them? Eleven months and less than two inches in height; Henry was slightly broader, but did that matter in a page? And look, he admonished Sybilla, how their intermittent quarrels had hardened down to permanent hostility. So sensible and logical.

By accident, Lady Astallon chanced to notice Richard and said, "Welcome back to Beauclaire, Henry."

Richard straightened up from his bow—both boys could be mannerly when they cared to be—and said clearly, "My name is *Richard* Tallboys."

The correction conveyed nothing to her, but the need to make it sparked off something in the mind of the boy who had already discovered that Beauclaire was not exactly as it had been pictured. Here, even more than at home, was the need to assert and prove himself. His name was Richard Tallboys and one day it would be a name to be reckoned with.

Nothing so crudely undignified as a tug-of-war for Henry went on in the now peaceful home; but Sybilla made conscious efforts to prevent Henry becoming a mere farm boy. The present state of affairs was only temporary; Godfrey would come home with money and Henry would take his proper place in the world. So her insistence upon a certain standard of manners became more stringent and, to Henry, tedious. Once she rebuked him for coming to table without washing his hands and he said, "Mother, I did. This is *ingrained* dirt." He sounded proud of it.

Perhaps, she thought, a little learning . . . But Henry, like his father, was content when he could write his name. She tried to entertain him with stories, myths, legends, tales from the Bible but to him they seemed poor, remote stuff compared with Walter's which always began in the same thrilling way, "I remember one time . . ." Walter had been *there,* seen with his own eyes, played his part.

The words, "Walter says," cropped up continuously.

"Walter says he's going to try his hand at brewing. He says his old mother made the best ale in Kent. Did you know that you start off with a dead rat in the mash?"

"How horrible!"

"But it is strained before it goes into the cask," Henry explained with something, a kindly condescension in his voice which made Sybilla say, "I hope, Henry, that you do not copy Walter and speak of me as your old mother."

He gave her Godfrey's candid blue look and said:

"Of course not. Walter always says, 'the lady, your mother' and I say, 'the lady, my mother.' Once I said, 'she' and Walter said, 'Who's she? The cat's aunt?' "

Walter, indeed, could not be faulted, except over his steadfast refusal to go to Mass, which made Henry demur occasionally.

Upon this one point Sybilla intended to have her way; Henry must be seen, properly scrubbed and scoured, properly dressed, every Sunday morning. So she spoke. "Walter, I should be much obliged if you would not speak of your Sunday morning plans to Henry—they almost always concern something he would like to do too."

Walter understood immediately, he gave her his rare, lop-sided smile.

"My lady, this coming Sunday I'll clean out the pigsty."

Father Ambrose, welcomed in few houses, struggling against apathy and indifference, had made a habit of having a word with as many members of his congregation as possible. Those who could dodge past unaccosted did so, for the kindly words often savoured of reproach. "I hope your mother's rheumatism is not worse." "Is Robin ailing?" Sometimes as the weeks went by Sybilla wished that she could sidle past and avoid the inevitable question. "Any news of Sir Godfrey, my lady?" And always the same answer. "Not yet, Father." Question and answer marked the passage of time, emphasised the distance, the immensity of the sea . . .

NINE

THE TOWER HAD BEEN BUILT as a fortress but it had not been used for years. The Count of Escalona had two powerful neighbours who were almost perpetually at war with each other, and, wanting no part in their quarrel, he had made a three-cornered treaty, promising to help neither in return for a promise from each of them to respect the neutrality of that part of his province adjoining the river.

Father Andreas did not wait to see knights and horses disembark; he went ashore himself, climbed the slight slope and eagerly examined the door of the fortress. The mark he had hoped to find, a newly scratched Cross, was not there. So the *Mary Clare* had not, as he had hoped, arrived first, and her contingent of knights would not be waiting at the little mountain town Santa Ana del Monte, which was regarded as Escalona's real frontier.

With his own knife he made the agreed sign, raw-looking amongst the graffiti of sentries long since dead, and breathed a prayer that the *Mary Clare* might be safe and not too far behind. And he added a prayer of thankfulness that *The Four Fleeces* had made the voyage without loss. Shambling about, finding their land legs, men and horses came ashore, the animals led by the donkey who preceded Arcol. Alone of the four-footed voyagers, the donkey had improved in condition, and now, fleshed up and lively, was, Sir Godfrey considered, capable of bearing his armour sack. Presently Father Andreas mounted his mule and led the way.

To everyone—except of course, Sir Ralph—this was a strange kind of country, rugged but not grey with, in sheltered

89

places, the green of trees in January! In the north only grass was really green at this time of the year; or garden plants like laurels. The warmth of the sun on their backs after midday, was strange too. Sir Ralph enjoyed pointing out orange trees and lemons and the grey-green olives, and Sir Godfrey, who knew the borders of Scotland and of Wales, wondered where were the people who tended the trees, gathered the crops. The borders he knew were scantily populated, more sheep than men, but they were not deserted, as this country seemed to be.

Santa Ana del Monte, when they reached it, was strange too —a small town completely walled and still contained within its ancient boundaries. The knights from the North knew that all towns had once been walled but four centuries of freedom from invasion had resulted in walls allowed to crumble, the gateways which led out of them only remembered by the names of streets which now ran into sprawling suburbs. Santa Ana del Monte was still as tight as a drum; red walls in good repair, a guarded gateway. Strange houses; in fact a street seemed to be one long wall, with no windows on the ground floor, a heavily grilled gateway or two giving entrance to several houses; upper windows protected by outcurving bars.

The curious street along which they clattered, their shadows now streaking long before them, debouched into a wide square with a fountain spilling over into a kind of horsetrough. A few women were washing clothes in the trough, beating the stuff against the stone verge. They were there, and then they had vanished. In such debatable land anything strange was suspect; go inside, close the gate, that was the custom, the inherited wisdom. So through the deserted square the knights clattered, out by another gate, and there were the silk pavilions.

"Now," Father Andreas said, "I can offer you welcome to Escalona."

Nobody, not even Sir Ralph at Navarre, had seen such a camp. Heated water, braziers lighted as soon as the evening chilled, as it did, rapidly, once the sun went down. Such food, much of it unfamiliar, but all delicious, and such wine.

They lingered, lounging about except while exercising their horses, for four days. Father Andreas was waiting, hoping,

90

praying for some sign of the *Mary Clare*. None came, and with the resources of the temporary camp exhausted they must move on; and it seemed that Father Andreas must face his patron with this handful of knights—all good; but so few!

The next day's journey was easier, the narrow trail sloping gradually downhill. There was another camp, again wonderfully well provided, and then towards sunset of the second day they came to the ferry. The water across which it plied was dark and still, not a river, a moat, but such a moat as none of them had ever seen, so wide, stretching so far to left and to right. It was in fact part of the vast irrigation system installed by the Moors who had occupied Escalona until the present Count's grandfather won it away from them, and drove them over the mountains to the west into Zagelah.

There was only one raft, poled by two men and capable of taking three horses and a few men, a little baggage at each crossing. It was growing dusk before they were all on the far side and Lord Robert said, "Just as I always imagined the Styx. And old Charon must have his penny." He gave each of the raft men a coin. Sir Godfrey had no idea of what he meant, but Sir Ralph said, "I seem to remember there was no return passage across the Styx." His suspicions about their having been brought for more than a mere tournament had hardened at Santa Ana del Monte. "Why not hold the tourney here?" he asked, gazing about the wide plateau on which the little town and the spacious camp stood. "Think of the time and expense it would have saved."

However, as they approached the city of Escalona itself, even he felt that any man who owned such a beautiful place would naturally wish to show it off. In the last sunset light they saw the rose-and-white city with its domes and towers. One dome struck a note of a different colour, turquoise blue against the evening sky. In its centre stood a great Cross of gold. The building under it had once been the main Mosque of the Moslems and was now the Cathedral Church of St. James. Seen from a similar distance London was a low huddle of drab-coloured buildings.

They approached the city through gardens and orchards, clattered through streets which, though secretive, were not stamped by the fear that had been plain in Santa Ana del

91

Monte and similar places they had passed through. Here and there the gateways to the houses were open, giving glimpses of courtyards, in which trees grew and fountains played. There were even—and this in January—some flowering shrubs. It was much warmer here, for the heartland of Escalona, of which the city was the heart, was a wide valley, sheltered on north, east, and west by mountains or high hills.

Lights began to sprout everywhere. "Oil lamps," Sir Ralph explained. "Oil from the olives. In such places the olive tree is as the pig is to us."

Their journey ended in a vast, brightly lit courtyard, swarming with servants, who led away the horses, carried away the baggage. Arcol went willingly enough, following the donkey, into a stable of great splendour, but once there refused the attentions of anyone but his own master; so Sir Godfrey was a little late at the bath house. This was a great hall, walled and floored with marble, with a sunken pool in its centre. The water was warmed, and perfumed. All the knights had been in the saddle for a long time—after a long time out of it—and they were all men who even when lodged in palaces and great abbeys had thought themselves fortunate to have a squire who could obtain a bucket of hot water. They shed their years and splashed and wallowed like schoolboys, calling to one another in voices which in this place had a curiously hollow yet resonant sound.

Servants waited with towels. But what towels, so soft and absorbent, so almost furry.

Sir Ralph said, "I retract. Plainly the fellow is rich enough to have brought us here simply for a tourney . . ."

Juan Enrique de Mendez, Count of Escalona, was indeed rich. Far, far richer than his own King, or any other European monarch. His grandfather had taken Escalona with all its accumulated wealth, had demanded vast sums in ransom from those who could pay and sold his poorer captives as slaves. He had been a simple soldier, but developed into a shrewd man of business, exploiting every resource of the conquered province, investing his money wisely and luckily.

Escalona's father had married an heiress of whom it was said

92

that she could ride from the border of Portugal to the border of Aragon without ever leaving her own land.

While the knights were enjoying their bathing and the expert attention of barbers, Father Andreas was explaining why he had brought so small a contingent.

". . . and of course, my lord, the other ship may yet arrive."

"She will not," the Count said, his voice light, almost merry, his pale eyes glinting with mischief. "Don Filipe saw her in his glass, wrecked on a desolate shore, all sand and pine trees. No survivors."

The Dominican felt a small chill at the back of his neck but he answered stoutly:

"My lord, you know what I think of such nonsense. Worse than nonsense . . ."

"That may be. But he was able to tell me her name. *Mary Clare!*" That slight chill again. "However, it is of no matter. I have maintained close contact with Hassan ben Hassan. All that is needed is a *show* of force, and that can be provided by twenty-five men. I assume you chose the best."

Father Andreas brought out his black book, evidence of enormous effort, miles of travel, hours of seductive argument.

"The best available. Even to recruit fifty was no easy task. My lord, something is brewing in England. No open breach as yet, but an atmosphere like that which precedes a thunderstorm. As a consequence any man with something to defend wishes to be there to defend it. Nobody said so: their excuses were most courteous, and, as one would expect of the English, devious. Of those who accepted your invitation about half are young men with their way to make. There is one exception. The rest are considerably older, men of small estate."

"One very lame." The Count's eyes sparkled again.

"I brought no lame man."

"Ah well, I suppose Don Filipe's inner eye is capable, like all eyes, of error. Or perhaps he misled me because I *asked*. He dislikes to be *asked,* he likes to *tell;* but naturally, my dear Father Andreas, I was anxious about you and your welfare, so I asked and he said that he saw you in a barely furnished hall with a knight who was very lame."

Father Andreas remembered how Sir Godfrey had limped into the hall at Knight's Acre, and later, seeing him to the door, had limped hardly at all. Without realising that what he said was almost an endorsement of the warlock's claim to magical power, he said:

"Sir Godfrey Tallboys is acknowledged the premier knight in England. He had suffered a slight mishap. But he is sound now. And of those here the best *man*. Indeed it is thanks to him and the young man whom I mentioned as an exception that all the horses survived."

"They shall have their reward. Land and resounding titles. You also, Father Andreas, anything you wish—except, of course, Don Filipe's head on a charger."

Father Andreas ignored the jibe. He and the Count were conspirators, their ambitions interlocked.

Serious again, the Count said, "Soon I must meet them. Tell me what you know."

What Father Andreas knew would have amazed—and in cases, annoyed—the men he had so closely observed. He knew which knight drank too much, was a womanizer, a gambler. When he came to Sir Ralph Overton he said, "A good knight, but a spendthrift. And the kind of wineshop gossip who knows all. He even claims to know you, my lord."

"How could he? I was never in England."

"Sir Ralph was in Navarre, in Pamplona."

Your turn to wince!

But the Count of Escalona bore the hurt of Navarre and Pamplona as calmly, outwardly, as Father Andreas had borne references to Don Filipe's magic.

"Indeed," he said. "I find these English names so difficult, so barbarous. I must ask you, Father to point him out to me. Sir Ralph Overton. Then I can pretend to recognise him—that is always flattering. I should also like my attention to be drawn to the man who was lame and now is not; and to the young man who did not come for money. What is his name?"

"He is Lord Robert Barbury. His father is an earl."

"I must remember that. May I see the book?" The names of those with whom Father Andreas had failed were deleted by a firm black line. "I will try over the names. My English has not

94

improved during your absence; the young man you left me as substitute tutor was far inferior to yourself."

Unflattered, Father Andreas listened and corrected the Count as he named his guests and then practised his little welcoming speech.

The knights were conducted to a great hall which was dazzling by its decoration as well as the plenitude of lamps. There were no wall hangings, the walls themselves were the ornamentation, all complicated, symmetrical, geometric patterns inlaid with ivory, various coloured marbles, silver, and glass. The ceiling appeared to be all of silver and from it, on silver chains, hung clusters of silver lamps which shed their light upon a table, all aglitter with gold. While they stared in awe and admiration their host, accompanied by Father Andreas, made his entrance.

"He has changed very little," Sir Ralph murmured. Escalona had been a very handsome young man and was handsome still, tall, slender, upright, silver hair and pale aquamarine eyes sharply, yet pleasantly in contrast with smooth, sun-tanned skin.

He addressed the whole gathering first, in the slow, careful English he had acquired in the last few years.

"Honoured sirs, welcome to Escalona. I hope you will have happy times here. I wish to make your visit to be enjoyed. I thank you for coming. Please ask for anything lacking." He then made his round, prompted by Father Andreas who murmured the name of each man. His memory was retentive; to Sir Thomas Drury he said, "You have brought your hound. We must find sport for him." He told Sir Godfrey that he was glad to know that he had recovered from his hurt. Pausing before Sir Ralph Overton he said, "We have met before. In Pamplona, was it not?" But whereas he had looked every other knight straight in the face, with a smile, he avoided Sir Ralph's eye. When he had passed on, Sir Ralph murmured again, "Quite a *royal* progress, is it not?" He was nearer the truth than he knew.

The Count took his place, midway along one side of the table, in a chair slightly higher and more ornate than the others, and the supper, a veritable feast, began. Dishes of every kind

95

of meat, cooked with no sparing of spices which in England were costly and used carefully even in rich households. To most of the English rice was a novelty, and the salads were much appreciated. Salads were available in England only in summer and even then in no great plenty unless one had a well-established garden. There had been Salett gardens on the banks of the Thames, but the spreading city had encroached upon them. The meal ended with dishes piled high with what looked like outsize jewels, fruits candied into semi-transparency by cooking in sugar—another luxury in the North. There was no lack of it here, for the Moors had brought sugar cane as well as rice and many other things to Europe. The green figs were emeralds, the apricots topazes, the peaches amber and the mulberries amethysts, the cherries rubies. Spiced or sweetened the food conduced to thirst, and the gold cups were filled before they were emptied.

Lord Robert said, laughing, "A few more meals like this and I shall need new armour." Sir Stephen Flowerdew, his tongue loosened by wine, said, "I will now confess that I thought the number and the size of the prizes rather too good to be true; yet I felt bound to take the risk. Now I see. The gold in these cups, platters, and dishes would keep the Royal Mint working for ten years."

After a few days they were mystified. Partly because their host, such a good organiser, seemed to have done nothing about the tournament to which he had invited them. There was ample room for practice and for exercise, but nothing even remotely resembling a tourney ground.

"Is it possible," Sir Godfrey asked Sir Stephen, "that he does not know how to lay one out?" After all, the Count, for all his wealth, his impressive appearance and personality, was a foreigner.

"Of course he knows," Sir Ralph said brusquely. "I told you, he was in Navarre."

"Then I wish he would lay out the ground and begin," Sir Stephen said. "With you here, Godfrey, I cannot expect to win any great prize, but the promised sum . . . I wish to earn it, quickly and get home. My Elizabeth . . . Waiting does not improve a girl's looks, or her temper."

Sir Thomas Drury fondled his hound and then made his

contribution to the conversation. "What strikes me as extraordinary is that he seems to have no knights of his own. Maybe here in Spain everything is different, but I should have thought that a Count would have some obligation to his King." It was something that had not struck anyone else, but it was true.

"Even the Abbot of Baildon," Sir Godfrey said, "supports twenty knights. I know, because I could have been one of them if I had been content to be hired and sit about kicking my heels."

In fact the Count of Escalona supported fifty knights, all well armed and well mounted, but they were stationed in one of the fortresses, far to the North. He had removed himself from the Court and immured himself in Escalona, dreaming his dreams and making his plans, but he was aware of his legal obligations.

For most of the knights this was an agreeable holiday. The Count organised deer hunts and boar hunts, expeditions to some of his outlying estates, lavish entertainments to enlighten the evenings. The only women in his household were servants, but there were houses in the city, too grand to be dubbed brothels though they served the same purpose.

Even those who most enjoyed his hospitality considered the Count to be eccentric; he seemed to have no neighbours, no friends. It was with surprise that his guests learned that their host had a six-year-old son who lived in a separate part of the palace and had his own household. "As though he were Prince of Wales," Sir Stephen remarked, when he, one of a favoured few, had been taken to see the peevish child, a tyrant in the making. It was assumed that the Count was a widower who had lost a wife so dearly loved that he had adopted an almost monastic way of life. The happily married men in the company could sympathise, and in part understand. Sir Godfrey felt that if Sybilla died, he would never want close contact with a woman again; and Sir Stephen agreed with him.

Sir Ralph, who liked to know everything, was a gossip, rapidly adding to the little Spanish he already knew in order to be able to gossip, but he never learned Escalona's history. How, baulked of his one love, the pretty, delightful Princess who could only be allowed to marry a *royal* person, the young

Count had become slightly mad; married—because a man must have an heir—a woman of low birth, likely to bear sons, being the one girl in a family of seven, used her as a tool, sired two daughters, utterly despised, and then a son. The two little girls had been put into a convent, on the far away northern border of Escalona; and once the boy was born, the Countess joined her daughters there. She had a peasant's down-to-earth sense and knew that as a rich woman, with a title, she would be better off in a worldly convent where such things counted, than in her husband's palace where she had never mattered at all, except as a breeding animal.

None of this was known to those who saw the one result of the Count's marriage, but some of them thought his attitude towards his son rather peculiar. There was no sign of fondness; and everybody knew that fondness was the basic reason why boys must be sent away from their own homes to be trained. The fond father, the doting mother were unlikely to provide the necessary discipline; nurses and other servants who had known a child from birth were still inclined to regard him as a baby. But until the boy was sent away from home affection showed itself in smiles and casual physical contacts. The Count of Escalona treated his son as though he were fully grown, a very important guest whose every wish must be respected, but with whom no intimacy was possible.

Real intimacy was impossible between the Count and the knights, for Father Andreas seemed to have vanished and the Count's English was unreliable. At the end of ten days Sir Stephen mentioned the tournament and behind the pale, smiling eyes a shutter seemed to come down. "He looked and acted as though he did not understand," Sir Stephen said, "and that *I* do not understand. After all, it is the reason for our being here. Sir Ralph, *you* must ask him, in Spanish."

Happy to display his knowledge, Sir Ralph did so; and gained no satisfaction. "He asked were we not happy," he reported. "And I said yes, of course we were happy, but that some of us were anxious to get home."

Neither in Spanish nor in English could the Count explain that he was waiting for two things, willing them to coincide. He must have a final word from Hassan ben Hassan; and a final

98

word from Don Filipe who was busily consulting the stars for a fortunate date.

Faced with Sir Ralph's lack of success, Lord Robert offered his explanation of the delay. "Of course!" he exclaimed. "He is still waiting for the *Mary Clare.*" Everybody said how stupid, how remiss of them not to have thought of that.

Then, one evening when they assembled in the great hall, there were differences. Father Andreas was present, attended by a young friar who carried a big golden Cross. Against the wall, behind the Count's chair a low dais had been placed, and fixed to the wall above it was . . . What? A picture? A map?

Most of them were familiar with maps of a rudimentary kind; this was very elaborate, many-coloured, showing buildings, mountains, even trees as they might appear to someone viewing them from an immense height. At the top, in the margin were two symbols, to the left a painted gold Cross, to the right, painted black, the Crescent of the Moslems.

For the first time since their arrival food was served without wine. The golden cups stood on the table, but they remained empty. One or two of the more bibulous knights drew the servers' attention to this fact and were ignored.

At the end of the meal, all servants withdrawn and the doors closed, the Count mounted the dais and took up a long, slender staff. Father Andreas stepped up and stood beside him, and the young friar went to the other side and stood like a statue, holding the Cross aloft.

"My friends and honoured guests," the Count began his well-rehearsed speech; "no wine has been offered this evening, because I wished you to make sober decisions. I will explain as well as I can. Father Andreas will answer questions."

He began by explaining the terrain; the point of the staff travelled. Here, buff, was Escalona, and here in the centre of the largest mass of foreshortened buildings was the place where they sat. Here were the mountains, at one point not high, little more than hills; and to the west of them, coloured pale purple, the Kingdom of Zagelah, Moorish territory. This blue ripple was the river Loja which had its source in the hills, which ran through the city of Zagelah and then on.

99

Even the least sensitive of his listeners felt the tension. The Count was plainly labouring under some strong emotion, strongly controlled. The hand that held the staff was not quite steady and, having explained the map, the man faltered and turned to Father Andreas who spoke swiftly in Spanish and then prompted him, in English, saying, "I will not insult you . . ."

"I will not insult you," Escalona said, "by asking you to give me your word of honour never to divulge what you are about to hear, but I would ask any man not willing to pledge himself to silence, please to go away."

Nobody stirred; curiosity alone held them rigid and attentive. Even when the sheer fantastic idiocy of his long-concocted plan was revealed to them, they sat almost stunned.

He told them that Zagelah was ruled by a young King, Abdullah, at twenty-four a monster of depravity; a pederast who kept a harem of young boys, a cruel, extortionate tyrant; and a bad Moslem. That was the turning point of the argument. All over Zagelah, in the main city, in the smaller towns, in villages, there were good, orthodox Moslems, and their leader was a lawyer, Hassan ben Hassan, a true follower of all the rules laid down by the Prophet. All these good Moslems had formed a sect—the Hassanites—and were willing to do anything, even make an alliance with the Christians, in order to unseat Abdullah. So what he was now asking of them was to take part in a small Crusade.

The word still held a kind of faded magic. Most of them had an ancestor linked to an earlier Crusade, a stone effigy in some quiet village church, every link in his chain mail faithfully reproduced and his legs crossed—proof that he had been to the Holy Land, warring against the Infidel. And of all the stories upon which little boys were reared, that of the greatest Crusader of them all, Richard the First of England, Richard Coeur de Lion was the most common and the most potent.

But that was a long time ago. Since Richard's time—he had actually been within sight of Jerusalem when his so-called allies failed him—there had been other so-called Crusades, all brought to nothing.

The knights now looked at one another, dubiously, questions in their eyes. And presently questions on their tongues.

100

Lord Robert or Sir Godfrey must be spokesman first, as they were by rank or seniority. The young man acceded the right and Sir Godfrey's simple question rang out loud and clear.

"My lord, why us? Why Englishmen?"

"That I can answer myself, I think," Escalona said. "They have not lately been fortunate in France, but English knights are still the best in the world. There at least we are in agreement, eh?" There was a little laughter. "I have also another reason . . ." He signed to Father Andreas to take up the tale in his more ready English.

The Dominican said the Count had always been much impressed by what happened in Portugal in 1147 when Portugal was small, only just recovered from the Moors and having difficulty in holding them at bay. A small contingent of English Crusaders on their way to the Holy Land put in at Lisbon, and the King of Portugal said to them, *Why go so far to fight the Infidel? Meet him here, on my doorstep.* They had done so and Portugal had been Christian ever since.

Giving the one explanation himself, listening to Father Andreas give the other, the Count hugged his third reason. He did not intend to employ, on this venture, anyone likely at the end of it to remember an allegiance to the King of Castile. The English would fight, take their pay and go home.

Lord Robert asked his question.

"Why should strict Moslems ask aid of Christians? They have Moorish neighbours in Granada. Why not appeal to them?"

"I myself asked that," the Count said swiftly. "Abdullah has sisters, all pretty, all clever, and all married to Kings. In Granada, in Murcia, even in Aquilleras. They would not allow their husbands to help rebels."

Sir Stephen put his question in the form of a statement.

"My lord, we are a muster of twenty-five men."

"It is enough. As you will hear." He used the staff again, and now it was steady. The Count felt that his testing moment was past. Nobody had said that the thing was impossible, what questions had been asked showed that his proposal had been seriously considered. With easy confidence he revealed the details of the trick that he and Hassan ben Hassan had planned.

It was possible that if Zagelah had been held by Christians some knights would have demurred, for although things were changing and the sternest ideals of chivalry on the wane, many men still regarded war as a kind of game, to be played according to the rules; but when you were fighting heathen who did not acknowledge Christ or His Virgin Mother, all rules could be ignored. It was also arguable that what the Count planned was a form of ambush, and even Christians ambushed one another.

(Walter had told Henry about ambushes and said how much preferable for such an exercise archers were to mounted men. "Horses will snort and snuffle and jingle their harness. And then look at the space. You can hide twenty bowmen in a coppice that wouldn't give cover for four like Arcol. I remember, one time . . .")

There were no demurs, but in case anyone had a doubt Father Andreas proceeded to speak, with all the force of fanatic conviction, of the benefits which a Christian victory would confer upon the conquered. They would all be offered a chance of conversion and of baptism. When the knights' work was done, his would begin. He was sincere; he had no doubt of his ability to convert even Hassanites; for there was so much that a strict Moslem had in common with a real Christian; regular hours of prayer, abstemity in the matters of food and drink, a disregard of possessions. He knew he would have one very tough problem, since Christianity meant monogamy and the Prophet Mohomet allowed a man four wives. But monogamy, Father Andreas knew, would come easily to the next generation, for the simple reason that once Zagelah was taken and very systematically looted, one wife would be all that any man could afford.

The looting was to be controlled. There was to be no robbery, no rape. A fair distribution of confiscated property. And Zagelah as a whole, the city, the kingdom reaching down to Andara where the river Loja emptied itself into the Mediterranean was for its size very rich indeed . . . Zagelah specialised in a woven cloth of silk, fine as a cobweb, and of colours nowhere to be matched. There was something about the water of the Loja River which allowed the dyers there to produce very subtle colours.

In the ears of a few of the knights the word now struck an echoing note—concerned with headdresses; privileged women

102

spoke of "my Zagelah." Sybilla had never owned a length of the filmy stuff; but Sir Godfrey, sitting there and listening, thought that he would take her a supply that would last her a lifetime; blue; harebell blue, bluebell blue, Canterbury bell blue, cornflower blue.

Escalona, with everything explained, said, "I leave it to you to think and talk over."

There was a great deal of talk, but at the end of it only one dissident—Sir Ralph Overton. As they stood about and muttered, balancing this with that, slightly fired by the word "Crusade" and the word "loot," thinking that having come so far . . . and not oblivious to the fact that to refuse this extraordinary challenge might smack of cowardice, Sir Ralph spoke:

"I'm having nothing to do with it. He tricked us once, saying *tournament* when he meant *war*. I'm going home. If he gives me the promised five hundred pounds, well and good. If not maybe my sister has relented or my creditors think me dead."

They all thought: Cynic! and remembered that they had never liked him much. In that muddled moment not one of them gave him his due and realised that it took courage of a sort to stand up, alone and say:

"My lord, I came to Escalona for a tourney. I now propose, with your permission, to go home."

"Sir Ralph, there is no question of permission. I want no *pressed* men."

The others were all of one mind for various reasons, and Sir Godfrey, forced to speak for all, said, "My lord, we ride with you."

"Then we will drink to our enterprise. Bring in the wine!"

TEN

"THE ENGLISH AS A RACE are nothing if not practical," the Count said. "And twenty-four out of twenty-five regarded it as a practical plan."

"I confess," Father Andreas said, "that when Sir Ralph Overton withdrew, I feared others might follow."

He looked back on the many acts of faith which had been made necessary; to continue recruiting in the face of such poor response; to embark with only a quarter of the number demanded; to face the Count with a mere handful. It had been a steady winnowing down, similar to that of Gideon, in the Old Testament story . . .

"Hassan ben Hassan says that he will be ready on the thirteenth. Five days' journey without overtiring horse or man. I have already set in motion the establishment of camps. Have you chosen your companions?"

"In my mind. I have not yet informed them. I think six—as a beginning. We do not wish to alarm Hassan until we are established."

During this waiting time, Father Andreas had fasted and prayed, and watched, selected, and discarded. The Dominicans who were to form the spearhead of Christendom in Zagelah must be young, malleable, yet strong and forceful—not a common combination. But he had six.

The Count would have enjoyed telling his fellow conspirator that Don Filipe's casting of horoscopes in order to find the most fortunate date had ended with the prediction that February 13 was favourable. But this was no time for teasing; so they parted in amity, yet each concealing something from the other. Father Andreas did not reveal to the Count that, once made Archbishop of Zagelah, he was not going to rely upon gentle persuasion to make converts; when persuasion failed, force would be used. And the Count made no mention of the fact that to his original intention of snatching Abdullah's kingdom and title an even more ambitious hope had now attached itself. Rumours reached him even in his self-imposed isolation, and the latest was heady in the extreme. Prince Henry of Castile was seriously intending to divorce Blanche of Navarre, giving as grounds that they were impotent together. The Pope was likely to regard Henry's petition favourably; sterile royal marriages led to squabbles about the succession. And if that happened . . .

In Navarre the immensely wealthy, handsome young man who had never been thwarted in his life had been curtly told that only royal personages could marry princesses. His scheme to make himself royal—in title at least—had stemmed from a desire to be avenged upon the world, from a determination that his son should never suffer such humiliation. His attitude towards the child, noticed by some of the knights, resulted from his regarding him as an instrument for his ambition, while feeling no affection for the product of a loveless marriage.

If, as now seemed possible, King Enrique I of Zagelah made suit to a princess who had been discarded, all his dreams might yet come true. And he would breed other sons, happy, healthy, merry, lovable children.

That he had a wife still living was no cause for concern; an unwanted woman was easily disposed of.

Parting from Father Andreas, the Count found himself irresistibly drawn to Don Filipe's apartments at the top of a tower in a remote part of the palace.

The old warlock, well aware of his worth, allowed himself a certain freedom of speech and manner. He gave a sigh of weariness and said:

"My lord, I have nothing more to tell you."

Unruffled, the Count said, "I have something to tell *you,* Don Filipe. You said that Zagelah would be taken by twenty-five of us. And you were right. One Englishman chose to go home."

105

"That is no news to me." Don Filipe's voice was peevish. "He will not get far."

"No, he will not get far." There was a short silence and then Escalona said, "I know you dislike being *asked* to see, but there is something I need to know."

Don Filipe disliked being asked to use his gift because he had spent so many years answering fatuous questions, eking out an occasional bit of genuine second sight with inventions, lies, evasions. Until he had been taken under the wing of this very sympathetic nobleman, he had led a precarious life as an itinerant fortune teller, caster of horoscopes, finder of lost property, a diagnoser of mysterious ailments. He had never been able to stay long in one place—the Church disapproved of his kind; and he had always been poor because he worked only just enough to keep himself alive. He believed in his gift and knew that every invention, lie, evasion, frayed it slightly; it was like taking a length of Zagelah gauze and using it to mop a rough floor.

"I worked out the date for you, my lord; I saw a great city taken by twenty-five men. What more can you ask of me?"

"What comes after?"

A great lord, a generous patron, but now almost on a level with country girls wanting to know if they would marry, whom they would marry. A man whose amiability was a mere veneer over arrogance, humble for once.

"How long after, my lord?" Useful to have some sort of guide, in case nothing came, though the inner eye had been more reliable since its owner had not been harried, forced to improvise, and often hungry.

"Whatever you see, Don Filipe."

"Very well, my lord. There may be nothing." At least to *this* patron it was possible to say such a thing without being called charlatan, wizard, warlock, scoundrel, heretic.

From amongst the clutter on the table, the old man dug out his ball of crystal, faintly clouded, faintly green. He moved his lamp a little, cupped the ball in his hands and stared.

"Nothing new," he said at last. Then his expression sharpened. "Yes! Wait. I can see your losses. Four in the open by the river . . . two in the gateway. And an eye will be lost. Another death, too, but of no importance . . . There, now it is gone. I see nothing." But he was pleased, in the circumstances, to have seen anything at all, and to have seen it so clearly. He looked to his master for approval.

The Count, who believed in Don Filipe absolutely, said:

"Interesting, only seven dead. You give me assurance. But what I want, Don Filipe, is some sight into the further future."

"It comes as it will, my lord."

"I know."

That was a thing that endeared the Count of Escalona to his wizard; he respected the art and understood that a gift was a gift, not to be commanded or harnessed. Because of this, and the way in which he had been housed and fed, given the courtesy title of Don, and protected from persecution, the old warlock, after some thought, said, unwillingly:

"There is another way, my lord. For you, if you wish, I will attempt it."

"I should be grateful."

Don Filipe had tried it seldom; only three or four times; it was dangerous. Despite what priests might say there was nothing evil in practising a God-given gift; in his crystal Don Filipe had done little more than to *see,* just as ordinary people saw their reflections in a puddle or a bucket of water; and in casting his horoscopes he was no more guilty of sin than any man studying a map. But this was different, and he knew it.

There was a priest-like ritual about his preparations; he cleared a space on the marble-topped table, lit and fanned a small brazier to a glow, took from the back of a shelf a stoppered flask. Then he said, "Sit over there, my lord," and indicated a bench as far from the table as the size of the room allowed. "Do not speak. Do not lean forward. And do not be alarmed if I appear to be—overcome."

From the flask he shook a little greyish-green powder into his palm, hesitated for a second and then spilled it onto the red charcoal. A dense, evil-smelling smoke arose and slowly formed the shape of a large mushroom, its stem rooted in the brazier, its cap level with Don Filipe's eyes. He put his hands to the sides of his head, like the blinkers of a horse, and leaned forward. His whole posture was different from that he adopted when looking into the crystal, taut and wary.

The smoke hung motionless, keeping its shape, but the stench

107

filled the room. The Count wished that he had brought a pomander ball. He wondered how Filipe could remain so close to it, could lean even nearer, staring, staring. He thought: He is doing this for me; he must be rewarded. But how? The only gold the old man cared about was that which he was trying to make from base metals.

Suddenly Don Filipe said, "No!" using the voice of one faced with something unbelievable, or utterly unacceptable. He moved his right hand and attempted to cross himself, but his head, deprived of half its support, fell forward, so that to the stench was added the smell of singeing hair. Escalona moved swiftly, lifted him—how light he was—and carried him to the window. Still holding the old man with his left arm, he threw open the window with his other hand. The night air, cool and fresh, streamed in.

Don Filipe looked dead. He had closed his eyes—against what sight?—and his lips were blue. Escalona thought selfishly: He died without telling me! But when he fumbled and found the old man's heart it was beating, though feebly, and after a second or two he took a gasping breath, enough to enable him to speak in a weak whisper. He said, "Such—great—slaughter." Then he said, "King . . ." not as an isolated word but as though a name should have followed. It did not. After that word he was silent.

The Count remembered that the warlock had told him not to be alarmed, and, unalarmed, he thought of wine as a restorative. There would be wine here, for Don Filipe was always, by order, well served. In fact, on a separate small table, supper was laid out and there was wine in a jug, and there was a cup. Escalona who had been holding Don Filipe's head against his knee, reached out for a huge book, pillowed him on that and crossed the room to the supper table.

In the short time that it took to fetch the wine, the old man died. And what he knew went with him. Just for a moment Escalona forgot that and surprised himself by feeling some emotion. Over the hollow old chest he made the sign which had not been completed; then, crossing himself, he said, "God rest you in peace."

He thought: He died in an attempt to serve me, and he shall

108

have Christian burial, no matter what Father Andreas and the rest of them may say.

Curiosity revived. Greatly regretting what had not been said, the Count examined the few words that had been spoken.

Such great slaughter. Well, naturally; Abdullah would have those about him who would fight fiercely, if only from self-interest; betrayed from within, they would be mown down. Escalona knew what his own loss would be, seven men. He also knew the Moors' method of fighting. They depended upon speed. Wearing light armour, or none, mounted on swift horses, they swooped to attack, slashing with their curved scimitars and yelling. Repulsed they turned, as if in flight, and then turned again, in their saddles, and used their other weapon, the bow, discharging, over their horses' tails, arrows dipped in deadly poisons. But Hassan ben Hassan had sworn that there would be no poison on any arrow; no man awake in any of the frontier fortresses. If only the Count could arrive on the given day.

King. Spoken like that, inconclusively, it might well be interpreted as the dying man's effort to give his sponsor his new title.

One word left unexplained, that horrified *No!* Perhaps he had seen in the smoke his own death.

The road along which the knights moved westwards had been made by the Romans, to whom Hispania had been one province; to the Visigoths, who had taken over from the Romans, the country had been one, also; and to the Moors who had driven them out. The splintering up into small provinces and petty kingdoms had begun with the Re-Conquest, but as late as the time when Escalona's grandfather had set out to carve a place for himself with his sword, Escalona and Zagelah had been one and the road that linked them had been much used and kept in good repair. It ran for the first day through fertile and well-populated country, scattered with little villages and a few larger places where some mineral deposit had bred industry. By evening, when they halted at their first camp, the range of mountains which the first Count of Escalona had been content to regard as the limit to his conquest showed, smudgily, against the sky.

Next day the road climbed, gently but inexorably; the olive groves, the terraced vineyards, the sheep-loud pastures fell away. They came to almost barren land, dotted with gorse bushes, here and there a stunted pine tree. Then all was rock, weathered red sandstone, the skeleton of the earth laid bare. But still the good road, and another comfortable camp.

After that Sir Godfrey rode, not uneasily, but alertly. The good road went on, but now it was often a narrow defile between two heights, places where half a dozen determined men could hold up an army. Outside his profession his imagination was not lively, but he could see that three or four well-aimed arrows or flung lances could throw their cavalcade into lethal confusion in such a place. Equally dangerous, to his mind, were the twists and turns which the road took in order to avoid sharp ascents or descents; how could you know what was just around a bend? And sometimes the road was merely a shelf with a steep wall of rock on the one hand and a drop into an abyss on the other.

But his fears seemed to be unfounded. And surely, if the Count had anticipated trouble here he would not have brought his son, who travelled sometimes in an ornate litter, borne by four men, sometimes on a very pretty pony.

"You may have observed," Lord Robert said, slipping into place beside Sir Godfrey and Sir Stephen, "that I am in deep disgrace. My turn to eat supper with his lordship, and not invited. Should I weep? Go ashamed and unfed to my bed?" He pulled a miserable face and then laughed. "Or dare I tell you the *hideous* crime of which I am guilty? Will you, too, avoid my company if I tell you that I *struck* that sacred child?"

They laughed and Sir Stephen said, "Long overdue."

"He was riding and kept stealing up behind other horses and giving sharp cuts with his whip. Imagine the confusion! Pluto and I almost fell into a ravine. So I approached the Count and complained and he said something about boyish high spirits. Not even a word of rebuke. I warned him; I said if Don Juan struck another horse, I should strike him. He did, of course; and I gave him a cuff he will remember—I hope."

Lord Robert did not know it, but by that one simple action he had lost all chance of a title and an estate when Zagelah was subdued. The Count did not love his son, was indeed prepared in certain circumstances to waive his rights, or even dispose of him, but at the moment he was heir apparent and to insult him was to insult his father.

The fourth day's march brought them, several times, into situations which Sir Godfrey had visualised, places where the road, running narrowly between two heights, or along a narrow shelf, was overlooked by fortresses which except for their colour, red instead of grey, and the shape of their arrow slits, their tops horse shoe-shaped instead of pointed, were not unlike the Peel Towers of the Scottish border. They were not derelict, like the one at the landing stage on the river, and they were in good repair, but they were deserted. Hassan ben Hassan was a thorough man. The contemptible little company of invaders passed into Zagelah without so much as a challenge.

The road, still avoiding steep gradients by curving, brought them down to tree level again; the beech buds were swollen, but still unbroken, some of the chestnuts showed flecks of green. "I never knew until now what trees meant to me," Lord Robert said. In what Sir Godfrey would once have thought an affected manner, he flung his arms as far as they would go around a grey beech tree and said, "Dear tree!"

"I like trees, too," Sir Godfrey said. "In fact I built my house around one." That was a statement unusual enough to evoke questions, but as always his inability to describe prevented him from giving his listeners any very clear mental picture. And his own mind wandered off to Sybilla and Knight's Acre. By now she should have received his first letter. And his second was on its way, written by Lord Robert and carried by Sir Ralph, who had promised to find a carrier for it the moment he stepped onto English soil. He had written cautiously, not to alarm her, no mention of going to war, simply that one tournament led to another and that he hoped to come home rich; that letter also— because it was not dictated to a celibate friar—was more loving.

The pity of it was that this more loving letter—almost poetical in places, for Lord Robert had a way with words— was never to be read. As Don Filipe had foreseen, and as Escalona had determined, Sir Ralph did not get far . . .

Their final camp was different from the others, secret, behind the last belt of trees before the cultivated land began. No

111

lights, no fires, no pavilions except the small one which sheltered the child and his attendants, the larger one where Father Andreas had set up his altar and the great golden Cross. Every man made his confession and was absolved. Many of them were reminded of the preliminaries of being knighted.

Then early to bed in a way which to most of them seemed more natural than the luxury of former camps. Not far from where they bedded the river Loja made splashing noises as it tumbled over the last of the falls on its way to the lowlands, through the city of Zagelah and then on, past another city, Andara, and so to the sea. From their darkened camp, knights who cared to look, could see faint lights in Zagelah.

They took up their positions in the grey, predawn light. Sir Godfrey and the eleven men who made up his company were concealed in an orange grove slightly to the south of the city's great gateway, with nothing but a few trees and the width of a road between them and the red and white walls. As the light brightened towards sunrise they could see that the gates were of bronze; inset was a smaller opening, wide enough to admit a cart or two riders abreast. The gateway was flanked by out-jutting towers, with battlements and openings that commanded views in all directions. Filled with men prepared to shoot arrows tipped in henbane, to lob down heavy stones, pour boiling water, the place would have been as nearly untakable as a place could be. It would have meant a siege. That Zagelah was dependent upon the surrounding countryside for food was proved by the number of laden donkeys and people carrying baskets who were beginning to line up in the road, awaiting the opening of the smaller gate. They were all preoccupied with their own affairs, getting and keeping their place in the line, prodding their donkeys, greeting acquaintances: Is the sole of my shoe flapping again? Shall I get home before labour starts?

The rim of the sun appeared on the eastern horizon. From the minarets the muezzins called and all good Moslems turned towards Mecca and prostrated themselves in the first prayers of the day. Then the gate was opened and they shuffled and jostled their way in. Not one of them had looked northwestwards across the valley and seen the unusual activity going on there, in full view. Those whose function it was to keep watch on walls and towers were either members of Hassan's party and deliberately blind or they had been dealt with, would sleep for twelve hours, perhaps never wake again. Hassan ben Hassan, like the Count of Escalona and Father Andreas, knew exactly what he wanted and held that the end justified the means.

Abdullah IV of Zagelah did not respond to the call to prayer, did not even hear it. In the heart of his rose-coloured palace—compared with which that of Escalona was a modest place indeed—in a bed of silver and gold and pearl, pillowed and covered with silk, he lay asleep, exhausted after a night of excess with his latest favourite, very pretty, very young, and at the moment very humble. He had actually gone to sleep on the floor at the foot of the bed, like a dog. It would not last, of course; it never did. All favourites sooner or later demanded favours in return, enormous gifts, remunerative posts; always given because, even when the first fervour had expended itself, something remained. And Abdullah delighted in giving. In fact his last thought before he fell asleep was that he would give the boy Sheba's ruby.

That was a drunken thought, for before, during, and after their parody of lovemaking, he and the boy had emptied two jugs of wine.

Nobody knew how the ruby, said to be the last present the Queen of Sheba had given to Solomon the Great, had come into the possession of the Kings of Zagelah. It was as big as a hen's egg, but more rounded; it was not set, simply pierced and slung on a chain of gold. It had had a curious history, about which nothing was known. A child in a black felt tent in Kurdistan had cut his teeth on it; an ignorant candle chandler in Damascus has used it as weight on his scales. It had been bought, sold, pawned. Nobody knew that it had been a gift made in anger not in affection or respect and that in the giving the Queen had thought: And may you and all who wear it suffer ill fortune. It had been lost sight of, regarded of no value, and then suddenly, at least half identified, in a legendary way by the same Arabic scholar who said that the oversized golden lion which now stood just inside the door of Abdullah's treasure house was one of those which Solomon had ordered for his temple or his palace. This extremely beautiful and lifelike thing

113

had never been displayed in Zagelah—to the orthodox Moslem as to the orthodox Jew representational art was forbidden. But Solomon had ignored such petty rules—and so, given time, would Abdullah. That was his last thought as he drifted into sleep; Solomon's golden lion and its exact replica, on guard beside his throne; and Sheba's enormous ruby dangling from the boy's slender neck.

On the momentous morning the boy, with the resilience of youth, woke and yawned and stretched; waited, became hungry and presently with diffidence—masters being so unpredictable —touched Abdullah on the shoulder.

"My lord, would you wish to wake and drink kaffe? Shall I fetch it?"

Fetch. In a week's time he would be saying: Shall I order it?

Abdullah groaned, muttered "Go away," and then remembered that today he must entertain his second cousin, Selim, a man whom he heartily disliked but must make some show of respect to; his father's cousin, the eldest surviving male of the family.

"Dear child, yes. You did well to wake me." He knew what Selim had come about: marriage. Selim was strictly orthodox, mindful of his duty towards his kinsman; disapproving of the wine, the kaffe, fairly tolerant of the boys but urging marriage as a political necessity; ready to say, "A boy for pleasure, if that is your fancy, but a woman for use. The meanest peasant needs a son to inherit his old donkey."

Stretching and yawning, fighting off a heaviness in his head —the kaffe would cure that—Abdullah thought that this promised to be an interesting day. He would agree to marry whomever Selim would come to suggest; then he would tease Selim a little; tell him that he should wear the patched clothes which fanatics wore; tell him about the plan to have the two golden lions; parade the new boy with the great ruby bobbing on his navel.

The waiting seemed interminable. With so much traffic on the road it seemed safe to talk, in quiet voices. Lord Robert said, "It is an old idea, you know. I believe it was Darius the Great who employed it against Babylon. But with a difference, of course." Nobody knew what he was talking about.

The Count had decided to trust half the operation to Sir Godfrey; telling him to choose his eleven.

He had a slight, nagging doubt. Father Andreas thought highly of Sir Godfrey and it was obvious that all his comrades respected him; but was there a certain almost dangerous simplicity, a naivety about the man? Unquestionably brave; given an order he would do his best to carry it out; told to hold a position he would probably do so until he died; but had he the flexibility, the quick-mindedness, the resourcefulness to deal with an unexpected situation? Asked to choose his company, Sir Godfrey had named Sir Stephen, Sir Thomas—both men of the same stamp—and then Lord Robert, younger, livelier of mind . . . Not that the unexpected was to be expected; everything planned and timed.

The river Loja rose in the hills, a waterfall, joined by others, and swelled and tumbled down into the valley; into and through the city, entering by one great archway in the red and white wall, and going out by another, and so down to Andara and to the sea. How soon would somebody notice that just at the point where it tumbled out of its rocky cradle and spread and slowed, it was being dammed? By rocks, loosened beforehand and needing no more than a push; by trusses of straw and the feather beds on which the knights had slept at their last comfortable camp, by folded tents, folded blankets, anything, everything which might for a little time halt the river's flow.

People who lived inside the city but worked outside in the gardens and orchards began to emerge. One of them gave the alarm. A great host, he said. Fifteen fully armoured knights on their great horses, backed by an army of workmen, looked formidable from a distance.

Panic began and spread, with shouting, with horns blowing. In no time at all the palace was loud with preparation.

Abdullah's first and main thought was, "No siege!" He had never lived through one, but his grandmother had survived one when she was a child and had retained the most vivid memories of its horrors. People had been reduced to eating dogs, those unclean animals, and rats. And the gasped out words, "They are damming the river," indicated a siege of the worst kind. The Loja was Zagelah's lifeblood; men could live with little food, even no food for several days; a city without water—

115

with the rainy season over for the winter—could hold out no more than two days.

Dissolute as he was Abdullah did not lack courage. He would himself lead the charge. He did not even stop to think of the safety of anonymity but flung on the robes of royal reddish purple which were handiest. As he raced down the stairs and into the courtyard—a scene of orderly confusion—someone with presence of mind flung over him one of the uniform white outer garments.

He had two hundred men here, all picked and proven, and although in his day there had been no real fighting, mimic warfare and constant exercise had kept them fit and ready. There were few among them who could not with a single slash sever a cow's head. This was a routine practice; it was according to the Law which decreed that an animal must bleed to death; and it saved the butchers a job.

He had other forces posted at strategic places throughout his little kingdom; had he had only a day's warning . . . No matter, no matter; he and his two hundred had an ally in Allah. Allah! He was aware that he had not observed the Law as laid down by the Prophet, but Allah was merciful . . .

He did not even notice that not all his two hundred had turned out.

The prospect of immediate physical combat did something to men—unless they were born cowards. Hearts beat harder and higher, breath quickened; nobody thought at such a moment of the wounds he might sustain, only of those he would inflict. When the great bronze gates of Zagelah creaked open, the Christian knights in ambush looked at each other and smiled, not one of them aware that his smile was wolfish—the old, age-old grimace of showing the teeth.

In one of his several preparatory talks the Count had said:

"Hassan considers that no more than a hundred, or a hundred and ten . . . will be in the first muster. Sir Godfrey, allow about forty to emerge. Then attack."

And who, at such a moment, could be bothered with counting? Four abreast at a time . . .

"Ready?" Sir Godfrey said. *"Now."*

Many of the Moors, attacked suddenly and heavily from the side, never saw what had struck them. Some swerved to meet this other enemy, and so lost the momentum upon which their form of charge depended. Others, some bleeding and dying, galloped on. Within two minutes, outside the gates there was the great slaughter that the old warlock had foreseen.

Up by the river where the dam was, it was worse. A white wave of warriors still, after all these years waging war as their desert forefathers had done, repulsed by so few—but each of that few a miniature fortress.

And Escalona had been extremely cunning. He had recruited his workmen from a class of men accustomed to defend themselves or die. Lonely people, shepherds who in winter must fight wolves or lose their gravid ewes; men who hacked from hillsides things like millstones and grindstones and, coming back from markets where such things were saleable, must be on guard against robbers who, unwilling to work themselves, were only too ready to grab the money which long labour had earned. They were all well chosen, stupid men, glad of an easy job with good pay and their keep. They had never bothered to ask what was the ultimate end of their activities. But when the Count of Escalona called, "Defend yourselves. We are attacked!" they knew what to do. Out came the slings. Just here the now dwindling river showed its bed, floored with water-rounded stones—and a rounded stone carried best. A chunk of rock, intended to be part of the dam, powerfully pushed, did damage to the delicate legs of the horses.

The Moors could not on this morning follow their usual procedure when swoop and slash failed; the Christians' rear was guarded by the river. They wheeled, loosed their arrows which should have been lethal and today were not. Something was wrong, terribly wrong. They turned, charged again, and then, with weakening impetus, a third time. Then it was over and the Count had lost exactly four men.

The walls of Zagelah were so incredibly thick that Sir Godfrey's company fought its main battle in a kind of tunnel between the gateway and the open space within. In such a place weight was an advantage and the sword a more effective

117

weapon than a scimitar. Once through the tunnel and into the sunshine of space beyond, they performed a manoeuvre so swift and so nimble as to be unbelievable with such heavy men and heavy horses. They lined up, knee to knee, offering the same solid, fortified opposition as their friends were offering by the river. There was an empty saddle, but the horse who wore it knew his job and lined up with the others.

Hassan ben Hassan had reckoned shrewdly. Of the two hundred only a hundred and ten had responded. Sir Godfrey, slightly impatient and no great counter at any time, had let thirty-two emerge before he said, "Now!" Eight or nine Moors had been killed in that sudden flank attack; more in the dim tunnel; and among those now left to throw themselves against the Christians there were many who were aware of something wrong. Where were those—the rest of the two hundred—who should now be supporting them? Where were the archers who should be manning the towers?

A Moor, practising the skill he had exercised on cows, took off the head of Sir Thomas Drury's horse in one marvellous stroke—destriers' necks being thicker than cows' and partially protected. The headless horse stood there, spouting blood just long enough to enable his master not to come down in the inevitable crash. Sir Thomas scrambled up into the empty saddle of Sir Alan Brokehampton's horse.

But we cannot keep this up forever. Rock against battering wave; battering wave against rock. Just as the next wave was about to break—had indeed gathered itself together and launched itself—somebody yelled and all the beautiful Arab horses rose on their hindlegs and pivotted and galloped away to the far side of the open space out of which three streets opened.

In the dim tunnel behind them, in the open, sunny space before them, there were dead men and dying men, dead and dying horses.

The Count had said, "At all costs keep the gates open." But who could close them? Wedged open as they were. By corpses.

As they drew breath one arrow flew and hit Sir Stephen Flowerdew in the left eye. The Count had promised, saying that Hassan had promised no poisoned arrows . . . but this was an arrow, and it might be poisoned. So he plucked it out, bringing his eye with it. Afterwards he said that when the arrow struck he felt pain, but none as the eye came away. "And my wife will look on me with even less favour," he said wryly.

They were waiting again, obedient to orders. No pursuit; hold the gate and await his coming. When he came he brought workmen. One perched behind every saddle. They jumped down and cleared the tunnel and the knights clattered in over the blood-washed stones.

As they did so a fountain in the centre of the square shot silver spray into the sunshine.

"Four," the Count said. "And you?"

"Two. Many Moors got away."

"Not far," Escalona said in a gloating voice. He moved his hand towards the fountain. "They were making for the water arch; escape by the river bed. Now . . . We make ourselves look as many and as formidable as possible and move to the palace, where Hassan will meet us." Three streets led out of the square; six men to each of two streets, seven to the third.

Presumably from behind the lattices and shutters eyes were watching, counting perhaps, but they might have been riding through a city of the dead. It put the final touch of strangeness to the whole fantastic operation. When towns were taken people watched, with sullen hostility, or dull resignation, or simple curiosity. Here nothing stirred except a few slinking, scavenging dogs.

Of the six in this narrow, balconied street, Sir Godfrey and Lord Robert rode side by side, and last. It was a short street, and shadowed; at its farther end lay another square, bright with sunshine.

Suddenly from a balcony some unseen hand tossed something. That was more natural and ordinary; hostile watchers threw stones, people who welcomed invaders threw flowers or favours.

This was nothing that either of them had ever seen before. It landed, quite softly, in the centre of Lord Robert's breastplate, clung there and began to glow. He tried to brush it off and as the unprotected inner part of his hand came in contact with it,

119

said, "God's blood! Red hot!" He then hit it with the gauntletted back of his hand, a few bits broke off, fell onto his armoured thighs and began to glow there. The original piece stuck fast.

A secret weapon! An invention of the Devil!

Sir Godfrey reached out and struck at it. A fragment fell onto Pluto's mane and there was a stench of burning horsehair; another fragment clung to Sir Godfrey's gauntlet and glowed and grew hot.

"Get down," Sir Godfrey said. "I must unharness you." He dismounted himself and pulled off his gauntlets.

His own armour was rather more than twenty years old and all that which he had worked on when he was a squire had been in the same style. Lord Robert—a rich man's son—had new armour and fashions had changed. All the straps in the wrong places, all the buckles unfamiliar and complicated. Oh God! God! Help me.

Inside his red hot carapace Lord Robert began to scream. His horse, aware of its smouldering mane, screamed too, and galloped away. Sir Godfrey, his fingers burned to the bone, went on struggling . . .

No fighting man could afford to be squeamish and in his time Sir Godfrey had looked, unmoved, on many an unpleasant sight, but nothing quite like that disclosed when at last the armour—still aglow—clanked into the gutter. Roasted alive, the boy he had loved like a son.

Overwhelmed by grief, stunned, single-minded as ever, he knelt—but not in prayer—by the charred thing which had lately been a lively, laughing boy.

And so it happened that Sir Godfrey was the only prisoner taken that day. By evening, the only Christian alive in the city.

ELEVEN

THE LETTER CAME IN APRIL. "Threepence" said the old fish-woman who had brought it from Baildon.

It was sealed in three places and marked with dirty finger-prints. With shaking hands Sybilla broke the seals and read the words in a single glance. Then she turned dizzy and had to lean against the lintel of the door. Did people faint from joy? She drew a deep breath, read the letter again, kissed it and gave the old woman sixpence.

Well, no doubt about it, when your luck was in it was in, and when it was out it was out. Her good luck had started with the sale of her old donkey for such an unbelieveable sum, had continued with the getting of a firm, regular order to supply fish to the place for bad women and the orphanage; and now, six-pence for delivering a letter. And seemed to be going on; for when she ventured to ask, "Will you be wanting fish today, my lady?" the lady said without looking up, "Yes. Yes. Two dozen of each." You could trudge about for an hour to sell so many.

I am safe and well and the worst is over now. He could be on his way home.

Such wonderful news must be shared—if only to make it seem real.

She ran out to the byre where Walter was milking, watched by Henry.

"Walter, Henry, I have news. A letter. He is safe and well."

Walter rose from the three-legged stool and said gravely, "That is good news, my lady." Henry slipped onto the stool and said:

"Now may I finish her off, Walter?"

121

"Yes, if you do it properly . . . My lady, is it over? Is he on his way home?"

His servant asked that; his son milked a cow!

Sybilla read the letter again. "That he does not say. He says he is safe and well and that the worst is over now. Oh Walter, I am so happy!"

To Walter's ear there was something a little strange about the words—the worst is over. A tournament. Would Sir Godfrey, who enjoyed tournaments, have written thus—unless he had had bad luck again. And if he had bad luck how was he safe and well? To Walter it sounded more as though Sir Godfrey meant the sea voyage was behind him when he wrote. But he would not say a thing to mar her pleasure.

"Does it say where it was written, my lady?"

It did, but she had taken no heed of that, and now, read out, the name meant nothing to either of them.

William, when he came as he did a few days later, was more knowledgeable and less considerate. He lived in a seafaring community and had never shirked contact with ordinary people.

"Mondeneno," he said. "Yes, I have heard of it. On Spain's northern coast . . . I think, my dear, that this letter indicates that Godfrey had survived the Bay of Biscay."

"Not . . . not that he is on his way home?"

"That could hardly be. The date—All Souls' Day in the Year of Our Lord 1452. I am no traveller, my dear, and my knowledge of geography is small; but I feel bound to say that no man could leave Bywater on St Michael's Day, go to the south of Spain, fight a tourney and be back at Mondeneno by All Souls'."

Was it possible to faint through disappointment?

"This letter," William said, "has been long on the road."

And that was true. Father Andreas had left the strictest instructions that the letter should be delivered into the hands of the captain of the first English ship that put in to Mondeneno's welcoming harbour; and he had been implicitly obeyed. The fact that the ship to which the letter had been entrusted was bound for the Canaries was merely incidental.

The year went on. Walter's fields grew green and the wind blew over them, a kindly, a rough hand smoothing hair. Lady

Randall's vigorous roses put out copper-coloured shoots which changed to green and changed again, a wealth of roses, two trees bearing red flowers, two white, and two mixed in the way called damask; all sweet scented. The lilies grew tall and beautiful and the bees buzzed about them. Sybilla cut an armful and carried them into the church—thus fulfilling one of Father Ambrose's dreams. She knelt on the cold stone, alone, as the Abbess had said all must be, with God. God keep him, protect him, wherever he may be; and in mercy, bring him back to me. There was, she realised with a start of surprise, something about the scent of those lilies. She had never been one for musk, or attar of roses—both extortionately expensive and both used artfully to attract men—but now the lilies smelt of lovemaking. A fierce longing gripped her.

Late-sown as Walter's wheat and barley had been, it had been sown on land that had lain fallow for years and by August he had something to harvest.

"I'll stook for you, Walter," Bessie Wade said.

"That's for her ladyship to say."

Walter was always administering such snubs and Bessie was either too dim-witted or too thick-hided to be deterred by them. She concocted excuses to go across the yard to his little house.

"Walter, you only had half a supper. I brought your piece of pie."

"I've had enough. Give it to Master Henry, he's always hungry."

"Ooh, Walter, you have made this place nice. Neat as a pin."

"More than I can say of your kitchen."

" 'S'not really mine, is it, Walter? Ooh, if I had a little place like this, of my own, I'd keep it neat as a pin."

The very way she said his name, the frequency with which she used it set his teeth on edge. Her devotion, her persistence insulted him. Just because he had a scarred face . . .

But in the field, anxious to please, she worked well. Sybilla had said that of course Bessie could stook and she would take charge of the kitchen. So Walter scythed, never hurrying and yet covering a great deal of ground in a day; Henry bound the cut ears into sheaves, and Bessie stooked. It was fine sunny

123

weather, perfect for harvesting, and she sweated a lot. Not a word of thanks or appreciation.

Yet Walter *could* give praise. He said he had never had such a good rabbit pie as Sybilla had made. He said, "I'm sorry you have to work so hard, my lady. Such a hot day, too." And he said that in the hearing of the woman who on that hot day had plodded up and down, up and down in the field behind him!

People who could afford to do so stacked corn and kept it until, late in autumn, prices rose. Walter, with some reluctance, decided against this, just for the one year. They needed the flour that could be made from the wheat; they needed the money which the sale of the barley would bring. He made a threshing floor and two flails, a large one for himself and a smaller one for Harry, and then . . . another large one for Bessie.

"Truly, Walter," Sybilla said, "I find it almost as easy to do things myself as to direct her. If she is of help to you . . ."

All this was makeshift; a holding on, a bearing up until Godfrey came back. The year tipped over and it was September again. On St Michael's Day he would have been gone for a year.

James, between his winter gout and his summer gout, had made conscientious visits and said vague, soothing things, about Spain being a long way away, and the necessity of patience; but he was self-absorbed, taking her news about the letter and what William had said about it with, "Good! Good!" and proceeding to talk about the betrothal of his gawky daughter to a young man of good family, but, alas, small fortune.

On William's next visit Sybilla said, "William, you hold high rank in the Church and the Dominican Priory is in Bywater. They have houses in Spain, too. If you asked, do you think they would make a few inquiries? It is such a *long* time. And if he could find someone to write for him in Mondeneno, he would have found someone in Escalona."

"And may well have done so. Remember how long the other letter took to arrive. But I will certainly ask."

He had a good memory but was inclined to be absent-minded, having so many things to think about; so she made him write a little note to remind himself.

It was now September, with just that hint of coming change in the air which was stimulating to sexual appetite; mornings came with a faint mist, like the bloom on a grape, midday was warm, and at night the harvest moon hung like a great bronze globe in the sky, making night-work possible for people whose reaping was belated. Walter was not one of them; by the middle of the month even the flailing was finished.

In a way winnowing was an unpleasant job; husks worked their way into one's hair and under one's clothes. On a warm late afternoon, scooping up the last grains of barley and tying the neck of the sack firmly, Walter said, "Well, that's over for the year. I'm going to take a bath. You, too." He spoke to Henry, not to Bessie. It simply wasn't safe to speak to her except to snap out an order.

Bessie decided to take a bath, too. It was in the course of it that she realised that Walter had never seen her one real beauty, the compensation for being too fat all over—a fine bosom with firm, well-mounded breasts, white-skinned and tipped with rose. She was thirty-two years old, and desperate . . . desperate enough to rip, deliberately, one of the two shifts she possessed.

Walter had heated a pot of water and poured it into a shallow bowl. Stripped to the waist he bowed over the bowl, washing his hair, face, torso. Then, discarding his hose, he stepped into the water.

Not a position in which a man would wish to be caught by an unwanted woman.

Enough to anger any man, but what was worse was the sudden, involuntary response of his body to the sight of those white breasts. A revolt against years of discipline and self-imposed celibacy. He snatched up the towel to hide his shame, said, "Get out," and broke into the language so foul that much of it was incomprehensible to Bessie who had spent her life in circles where even abuse was limited. But she understood that, despite a second or two of promise, she was being rejected again. There could only be one reason, and she spat it out at him.

Holding the towel about him with his left hand, Walter used his right to slap her, forehand, backhand, across the face.

The people of Intake, freed of feudal domination, had re-

125

verted to an earlier, more truly English institution—the Council of Elders.

Sybilla faced the deputation, four venerable men in their tidy Sunday or market-day clothes and said:

"I cannot believe it."

"But the girl's face is swollen and bruised, my lady. She got a black eye one side, a split lip the other. And what about the torn shift?"

"Granfer Wade"—he had been excluded from the deputation for various reasons, too closely concerned in the matter, liable to get angry, certain to feel shame—"Granfer Wade said Bessie went to his place, near naked, and bawling like a calf just taken from the cow. And all hurt about the face."

"I was here," Sybilla said. "Should I not have heard? Bessie said she would take a bath—after supper, in the kitchen. Where was this assault supposed to have taken place? And when?"

About that Bessie had not been explicit. But shift implied bed.

"In her bed."

"But she slept above stairs." Bessie had indeed been privileged. In many places, even now, and even in magnificent places servants, male and female, slept all hugger-mugger in the hall or the kitchen; Bessie had had a room.

"I sat here," Sybilla said. "Bessie took her bath. I went up, as I always do, to look in on the children, to see that they were covered. I thought that while I was looking at them, Bessie followed me up and went to her bed. It was not until this morning . . . All her outer clothes there in a heap in the kitchen and I thought—when she did not appear—that she was taking a rest, well-earned. I can assure you, this alleged attack did not take place in this house. What is more, Walter Freeman has been with me for many years. In places where sonsy girls were on display and fully available. And never in all those years have I heard one word against him—in that respect."

"He set about Bessie last night, my lady."

"Not in this house. Her clothes are there in the kitchen where she left them. Her grandfather says she went to his house almost naked. If Walter laid a finger on her last night it must have been in his house; and she went there. *In her shift.*"

126

They thought it over. Bessie Wade lost some of the aspect of an innocent victim.

"If she done that," old Martin said, "she were asking for trouble."

"Did you hit her, Walter?"

"Yes, my lady."

"Why?"

"She broke in on me while I washing myself. I told her to get out and she just stood there."

All too often Bessie's response to any order or suggestion was just to stand there. Almost asking to be smacked.

"You seem to have hit her very hard."

"Not hard enough . . ." Suddenly, under the weathered tan his face crimsoned as he remembered the vile thing Bessie had said. Suppose she went saying it about the village. He thought: I should have *killed* the bitch!

"Those old men seemed to think that she would not work here any more."

"I'll find you another woman, my lady. A better one."

"That should not be difficult," Sybilla said.

Yet it proved to be. Bessie's story might not ring quite so true as it had done at first telling, but it confirmed something that everybody had felt all along—there was something not quite right about Knight's Acre. Big should be big and rich should be rich; Knight's Acre was neither one thing nor the other; a servant who did not behave like a servant ruled there, and her ladyship stuck up for him. Even at the Michaelmas Hiring Fair several likely young women who would willingly have gone to be bullied by Lady Emma at Moyidan, or to be half starved in William's palace at Bywater, shrank away when offered employment at Knight's Acre. The woman Walter finally found was stone deaf as a result of having had measles when fully adult; but she was a good cook and a conscientious cleaner. Anxious to please, too, and gifted with a kind of extra sense as the afflicted often were.

Downhill into winter. In the house one woman who heard nothing, and one whose ears were constantly alert for a footfall or a hoofbeat, for the news that never came. Henry growing every day more and more like his father in appearance—some-

127

times the likeness smote her to the heart; Margaret growing a little in size, but in no other way, and John as precocious and sturdy as Henry and Richard had been.

From Beauclaire good news of Richard. Hateful to think that at the moment of arrival the two letters from Alys— written by one of her waiting women—had been sad disappointments in a way. Lady Astallon, through her henchwoman, wrote that Richard had settled down very well and was well behaved. Richard was in fact not only behaving himself, he was enjoying a backwash of public opinion; if the young Tallboys didn't kick and bite, then he was a good boy.

Lady Astallon's second letter informed Sybilla that Richard had outgrown his first outfit of the Astallon green velvet and that he had, of his own accord, taken lessons in reading and writing. Proof of that was at the foot of the page: RICHARD TALLBOYS, carefully and plainly written.

I should be glad. I am glad. But this is not what I am waiting and watching for.

TWELVE

GRAVELY, for both were men of dignity, Selim the new King of Zagelah and Hassan ben Hassan laughed in their beards and congratulated themselves. They had hatched and put into action the perfect plot. There would be no civil war—as might have resulted from an uprising; no interference from Abdullah's brothers-in-law which would have resulted from an assassination. The Christians had attacked Zagelah, killed Abdullah and most of his loyal adherents—all bad Moslems; Selim of Andara had simply happened to be in the city at the time, and strong enough to rally the Faithful and gain a great victory. And Selim's inheritance by conquest was backed by his legitimate claim. He was kin to Abdullah.

And this was only a beginning. A reformed and purified Zagelah would presently move against Escalona and reclaim it.

"And that," Selim said, "will bring the Christians against us."

Against his will he had been impressed by the performance of the Count and his small company. Fools, all of them; but for so few they had done a vast amount of damage. A matter of training and equipment. He had begun, even on that first day, to toy with the possibility of forming a squadron of his own, similarly trained and armoured. With this in view he had issued an order to take prisoners when possible, to house them and feed them well. Despite this only one had survived—the man with the burnt hands.

Just upriver from Andara, Selim owned a marble quarry, worked by slaves of almost every nationality; most of them

129

were seamen who had been captured by the Barbary pirates and offered for sale in the port's slave market. Selim, as a strict Moslem, would not own another as a slave, and since despite comparatively good treatment his slaves seldom lived long, he was always in the market for able-bodied men. He now sent a messenger galloping to Andara with instructions to bring back an English slave.

Sir Godfrey's hands were beginning to heal. The Moorish treatment for burns was very peculiar. In England the practice was to smear a burn with some kind of fat and then to exclude the air. Here it was immersion of the burnt part in cool, slightly salted water. At first touch the water stung, then the coldness seemed to numb the pain. The burns were then exposed to the air, immersed again. An endless repetition.

The pain was the least of his woes. He was bereaved, and he was a prisoner in a heathen land. In a Christian country his ransom price would by now have been fixed and James and William and Alys—and maybe a friend or two—would be getting the money together. Here there was no hope. He lived in a state of utter dejection, not even noticing that he was being well treated. His thoughts went round and round, like an ox treading corn. I shall never see Sybilla or the children again. I shall never go home. Robert is dead. His death was horrible. I shall never see . . .

The English slave—his name was John Barnes and he was one of the few men who worked in the quarry without developing the cough which was a death sentence—wore the quarry uniform, a pair of short drawers, a sleeveless shirt and a pair of rope-soled sandals. His grizzled hair was neatly trimmed, his face freshly shaven. He looked well fed, but his face had the tallowy pallor of long exclusion from fresh air or sunlight. Sir Godfrey looked to be in worse case. They had taken away his armour and the quilted garment he wore under it and given him a long Arabic-style gown, once white, now soiled. The good treatment that Selim had ordered had meant to his Arab gaolers enough to eat and no active ill-usage, but not the use of a comb or a razor. His hair was rough and clotted and he had just enough beard growth to make him look dirty.

"Th'art English, lad?"

130

"Yes. I'm English."

John Barnes said hastily, furtively, "Do what th'art towd, lad. No matter what." Then they both waited. Selim, in Arabic, spoke to John Barnes and he in turn spoke to Sir Godfrey.

"What's thy name, lad?"

"Godfrey Tallboys. Sir Godfrey Tallboys."

Deep down in the marble quarry near Andara, John Barnes had heard nothing about the doings in the outer world. All he knew was that he had been brought out into the open, had a ride on a horse and several very good meals because his services as a translator were needed. But he knew what it meant when a man prefixed his name with *Sir;* and he did not use the familiar *lad* again until the very end.

He obeyed his master's instructions. Selim was offering Sir Godfrey an honourable post. All he had to do was to train men to fight in the Christian way; overlook the making of armour, copied from that taken from the bodies of dead men; show men how to school horses. Arcol had made his mark. In that narrow, balconied street with Sir Godfrey crouched in the gutter beside the armour, removed too late, and the charred body, Arcol had behaved valiantly as a destrier was trained to do if for any reason his rider was smitten down; four iron-clad hoofs, strong teeth. It was in fact to Arcol that Sir Godfrey owed his life. His spirited resistance had gained that moment of time for the order from the centre to penetrate—a few prisoners . . .

"No," Sir Godfrey said, hearing the proposition but not giving it long thought. Connive with these Infidels, against his own kind. No!

John Barnes said, "Best think it over, Sir Godfrey. They have a whip . . . I've tasted the rope's end, twice. It's nothing compared. Save thysen."

"Tell them, No."

"Th'art a fool, Sir Godfrey. They'll beat thee. Me too, they'll say I didn't tell thee proper . . ." The man's tallowy pallor took on a greyish tinge and out of Sir Godfrey's despair, deep enough to welcome death in whatever form—I shall never see Sybilla and the children again; never go home. Robert is dead—and so many more; all my friends—a tiny bud of something else started.

131

"If you stand still," Godfrey said, "I'll show them otherwise."

He clenched his fists and the new frail skin on the inner side of his hands crumpled and split. He hit John Barnes twice, light, but telling blows; right fist to the left of the chin, jerking the head back, left just under the right ear.

It was the only indemnity that he could give his fellow countryman. And as, under the first blow, John Barnes's head jerked, he said, "Thanks, lad."

"A spell in the quarry may make him think again," Selim said.

The quarry just outside Andara was an awesome place. When God made the world out of darkness and chaos He had laid down a streak of pink marble at the base of a limestone ridge. It ran sideways and underground. The Romans, in their day had tapped its upper outward end, and done well, for this marble was of peculiar beauty, pink, its colour shading from palest rose to deepest, not flecked, or striped. It had been greatly in demand for palaces and temples. Later for churches and ornate mansions. Besides its colour it had another unique feature, it was layered, slab on slab, like the leaves of a book, and interleafing limestone layers often produced garnets. As the centuries went by, the productive working face of the quarry retreated into the hillside, and by the time Sir Godfrey went to work there, there was, between the ordinary daylight world and the pink marble, a series of caverns and tunnels, emptied of their treasure, providing excellent living accommodation and work rooms for slaves. There were air shafts, conduits for water, plentiful lighting by means of lamps that burned olive oil. It even had a climate of its own, equable and unaffected by either winter's snows or summer's baking heat. From a slaveowner's point of view it had yet another advantage; it had only one entry.

Into this subterranean world Sir Godfrey Tallboys was conducted, as hundreds of other men had been, to live and to work and to die. Perhaps, in his case not to die; for an order came with him. Light labour only and no ill treatment; the King might have another use for him.

132

He was set to work with some old men, a few survivors of the régime, or weak men, racked by coughs, or men who in more vigorous work had suffered accidents. The "light work" consisted of polishing small pieces of marble, the debris of the quarry's produce. The marble was brittle; sometimes a slab broke as it was heaved out of its matrix, sometimes one was dropped. Nothing here was wasted. A little jagged piece no bigger than a thumbnail was marketable for use as part of a mosaic floor or patterned wall. The polishing was done with a woollen rag, dipped first into oil and then into a grey powder.

His arrival aroused no interest—less in fact than a strange cow would arouse in a field of cows. There was here the apathy of hopelessness which he fully shared. Wait for the next meal, wait for bedtime, wait for death.

There were two meals a day, always enough for everybody. In the morning rice with small chunks of meat; in the evening rice with sugar and bits of dried fruit.

There was provision for nature's other need, not unlike the garderobes of castles, except that here the outlets were small.

There were guards or overseers who carried whippy canes and used them freely on anybody who had not turned enough jagged bits into smoothly polished pieces. Each man's finished work lay by his feet at the end of the day and every day Sir Godfrey's pile was smaller than any other, but he was not caned.

There was nobody to whom he could speak. No Englishman here. The guards shouted or scolded in Arabic which Sir Godfrey did not understand, or intend to learn. He did what the others did.

For a full fortnight.

At the end of the second week, in accord with the deadly, soul-killing routine, he was taken out into the air, blinking and blinded as they all were by the sunshine. But he saw . . .

There, dark and yawning, the great arch, entry and exit to the quarry, and immediately before it the hard-trodden ground, a space where laden men and laden donkeys delivered what the quarry needed and took away what the quarry produced. Herded by the guards, shouting in Arabic and using their canes freely, Sir Godfrey and those who worked with him turned to the left. And there was half a meadow and beyond a

133

stretch of river. Half a meadow, because it had been carved away, made into a pool, curving inwards.

For the first time since he had been taken in that narrow, balconied street, Sir Godfrey's eye for terrain went to work.

The pool was a semicircle carved out of the riverbank and separated from the river by an iron grill, slightly wider than the opening of the pool into the river. Upstream, downstream the iron grill, very spiky, reached into the green meadow.

If I could swim!

With that thought he began to live again.

The biweekly bath was a ritual. Gang by gang, on differing days, all the slaves of the Andara quarry were taken out, stripped, made to go into the water, brought back, clad in clean clothes, given into the barbers' hands to be shaven and shorn. Not for their comfort, who cared? A guard against lice and all the other things which unwashed bodies produced.

The pool, Sir Godfrey thought in the mind that had begun to work again, is shaped like a C; the grill that separates it from the river extends, ten, twelve feet upstream, downstream. Are those points guarded?

It seemed not. So he worked it out. All that he needed to do was to go into the far edge of the pool, step out onto the bit of grass confined by the iron grill, run across it, plunge into the river and *swim*. Swim down to Andara, find a ship with an English name. The masts and spars of the ships in the harbour were visible from the pool.

His time in captivity in Zagelah, his fortnight of sedentary work had slackened his muscles. That must be put right. He started his surreptitious exercises; stretching and bending, swinging his arms, flexing his legs, first thing in the morning, last thing at night. Not enough. He took to wolfing his food and thus gaining a few seconds in order to perform his antics which his fellows watched with complete lack of interest, and every time he went to the garderobe place he stayed a little longer than was necessary. He observed that every now and then one of the men he worked with was assailed by cramp, and with yelps and grimaces of pain would stand up from his cramped

134

working posture and stamp about to relieve it. He had not yet suffered this affliction himself but he now pretended to, as often as four or five times a day. His pile of finished work grew even smaller, but he was never caned. In this place as in all others under Selim's control, an order once given remained in force until it was rescinded.

There was a legend in the quarry that once upon a time a slave had attempted to escape on the way to the bathing pool; on the trodden forecourt he had turned right instead of left, thrown himself on a waiting mule and galloped off. It was a long time ago, but the guards were always particularly vigilant at that point. Once the slaves were in the water they relaxed a little, nobody could escape from the pool; all they had to do was to see that the slaves went far enough in and really washed themselves. On his second visit Sir Godfrey investigated the depth of the water. It grew deeper as it neared the grill. He waded out until it was chin high—that was about the centre; another step and he could feel the buoyancy of the water. He had never swum himself but he had seen it done. You kept your nose and mouth above water and made certain movements with arms and legs. He began to practise such movements. It was slow work, it was hit and miss, but his whole heart was in it and he made progress.

He was still dissatisfied with his physical shape; despite all his exertions it seemed to him that day by day his belly, which had been flat as a board, bulged a little more, while his chest shrank. He began to wonder whether the food had anything to do with it. Most slaves in the quarry looked well fed, though two meals a day was not really very much and if you looked closely at the unvarying dishes—as he did—the amount of meat in the morning meal was very small indeed, and the fruit pieces at evening were equally sparse. Was it the rice which made his belly bulge? He didn't know, but he could find out. He began to pick out the meat and the fruit and eat only a spoonful or two of the plentiful rice. For some days he suffered hunger pangs, then they eased; but the bulge was, if anything, even more pronounced.

In this place there was no day and no night; nor any way of telling one day from another; only the fortnightly cleansing

135

marked the passage of time. The guards changed from time to time, but they all looked and sounded alike, and their behaviour varied so little that they might have been one man.

Outside the seasons progressed; the weather became warm, then hot, so that the bathing became a pleasure and there was no need for the guards to shout, "Further!" The grass in the meadow became yellow and brittle. July? August?

Sir Godfrey knew that the attack on Zagelah had been made in mid-February. After that he had been too dejected to bother about time. Say he had come to Andara early in March. And say this was July. Five months. He should have been home by now. Sir Ralph had promised to go and see Sybilla and take her a message. He was *not* to say that it was war, not tournament, and for his own premature return he was to use the excuse of ill health. Sybilla knew how long a tourney lasted. She would be worried now.

He must make his attempt as soon as possible, not wait until he swam better. Another consideration was that shipping was more plentiful in summer, and voyages speedier.

The guards, more observant than they appeared to be during the washing time, were now accustomed to the sight of one man venturing into the really deep water and performing antics. They were not worried; he could not escape by the grill which was heavily spiked and at its top turned inwards.

It was an afternoon of somnolent heat; not a time for swift movement or swift thinking. He splashed about a little, sure now that it was just possible. He had only to heave himself out of the pool, run like a hare to the end of the grill, throw himself into the river.

Now!

He did it. As the water closed over his head he heard the shouting. He surfaced and clumsily struck out.

What he did not know, and couldn't know, was that some of the pink marble was transported downstream to the port in small boats. Somebody in one of these hit him over the head with an oar and dragged him aboard.

Far less heinous offences than attempted escape were punishable by flogging, but this man could not be flogged without the

King's direct permission. And Selim had lost interest in Sir Godfrey. For one thing Hassan ben Hassan, a firm traditionalist, had been opposed to the idea of newfangled methods of fighting and found the thought of aping the Unbelievers most repulsive. For another, when, as he planned, he moved in on Escalona nobody had made so much as a murmur of protest. The nearest two great Christian lords were busy with their interminable squabble; and the King of Castile had other things than the loss of a small province to think about. Divorce, remarriage . . .

In due time the new order came: Treat this man as you would any other.

Sir Godfrey had regained consciousness in a place so dark and so narrow that when he had felt about a bit he had been seized with panic. He had drowned and they'd buried him alive.

It was a rational assumption. During his time in Andara he had seen two men die and seen how casually their corpses had been treated—literally dragged out feet first, with no more ceremony than would have been given a dead dog. His head hurt. He had no memory of the blow that had stunned him and thought that his head had been injured by similar rough handling.

He felt about; stone under him, stone on both sides; then wood. Wood? Yes, wood. The lid of the coffin? The door to the vault? He hammered on it and shouted. There was no answer.

A man not yet dead, but buried alive and soon to die, should make his peace with God.

He had never been a very pious man; he had accepted the teaching of the Church, kept the rules. He had been faithful to his knighthood vows and to his marriage vows, he had never cheated or told an unnecessary lie, but his religion had always been a matter of form rather than of feeling; except when he knelt there in that narrow street and asked, from his heart, for help in getting Robert out before he roasted. That help had not been forthcoming . . . How then approach God now, except to say, as to some remote, indifferent overlord, "My God, I am sorry if by word or deed I have given offence. I beg forgiveness."

A creak, a narrow streak of oil-lit light. Something pushed in and a voice. "Take this, you swine!"

137

Without knowing, without wishing, Sir Godfrey had picked up a small knowledge of Arabic. Terms of abuse were always the most easily acquired in any language.

He had not been buried alive; but he was still a prisoner. He had failed in his attempt to escape and was back with his hopelessness. Sometimes in the darkness, he wept.

Floggings were not frequent in the quarry, partly because they disabled a man for work for some time; but it was good for everyone to be aware of the existence of the dreaded whip and to see it in use from time to time. The procedure was therefore made as public as possible, with the offence which had occasioned it chanted. "Look well and learn. See what befalls one who would run away. See the punishment for defiance."

Sir Godfrey would have said that he was hardened to pain; to bear it without fuss was part of every boy's training. At the first stroke of the many-thonged, metal weighted whip he bit through his lower lip in order to keep silent. At the second both bowels and bladder failed him and he screamed like a trapped hare. Then he lost consciousness again.

He was now, in every sense of the word a marked man. Even an abortive attempt at escape was resented by the guards as a reflection on their vigilance, and this man had for months been immune from even the most desultory punishment. As soon as his back and shoulders and ribs and buttocks were half healed he was moved to heavier work, at the rock face itself.

Had he, in this new misery, been capable of finding consolation in anything, he would have found it in the fact that he now worked alongside John Barnes, with whom he could at least exchange remarks now and then. Much talking was not allowed. The atmosphere here was also less dour and sullen than in the mosaic chamber where everyone was half dead of age or ill health; this was the place for the younger and more able-bodied slaves. Their plight was just as hopeless, but they chose not to recognise it quite as fully as the old, sick men had done. They were of many nationalities; Italian, Dutch, French, Norwegian, German, but they had developed a kind of polyglot language with a good deal of Arabic in it.

One day when Sir Godfrey had been at the quarry face for

some time there was a new arrival; a Greek who also spoke Latin and quickly made himself understood by the two Italians, who managed to impart the news he brought to the rest of them. The Turks, he told them, and they told the others, had taken Constantinople in May.

"And that should stir up the Pope and the rest of 'em," John Barnes said. "There'll be big war now, Christian against Infidel all over t'place. We might yet see t'light of day; if we bear up."

It was a frail hope, but anything, however small, was better than nothing.

THIRTEEN

AT THE POINT where the road to Moyidan met the lane to Intake, Bishop William halted his horse. James was head of the family, after all. And breaking bad news to a woman was a woman's job. He was tempted. Then he admonished himself for wishing to shirk, and rode on down the lane.

Sybilla, at the sound of his horse, ran out, her headdress blowing in the gay April wind. At the sight of his face, she said:

"Bad?"

"I am afraid so."

"Dead?"

"Nobody knows. It seems likely."

She did not break into the storm of tears which he had feared. Her face blanched and hardened, that was all.

Inside the hall she said, "I have felt for a long time . . . from the very first . . . I was against it. What does it mean—nobody knows?"

He took out the letter which the Head of the Dominican House in Seville had written.

The Count of Escalona, the knights who were with him, Father Andreas, and six other Dominicans had simply vanished. They were known to have gone into Moorish territory in February 1453. No word of what had happened to them had ever been received. In March 1453 the Moors had overrun Escalona itself, and so far as could be ascertained there had been no refugees. All hope for the priests had been abandoned and the chance of any man's survival was small; the Moorish custom was to take only women and children as prisoners.

Sybilla sat perfectly still with her hands pressed to a point just below her breast as though easing a pain. Stunned, poor woman. Now he found himself wishing that she would cry.

He noticed for the first time how thin she had grown during these months of anxiety. He remembered, with startling clarity, a dress she had worn on one of her early visits to him. Not a modest dress, he had thought at the time, either in colour or style. It was bright scarlet, cut low and with sleeves that were so wide and loose that every time she lifted her spoon, her right arm had been revealed to the elbow; white and dimpled.

To be honest, in those days he had not either liked or approved of her much; too worldly and given to fashion; and then when the children came she had spoiled them shamelessly and tried to interfere with his household arrangements which suited him perfectly. But now he was genuinely sorry for her, as he was for all the afflicted, and his words of comfort, though well worn, came from his heart.

Godfrey, he said, was now in God's hands and safe forever. Dying in a battle against the Infidel—as must be assumed—he had died in a Holy War. And it could be certain that he had died bravely. "He was a brave knight, and a good man."

In his experience, praise of the dead, however little deserved, provoked more tears in those already shedding them but applied comfort at the same time.

"He was a brave knight and a good man. *And he died because I must have a house!*"

"He died," William said, "because this Count of Escalona, having gathered knights for a tournament, snatched an opportunity to lead a small Crusade. In effect, Godfrey took the Cross—an act which, even with men of evil life, shortened the the pains of Purgatory. Godfrey is now in the presence of God."

He then bethought himself of his last talk with his brother. There would be no money now to be brought home and looked after.

In his own way William Tallboys was brave, too. He had broken the bad news, given what spiritual comfort was available and now took a decision that was likely to cost him dear.

He said, "My dear, I should be very happy if you would come and make your home with me."

And if ever a man told a lie, he told one then. For more than the mere disruption of his household was at stake, though

141

that would be bad enough . . . Henry was old enough to go to the monks' school, but even so it would leave two, and John bade fair to be as noisy and hungry as his brothers. But there was also an undertow; the Lollards had been put down, but some of the things they had said during their attacks on the Church, had echoed . . . the words "housekeeper" and "nephew" had been smeared; and something of the smear clung. Conscientious clerics were careful to have only old, ugly women about them; and seemed to have fewer nephews . . . Still, if at his age and with his umblemished reputation he couldn't invite his brother's widow to share his home, things had come to a fine pass.

"William, that is very kind. I am grateful. But I must stay here."

"Alone?"

"Except for those few short months I have always been alone here."

"But with hope," he said gently. "Now you will be . . ." He left that sentence unfinished. "I am sure we could make some very comfortable arrangement. Those rooms that face the sea. A kitchen of your own."

"Thank you. That is most kind and generous. But I must stay here; in the house that Godfrey made for me. His last gift."

"The offer will remain open, my dear." She was in no state to be pressed. He felt that she was making a wrong decision: and although to make the offer had been an effort he did not like to see it rejected so promptly. Nor did he like the idea of leaving her here alone. Such unnatural control must surely snap. On whose shoulder would she weep?

He offered to stay overnight. Offered to send Emma from Moyidan. Offered to send a well-mounted messenger to fetch one of Eustace's sisters. She said, "I need nobody, William. I have been prepared for this. For many months now."

But then, he thought, so were women who had watched through hopeless illnesses—yet they wept. For the first time William understood what his sister Mary had seen in Sybilla.

James came next day and made an offer similar to William's and that had cost him even more of an effort—hours of argument with Emma who did not favour the idea at all. And he had come a cropper. In the course of the argument he had pointed out—meaning no ill—that in June Margery was to be married and that Sybilla could, to an extent, take her place. Emma took that much amiss. "Are you telling me that I am old enough to be Sybilla's mother? I thank you for nothing! She is full twenty-six, maybe more if the truth were known." He had tried to explain; he only meant that Sybilla would do the errands, the running about, the waiting on. Emma refused to be pacified, refused even to discuss the matter further until, by one of those curious twists that a quarrel takes, they came back to something she had long wanted and James had been reluctant to give, holding as he did that as he inherited property so he should pass it on. And there was something—unpleasant—in this assumption that she would surely outlive him, obvious as it must be considering their ages. And she had been well dowered; but her argument was that values were changing so rapidly. A noble, once worth, in words six shillings and eightpence, was now, in words worth eight shillings and fourpence, but it bought less; and she could not really trust Richard to look after her—good mother as she had been to him. He was so *weak;* even in the midst of this quarrel she could not bring herself to say simple-minded; weak and stubborn. He'd choose his wife—as Godfrey had done—and then live under her thumb, and where would Emma be?

By the end of the quarrel, Sir James had pledged his word. Emma should have land and money enough to build a house when she needed it; not as a bequest in his will but now. A bribe for doing what was merely a duty—offering a home to a widow and her children.

Sybilla gave him the same answer as she had given William. Kind. Generous. But she must stay here. And she could manage. Knight's Acre was even now virtually self-supporting, next year it would do even better. She could manage. Sir James was so much impressed by her attitude that he made another effort; he said that if ever she needed money—or advice—she had only to ask . . .

Time now seemed to change pace. While she had awaited news, it had been both speedy and slow. A week of waiting an

143

age and yet the Sundays seeming to crowd one another. Different now.

She had broken the news to Henry. "Henry, I have something sad to tell you; I heard today that your father is dead." No impact. Henry said politely, "I am sorry, Mother." He would have been more concerned if she had cut her finger.

Walter struck a truer note. "I am sorry, my lady; but I had begun to think . . . And he died as he would have wished. If's that any comfort."

There was that to think of. She had not wanted him to go, but he had wanted to, and had whistled, merry as a blackbird as he scoured his armour and rubbed neats' foot oil into its straps. He had gone happily to death. And since death must come to all men . . .

Father Ambrose asked, "Any news of Sir Godfrey, my lady?"

Senile; she had told him in those first bitter moments, and he had said, "I am very sorry. I will say a Mass for his soul."

But he asked the question every time he saw her; not on Sundays only; as the days lengthened and even the twilights were warm he would come, knock on the door, ask the same question, receive the same answer, make the same promise. She outlived the stage of being exasperated and was able to think: Poor old man!

In that April William of Bywater had had another thought. What of the rest? Who else should be informed? He plodded up the hill to the Dominican Priory, and because Dominicans were scrupulous about records, he was given the names of fifty knights, half embarked on a ship named *Mary Clare* which, after so long a time must be assumed to be lost, and half on *The Four Fleeces* which had been luckier.

He went back and sat at his wide table and cogitated. Urged by Sybilla he had put inquiries afoot; and been answered. Other women, living with anxiety and suspense that ate the flesh from the bones, still knew nothing. It was his duty to write and he did it, until the repetition dulled his mind and the writing cramped his hand. He had a perfectly adequate clerical staff, but he felt that such a letter should be personal.

The mystery surrounding the event kept interest alive and it

144

was still being discussed when Sir Simon Randall went to the Lammas Tourney at the Abbey of Bury St Edmund's. There he disported himself less well than usual because his mind was distracted: Should he or should he not pay a visit of commiseration to Sir Godfrey's widow? It would be a perfectly conventional thing to do; he and Sir Godfrey had been comrades-in-arms during the Welsh war; so why not make up his mind and go? Because, after only five months, bereavement would still be raw and he shrank from seeing her in a lachrymose state. He'd been a child when his father died but he had a vivid recollection of how his mother—a strong-minded woman, too—had behaved for a full year. (He could also remember how his parents had quarrelled; but he had not associated his mother's violent grief with feelings of remorse and guilt.)

In the end he decided to go; sent his squire home with his great horse, and a message to his mother, rode to Baildon and spent the night there and arrived at Knight's Acre at midmorning.

Sybilla was in the kitchen. Madge, the deaf woman, was helping with the harvest: she worked less ostentatiously hard than Bessie had done, being older and not inspired by a wish to impress Walter, but she did well enough. John and Margaret were also helping this year, gleaning stray ears for the hens. Their development had reached the stage where whatever John did, Margaret would attempt to copy.

Sybilla no longer listened for horses' hoofs and when the knock sounded on the door, she thought: Father Ambrose again! She stopped only to throw off the coarse apron. She had abandoned headdresses now. Even in those days of declining hope, or near hopelessness, while there had been the slightest chance of Godfrey ever returning she had been careful of her appearance. Now there was no reason to suffer inconvenience.

The hair thus fully exposed had changed colour; Sir Simon remembered it as being the soft amber of fresh-run honey. Now it was primrose pale. And that look of youth which had made her so surprising a mother to four children, two of them big boys, had vanished. He felt something twist inside him as she greeted him. Poor lady, she has felt her loss keenly.

There was, however, nothing tragic about her manner; she

145

actually smiled as she said, "Sir Simon, how very kind of you to visit."

"I was nearby," he said a trifle awkwardly.

"I have for so long been meaning to write to your mother. To thank her. *Everything* she sent me flourished and gave me much pleasure. The roses are over now, but I believe, I really believe that one tree, one of the damasks, is preparing to bloom again."

"That does happen sometimes—with damasks."

She still had no wine, no saffron cake for midmorning hospitality. But she had ale.

"Walter," she said in a light, sociable manner, "has taken to brewing—and does it as well as he does all else. And I have learned the art of making harvest buns."

Harvest buns were meant to be eaten in the field; they contained a little finely chopped suet which prevented them drying out as slices of bread did. They were flavoured, too, a pinch of nutmeg, a pinch of cinnamon and just before harvest started Walter had "happened upon" another of his extraordinary bargains, a little old battered chest, regarded as rubbish by those who had inherited it and hoped to find gold . . . The spices in its small compartments, which ignorant heirs had opened with hope and shut again in disappointment, had found their way to what Walter called "the rubbish market" at Baildon.

Sir Simon was at a loss; he had been properly reared and taught what to do in most circumstances; but how could you mention a dead man to his widow who talked about roses, about ale, and harvest buns. It was like seeing a woman, and talking to her, through a window.

Finally he forced himself to say what he believed he had come to say. "Lady Tallboys, I was most profoundly sorry to hear . . ."

The glass between them should have shattered then; but it did not. She said, "Yes, it was a terrible thing. My only consolation is that he went happily. That is true. He whistled as he made his armour ready, and as he prepared Arcol. To be honest I was never in favour of that enterprise; I sensed something wrong . . . from the very beginning. But he went happily . . ." There was a sombreness now in her voice, and on her face the look of sorrow which had hollowed the youth away. But almost immediately she was again a hostess entertaining

146

a welcome visitor; asking what he had been doing since they last met.

How astonished she would be, he thought, if I told her the truth: Sedulously avoiding my mother's matrimonial lures! He gave her a brief account of his recent activities, one half of his mind intent to be as entertaining as possible—the other deeply concerned for her. Poor and alone. And sad—for all that brave front! Finally, feeling self-conscious about it, he managed to get in his question; did she propose to stay in this house? Oh yes, she said, everybody had been exceedingly kind; she told him about the homes she had been offered. "But I prefer to stay. I am not lonely. I have three children, and Walter, and Madge. At the moment they are all in the field." Where shortly, she should join them, carrying ale and harvest buns. The corn was thicker this year and no part of a good working day must be wasted by dallying over dinner. Supper was the main meal at this busy time of the year; she had been in the act of preparing it; a mutton and apple pie . . .

When he rode away Sir Simon was deeply, and now legitimately, in love. *Thou shalt not covet thy neighbour's wife:* and Sir Godfrey had been in a way his neighbour in several bloody little affrays. Now he was dead—God rest him in peace—and Sybilla was not a wife, she was a widow.

Lady Randall *knew*. For Simon who had always shied away from anything that was not completely pleasant, to go out of his way . . . This Lady Tallboys . . . Typical widow . . . she had known several, one man lost; all agog to catch another. Experienced. Wily.

She had an erroneous picture in her mind. After Simon's first —and completely explicable—visit to Knight's Acre he had spoken of Lady Tallboys, mentioning the four children, two big rather naughty boys, mentioning also her youthful look. That implied a liberal use of cosmetics.

Now, after his second visit, he sounded concerned about the woman in a way that could only mean one thing—concern for others not being one of his outstanding virtues. Knight's Acre was such a remote place, and although Lady Tallboys denied that she was lonely, she must be, left with only children and

147

servants for company. Had she no relatives? Yes, and both Sir Godfrey's brothers had offered her a home, but she preferred to remain in her own. A woman out to catch another husband, Lady Randall reflected, would enjoy far more freedom of action under her own roof.

Open opposition would be worse than useless, all mothers knew that. Lady Randall could only hope that this infatuation would wear off; that some man nearer at hand would forestall Simon; that if the worst came to the worst, Lady Tallboys was capable of bearing another son. She had a great longing for grandchildren, but was prepared to make do with one, if a boy.

In October the Cressacre orchards yielded their final offering for the year; particularly excellent pears, long-keeping apples, walnuts. "Lady Tallboys has no such things," Simon said. So the gaily painted cart was loaded again, and into it went two casks of good wine as well. Sir Simon followed his gift and was prettily thanked and given a good dinner, for Walter had killed a pig that week.

That morning there was a good fire in the hall, but partly because it was so sparsely furnished, it still struck cold. Of course, no rushes on the stone floor. On his way home he turned aside and went to a place called Shimpling where a special kind of reed grew; scented, so that every time a step was taken, a pleasant odour was emitted. He paid for a load to be delivered to Knight's Acre.

It was that gift which wakened a suspicion in Sybilla's mind.

Presents of surplus produce were usual enough, costing the donor nothing; but she knew this particular kind of rush and how much in demand, how extremely costly, it was.

Dismiss the suspicion as ridiculous! Take a look in your mirror! A boy, twenty-three at most. And are you so old? Twenty-seven. But one ages not only by one's birthdays. In all but years' reckoning I am old enough to be his mother!

He is a young man with a kind and generous heart; he had a fondness for Godfrey. I wrong him. I flatter myself.

But he came again, just before Christmas, bringing not only gifts but an invitation which Lady Randall had extended in a spirit of resignation. If Lady Tallboys had no previous engagements, Lady Randall would be most happy if she and her family would come to Cressacre for the festive season.

"And I thought," Sir Simon said, "that if you travelled with the younger children in the wagon, the cloak would keep you warm."

It was of sable; the costliest fur known, coming, as it did, all the way from Muscovy.

The Abbess of Lamarsh, training a promising girl, had said, "Of two possibilities, think of the worse first. One can always retract."

Time to make things clear; but gently. She used his name without its prefix for the first time.

"Simon, such a gift no honest woman could accept—as you must surely know—except from a wealthy kinsman, or a husband."

Playing straight into his hands. "And that is what I wish to be to you, Sybilla. I fell in love with you at first sight."

The very words Godfrey had spoken in the cold convent parlour. And then, all innocence and defiance and with a feeling of being let out of a trap, she had been able to say with all sincerity, "And I with you." That was not possible now.

"You must put all such thoughts from your mind. I shall never marry again."

"I spoke too soon . . ." He had indeed been precipitate; he had intended to make his declaration at Cressacre.

"No. In ten, twenty years, I shall still be of the same mind. A proposal is always a compliment, and I value yours, Sir Simon. But I cannot accept it."

"Why? What have you against me?" What indeed? He was young and handsome and rich and had gone out of his way to show fondness; he was prepared to treat the children as his own.

"Against you? Nothing! Nothing. But it would be impossible for me to marry any man."

They were now talking at cross purposes. He felt that he had blundered—though she had known of her widowhood since April. He attempted to defend himself.

"Sybilla, I should have waited. But, beside my love, there is another reason . . . Time may be short . . . The threat of civil war hangs over us all. Next year, or the one after at latest.

149

If you do not love me"—as plainly she did not—"consider your safety and that of your children. Cressacre is well fortified; moated. It could withstand a siege. Also, married to me, you would be on the winning side. York!"

Sybilla had heard talk of civil war as long ago as when she was staying at Beauclaire: her brother-in-law, Lord Astallon, had been sure that it would come and equally sure that a cautious man could remain neutral. He never went to Court— much to the chagrin of his lady; he did not allow political talk in his hearing; he avoided people with strong views.

"I shall be safe here," she said. "I take no sides and I have nothing that anyone could covet."

In any other woman he would have regarded such reasoning as idiocy; in her it indicated a touching innocence.

"I beg you," he said, "reconsider. Do not refuse out of hand. I will accept that you do not love me—but you might come to do so. Marriages are made every day with no fondness on either hand—yet love comes. And I love you so much. I could *make* you love me, given half a chance."

She shook her head. "I loved Godfrey. I love him still."

He *had* spoken too soon!

"Think it over," he said again. "I will come again, after Christmas."

"That would be foolish. You must forget all this. There must be so many girls, with love locked in them, waiting to be freed. So it was with me. Find one of them. And I wish you happy."

Their leave-taking had, on her side at least, an air of finality.

He did not ride home directly. Temporarily defeated, he felt the need of allies—and found them.

James at Moyidan said, "It would be the most wonderful thing for Sybilla. She has, as you know, so small a substance. Four pounds a year in rent and what the farm—it is only a farm—brings in. We do what we can, of course," he said deprecatingly, and in fact when their bees swarmed they had sent Sybilla a hive, "but times are bad and getting worse."

(You are a fat selfish pig, Sir James Tallboys, and every twinge of your gout is well deserved, Sir Simon thought.)

But he was an ally, saying yes, and yes, he would make the

great effort and some time over the Christmas season go and have a talk with Sybilla.

William at Bywater was equally obliging if less outspoken. In his long and on the whole, sorry, experience, women who had once known the joys of love, as they called it, needed it again. Time after time a woman, betrayed, rescued, and placed in a position which promised security, had fallen again. And he knew about widows, too. Only a few, disappointingly few, were content to live on in loneliness and leave their goods to the Church.

"It would be an excellent thing for Sybilla," William said. "If you could be patient, Sir Simon. I think she has not yet realised what loneliness—without hope of relief—can mean. And she is a comparatively young woman still."

"She has requested me not to visit her again."

"And that, surely, is discreet. But you may rely upon me—and upon James, I am sure—to advise her for her own good."

"She refused me," Sir Simon told his mother. "And also your invitation."

To her already unpleasant vision of Lady Tallboys, Lady Randall added another stroke: Coy! She then made a blunder.

"Perhaps, my dear boy, it is as well. A widow, with four children. Not an ideal match."

"The only woman I ever wanted to marry—or ever shall. I can tell you this. Unless Sybilla changes her mind, I shall never marry."

"Nonsense," his mother said briskly. "If you can stay away from her for six months you will forget all about her."

Lady Randall was a practical woman and, anticipating that Lady Tallboys, falsely youthful, would be spending Christmas at Cressacre, had invited also two very pretty young girls.

"And you cannot *not* marry, Simon. Cressacre needs an heir."

"My uncle of Malvern remained a bachelor. I have no nephew, but doubtless I shall find a godson."

Christmas passed; the pretty young girls doing their best and winning from their host nothing more than a host's due civility. In his lordly surroundings Simon Randall awaited the coming

151

of a messenger just as Sybilla had waited. Sybilla could have changed her mind; the persuasions of her relatives could have been effective; but there was no word from Knight's Acre, Moyidan, or Bywater. January, by measure of days one of the long months of the year, but of itself the longest, painfully climbing out of the trough of winter, came and went. Early in February a baby born at nearby Bradwald was christened—with Sir Simon Randall as his godfather; and Lady Randall, looking with unfond eyes at the squalling, red-faced, scrap of humanity, asked herself: Was it for *this* that I managed during Simon's minority?

Oh, better a widow—still of child-bearing age, one hoped.

Bang, bang, bang of the iron ring on the solid door. Father Ambrose again. A form of discipline. "Any news of Sir Godfrey, my lady?" "Yes, Father, he died in Spain." "I am sorry to hear that. I will say a Mass for his soul." Again and again, impatience becoming tolerance and tolerance melting into impatience again. This time she would not even remove the apron, then he would see that she was busy and not make some remark about the weather and then repeat the question. Madge, taking advantage of the fine, bright day, was at the washtub, and Sybilla had been dealing with a piece of bacon which Walter had taken from the smoke hall in the kitchen chimney before taking a sack of wheat to be ground at the mill.

A poor household indeed, Lady Randall thought, where the door is opened by a little kitchen slut with black hands and a smut on her face.

"I wish to see Lady Tallboys."

"I am Lady Tallboys. And you, I think, must be Lady Randall."

Dumb from astonishment, Lady Randall, who had walked straight into the hall, turned and stared at Sybilla who was closing the door. Outside, on the wide path flanked by Lady Randall's roses, Lady Randall's attendant stood holding Lady Randall's two tall horses.

"There is such a strong resemblance," Sybilla said, and smiled.

Since Simon had always been considered handsome and Lady

152

Randall, even in youth, not even pretty, this was a compliment indeed.

"I beg you, excuse my appearance. Had I had warning . . . I was doing a rather dirty job. Pray be seated." With one soiled hand she indicated the cushioned settle. She then divested herself of the coarse apron. On the cleaner parts of it she rubbed her hands, taking off the worst, but leaving them still far from clean. She rolled the apron and dropped it out of sight behind the settle and then seated herself on the plain wooden bench. And then, since Lady Randall was still speechless, Sybilla said:

"I am so happy to see you and to be able to thank you, in person. I asked Sir Simon to tell you that everything had flourished most wonderfully—but a message is not quite the same."

Lady Randall recovered sufficiently to say that it always gave her great pleasure to give a few plants to appreciative people. But as she spoke she was taking stock. What *can* he see in her? Somewhat over thirty; colourless; no figure to speak of. A kind of grace, yes, a pleasant voice, a composed manner, and dignity —despite the smudged face and the rolled-up sleeves. Nothing to account for the boy's infatuated behaviour. Nothing that could not be matched a dozen times, with youth and prettiness thrown in.

"I am—thanks entirely to your generosity—able to offer you a cup of wine, Lady Randall. If you will excuse me. My maidservant is completely deaf."

While she was alone Lady Randall could study the hall, the bare cupboard, the single wall hanging. Her mystification grew; and curiosity alongside.

When Sybilla returned she was clean. She had dabbled her hands in the washing tub, and Madge, saying "Excuse me, my lady," in the harsh toneless voice of one who had been deaf for years, had removed the smudge.

"I came," Lady Randall said, accepting a cup of wine and a wafer-thin slice of something that was neither bread nor cake, "to talk to you about my son. I understand that on his last visit he made you an offer of marriage, and that you refused it. And said you did not wish to see him again."

153

"I hope—no, I am sure—that I did not speak so harshly. I refused his offer. I advised him to go away and forget me. I advised him to find a young woman who would love him as he deserves to be loved."

"As you cannot?"

"As I cannot."

"Why? If you think him worthy of love?"

"Because I loved my husband. It is too long a story to tell . . . He loved me and I loved him. What feeling is left in me is for his children, *because* they are his. I have nothing to spare, even for someone so charming, so kind, so handsome, so altogether delightful as Sir Simon."

Lady Randall, who had come in desperation to plead with a coy, flighty widow who might—one never knew, men being so stupid—have another, even more eligible man on a hook . . . Now, again confounded, she said:

"Perhaps Simon spoke too soon. I know. I have myself been widowed . . . I wept every day for a full year. But my dear Lady Tallboys, life must go on."

"It goes on here. Every day."

Lady Randall brought her hands together in an ungraceful way, the right fist clenched and banging into the palm of the left.

"Listen. Within a year there will be war. My brother-in-law, Lord Malvern, informed me privately, only the other day. The present situation cannot outlast the summer."

And God knew that she had meant to mention Lord Malvern in another connotation, bait for the coy, flighty widow. But this was bedrock stuff. If this stubborn, stupid woman persisted in her refusal, and Simon, stubborn and stupid, persisted in his determination to marry nobody else, and the war came . . .

"Has a reluctance to give your children a stepfather any bearing on your decision, Lady Tallboys? I can assure you that Simon . . ."

"Far from it. I know very well that they would benefit. Indeed, I am not very happy about Henry—that is my eldest. He is eleven and has had no advantages at all. But . . ."

"You must have married very young." A cunning interruption.

"I was just sixteen and Henry was born within a year."

154

Twenty-eight then; and four children living: A good breeder!

"Naturally any son of Simon's own would inherit Cressacre. But—not to put too fine a point upon it—Simon is very well-to-do. My husband was rich; I brought him a good dowry; and in the years before Simon came of age, by thrift and good management I added to the estate. There would be enough for all; even without regard to the fact that Simon will in all probability inherit Lord Malvern's lands—and *title.*" Surely as glittering a bait as was ever dangled before a poor widow with four children.

"There are times," Sybilla said, "when one's mind moves quickly. I thought of all the advantages as soon as Simon had spoken. But even as I thought I knew that it would be impossible for me to remarry. I regret the impossibility—but not the decision."

"I fear that you will, Lady Tallboys. Privation lightly borne in youth become burdensome as one ages."

"And some ease," Sybilla said—again that smile. "A few years ago it would have mortified me to wear such a dress. I should have sat up all night to refurbish it. Now I do not even notice."

To Lady Randall the most infuriating thing was that she found herself liking the woman, positively *wanting* her as a daughter-in-law—a very different thing from the grudging acceptance, the better-this-than-nothing mood that had brought her here. She was now even prepared to admit that Sybilla had beautiful eyes and an entrancing smile. She tried persuasion; Cressacre with its castle and all the more habitable living accommodation that had been added was big enough for four or five separate households; Sybilla need not fear any interference or overlapping. She made the final, sacrificial offer. Sybilla could have her garden, she would make herself another, begin from the beginning again.

And all Lady Tallboys said was, "I am sorry. I am very sorry." Lady Randall, like her son—and like the Abbess of Lamarsh—was accustomed to getting her own way. In the end she was angry and said some very unkind things. But long ago, as a child at Lamarsh, Sybilla had learned not to meet anger with anger. The soft answer was supposed to turn away wrath. The Abbess had said that—a quotation from Holy Writ—early

155

on, before she had need for wrath or Sybilla need for soft answers. Later Sybilla had learned that when the soft answer turned wrath to rage, a harder one served, provided it were politely phrased, and towards the end of this extraordinary interview she said, "Lady Randall, you are wasting your time."

FOURTEEN

THE WAR WHICH FATHER ANDREAS had foreseen in 1452, and which in England had been a matter of talk for years, came in 1455, in the beautiful month of May. It affected the part of Suffolk of which Baildon was the centre hardly at all, for it was a war between great lords with their own private armies and this was an area of manors, large or small, of fields and sheepruns run by people who had no political ambitions. At one point of the long seesaw struggle there was a possibility that the French might send aid to the Queen and that French troops might attempt to land at Bywater. Then even the Abbot of Baildon, Lancastrian at heart because King Henry was such a friend to the Church, remembered that he was English and turned Yorkist, temporarily, sharing the general feeling: *We want no French here.*

Apart from this short-lived scare, the war meant mainly a rise in prices, and for people who produced things this cut both ways; if you paid more for what you bought, you gained more for what you sold.

However, as time went on and the seesaw tilted this way and that, and there were truces, followed by fresh battles and other truces, even this peaceful corner was touched by war's aftermath—footloose men, some wounded, some simply dismissed, turned off to make their own way home, if they had homes. Some merely begged, some demanded what they wanted, with menaces. The civil war weakened the structure of law and order, and the bands of "sturdy beggars" as distinguishable from the pitiable were much dreaded.

Intake, for two years, escaped even such visitations; it lay

157

at the end of a lane which led nowhere and on the whole the sturdy beggars infested busy roads where travellers and merchants could be robbed. Isolated houses of medium size were also a target; larger establishments with able-bodied menservants about were avoided.

The six men who came to Intake towards the end of a March day in 1457 did so by accident, misled by one of their number who claimed to have knowledge of the area and said that the narrow lane was a short cut which would bring them out onto the road to Colchester. And was a sheltered road, with thick woods on both sides.

On an ordinary March day, to hardy men, that would not have been much of an attraction. But this was no ordinary March day; a blizzard was blowing, laden with something midway between snow and sleet. Hungry weather. They were all hungry men. Behind them, three bad days. A long tramp up a long drive to a house that looked likely, only to find it a blackened shell. An attack on Baildon market, where almost everything was for sale—or for the taking, even hot pies, kept warm on a charcoal brazier, but as they moved in, preparing to take what they could not pay for, the pie-woman screamed and immediately all the other stall-holders formed a ragged, but effective, amateur defence force. Out from under a stall offering butter and eggs came the club, from another the long knife, the hammer . . . even a pottery bowl, aimed well, was capable of breaking a nose.

At the miserable end of a miserable day, Intake looked promising; a house, big enough to promise food, not big enough to offer much resistance. Food and shelter for the night.

Civility first.

"Lady, we're hungry. Got a bite to spare for old soldiers."

Walter had spared her from the harrowing tales he had heard, and he had not been to market that day. Supper at Knight's Acre was over, and had been an eked-out, somewhat meagre meal. The farmhouse routine had been adopted here; when work in the fields was possible dinner was makeshift, supper substantial; in winter the business was reversed; dinner was the main meal and supper simply something to stave off hunger until morning.

"You are welcome to what I have—bread and cheese."

158

There was no question of asking them in; they were in, looming large in the kitchen. Margaret, as always when faced with any unusual situation, went rigid. The deaf woman looked startled, having heard nothing; she stared at the six men as though they had sprung up out of the floor.

Sybilla made the signs which Madge understood, pointing to Margaret and to John and then to the floor above.

Sybilla brought out the bread and the cheese; not much for six hungry men and now she half understood the situation. Hungry beggars stood humbly by the door waiting for whatever was handed out. These men, uninvited, had walked in.

"This all you got?" one of them asked, cramming cheese and bread into his mouth.

Another said, "We're meat hungry."

She had the courage, partly inbred and partly acquired, of her class. This was, she now realised, a raid, but the idea that anything untoward might happen to her never once occurred to her. But she might be robbed—was in fact already being robbed insofar as the men were devouring a month's supply of cheese, a week's supply of fresh baked bread. One of them had even followed her into the larder.

"You live poor, lady, and no mistake."

"I am poor," she said.

Henry stood staring and a thought occurred to her.

"I could offer you ale . . . Henry, run across to Walter; tell him we have guests—old soldiers. Ask him to bring a jug of his ale."

"How many, Harry?"

"A lot. Six or seven."

"Now listen. Where are they?"

"In the kitchen. Eating."

"Then you take this . . . And these . . . Think you can manage? That's my boy. You go in at the front and lodge them all handy, in the hall, near the door to the kitchen. And then go to bed."

"You going to shoot them, Walter?"

"Not less I must. I'll try getting them drunk first."

The bleak, bitter, near-freezing day had ended in a clear, frosty night. Carrying not a jug but a cask of ale across the

159

yard, Walter calmly made his plan. He could not fight six men within the narrow bounds of the kitchen; but with any luck he could get them drunk and incapable. What happened after that somewhat depended upon the men themselves—or upon his judgement of them. To a degree he had sympathy with the plight of soldiers, turned loose upon the world, unwanted as soon as their masters had come to terms. He proposed to drink with them and talk to them; those he considered fundamentally honest, driven to villainy by circumstance, he proposed to drag by the heels and deposit in various parts of Layer Wood, and he would leave them their clothes. Real rogues he would strip, and men so exposed, full of ale, on such a night, would die.

He entered the kitchen with an air of conviviality.

"Brought you some ale, mates. I know what soldiers like. Been one myself."

To Sybilla he said quietly, "Go to your room, my lady. Bar yourself in."

He sat, plying them with ale and pretending to drink with them. The first effect, as usual, was to make them garrulous. Even in this stage they all seemed decent fellows enough; boasting a little of brave deeds, desperate engagements, narrow escapes; but not of cold-blooded murder, or rape. They seemed to be united in their hatred of Lord Delamount, whose men they had been; he'd switched sides so often that in the end neither Lancastrians nor Yorkists could trust him and he'd run off to Scotland without paying the money he owed them.

Presently they were all drunk, laughing, singing bawdy, scurrilous ditties. But the next stage, the one for which Walter was waiting, seemed long in arriving. No heads sagged forward on to the table. Nobody fell to the floor. Strange! They had come in from the cold to the warm kitchen, they had eaten— for the first time in three days if they were to be believed, and they had consumed a vast quantity of ale—October ale, always considered the best and most potent.

Walter took a meditative sip of his own cup. Yes, good ale.

Yet they seemed to grow livelier. And hungrier.

They now accepted him as one of their company.

"We're hungry for meat, mate. You got pigs around here."

160

Useless to deny the presence of pigs. They had only to go into the yard, take twenty paces and use their noses.

"Old sow. Tough as the Devil," Walter said, thinking of the seven piglets snuggled in the straw beside their mother. Anything to save them! "Tell you what, though; there's pickled pork in a barrel."

"Then why dint that bitch bring it out?"

"And why dint you spot it, Joe? You follered her in."

"We don't want no pickled pork. Lived on it for months."

"That weren't pork. That were horse. Went into the cask shoes and all."

"And harness! Believe me, mate, what we ett, and fought on. Owd sow'd be a treat."

They were good humoured enough, but ready, Walter knew, to turn otherwise. He made one last effort.

"Take an hour to get ready, she would; and three to cook. I could boil us up a bit of the pickled in no time at all."

But now their minds were all set on fresh meat, the fat translucent and sizzling.

Somebody said, "Make up the fire." He tossed a stool on to the embers. Somebody threw on two of the wooden plates. They were all on the move now. And potentially dangerous. Likely to set the house on fire. They were drunk, but not in the way he wanted them to be.

"Where's this owd sow?"

Walter's aim now was to get them out of the house. And he had one small hope left. Sometimes men not ostensibly drunk in a warm room went into the cold and were suddenly very drunk indeed. It might happen now.

The clouds had blown away; a thin layer of snow lay on the ground; in the sky the stars and a half moon shone frostily bright. It was very cold.

The men, laughing and shouting, keeping together, jostled out into the yard.

"Over there," Walter said, "to your right. I'll just make the fire up properly." He stooped and picked up some wood from the pile just outside the door and stood for a second, watching. The cold did not have the desired effect, but they were drunk in a very peculiar way, they seemed to be dancing, making little leaps into the air.

161

Very quietly he closed the door and barred it.

His long bow and the six iron-tipped shafts stood just where he had directed Henry to put them. Taking that precaution he had not been able to visualise clearly how he could use them, now he knew. Passing the front door he barred that, too; and then climbed the stairs. Outside Sybilla's door he called: "My lady, it's me. Let me in." Her big bedroom had two windows, one overlooking the garden at the front, one the yard at the back.

"Have you got rid of them, Walter?"

"Far from it. But I've got them out. It'll cost us one of the sucking pigs; maybe two. Men like that are wasteful."

"In that case we shall have escaped lightly," she said. She seemed unperturbed still. She had retired when Walter told her to because ordinary men, with ale in them, would use language unfit for female ears. His other instruction, to bar herself in she had ignored—in any case, with what? And when the noise in the kitchen increased, Margaret had waked and screamed, and John, for once copying Margaret, had yelled too. Sybilla was so uninformed, so unsuspicious, and so confident . . . Six men, plainly hungry, had come and asked for food and she had given them not all she had, but all she could spare. In the larder she had purposefully placed herself between the rather rude man who had followed her in and the cask of pork.

"I hoped," Walter said, taking his stand by the window, "to get them drunk. Then I could have dealt with them. But it didn't work . . . My lady, there'll be a bit of trouble when they find the door barred . . . Better stand away."

Still with that extraordinary dancing, prancing gait they came back from the sty. Joy, joy, joy. Not an old sow, tough as the Devil but that rarest of delicacies, a sucking pig. A dish which only the very rich could afford. Ordinary people who reared sucklings never ate that tender meat, because a young pig must be fed and coddled along until its weight outran its edibility. Sucking pig . . . no dressing needed; no bristles to be singed off; no real hide to be scraped. And taking no time to cook. The old sow would have been a different matter but even for her they had been prepared to wait. Within an hour this young, but sizeable body would be edible. They pranced and danced, tossing the little corpse from hand to hand.

And now, between them and the cooking fire a barred door. The seemingly old comrade had betrayed them.

They hammered on the door and shouted; unless Walter opened the door at once they'd ram it in.

From overhead Walter's voice, cold and level, said:

"The first man to touch that door, I'll nail him to it."

From another window a younger but equally confident voice called, "And so will I."

They drew off a little. They were used to making shift. There were outbuildings. Easy enough to make a fire anywhere.

At that moment a log on Walter's untended fire shifted and blazed up, making the window bright in his little house. A cottage! Leaping and laughing they made towards it.

"They've gone to my place now, my lady," Walter said. "But better there than here."

They'd ransack the place, of course. They'd find in the second little room, his other cask of ale. His original plan might yet work.

He watched and saw the window glow more brightly as the intruders broke up his bed, his chair, the big stool which served him as a table, the shelves he had made to hold his few belongings. Presently sparks as well as smoke emerged from the clay-lined hole which served him as chimney. Distance slightly muted the noise, but there was a lot of it, and increasing.

As though speaking to himself, Walter said at last:

"It must be the rye."

"What rye, Walter?"

"I used rye for my brewing this year, barley being such a price, my lady. It looked all right and tasted all right. The ale, I mean. But it made them drunk in a funny sort of way."

"Do you think they will leave tomorrow?"

"I can't say. Probably not. Maybe not till they've eaten all we have—including the horse. The one thing I can say is they won't set foot in this house again. You're safe enough, my lady."

"I always feel safe with you," she said simply. "Of course, I

163

should never have let them in. But they said they were hungry; and I felt sorry for them."

"So did I—at first. But not now. I took against them as soon as they mentioned the pig."

Sybilla moved about. She looked in on Margaret and John, both sound asleep again. She took a blanket from her bed and offered it to Henry who scorned it. "Mother, I must have my arms free." Walter refused it too, so she wrapped herself in it and sat huddled at the foot of the bed, cold even so. As the night aged the cold grew sharper.

Suddenly Walter exclaimed, "God's eyeballs!"

She ran to join him at the window.

"Walter, what is it?"

For a second he struggled between his two languages, foul which came naturally at such a moment, and decent because she was here. There was a stammer and a choke before he managed to say, "They've set my place afire." She pushed beside him in the narrow window opening. It was true; sparks from the recklessly heaped fire had ignited the thatch at a point where the thin covering of snow had already melted from the heat within.

"And I hope they all roast," Walter said.

For quite a long time those inside Walter's little house were unaware of what was happening overhead. The little pig was not well cooked, but even its slight rawness was pleasurable. They dragged it from the fire and set it on the floor, pulling it apart with their fingers, cramming the charred, crisp outer skin and the tender, only just heated flesh into their meat-hungry mouths. They were men of varied experience—the veteran of the party had been able to match almost word for word Walter's experiences in France, the youngest was only six months away from the plough, but not one of them had ever known such happiness, such elation, such a desire to dance, to sing.

Walter's house, like all the others in Intake except Knight's Acre, was built of clay clods. It had a beam or two, and its thatch, vulnerable to fire; at shoulder level for a tall man, head level for a shorter one it offered more resistance. When the roof and the beam that upheld it collapsed, four men were engulfed in smoulder and flame. Two, nearer the door, tore it open and escaped. The incoming draught fanned the conflagration and gave the others a mercifully swift end. The two survivors, out in the yard, went through some antics. It was as though a puppet master had muddled the strings. And to the stark black and white of the moon and starlight reflected from the now frozen, diamond bright sprinkling of snow was added the red glare of the burning house, and in the yard two madmen danced and then disappeared, into the shadow cast by the outbuildings.

"But Walter, should not they all—even the ones who burned —have Christian burial?"

Four charred corpses—even their mothers would not recognise them, and two, frozen stiff—no need to strip them, in their dancing frenzy they had stripped themselves, just by the pigsty.

Walter said, "There's a bit more to it, my lady. Oh, I know Father Ambrose would get busy. He's lost his memory for nearby things but he holds to the rules. He would very likely say suicide and he wouldn't be far wrong. And then the Coroner's Court . . . and talk . . . A place like this; one man and a boy . . . it could be a temptation to others. Better do it my way. And the first thing to do is to find out if they were seen. That might make all the difference. I'll go down to the village and ask."

He put his questions craftily. "My place got set on fire last night. Did anybody see anybody lurking about?" In every case the answer was "No." And Walter believed it. Had anyone seen the strangers he would have said so, if only to make plain the exculpation of any mischievous Intake boys. The men had arrived at dusk and in such weather everybody was within doors and the shutters closed.

Reporting back, Walter said, "What's left in the house I shan't bother about. I'd bury the other two, but the ground's too hard for digging. I'll get the barrow and dump them in the wood."

"Will that be safe? Suppose they were found . . ."

"There won't be much left to find, my lady. This is hungry weather for foxes and weasels and such."

Sybilla gave a little shudder. "It sounds such a horrible . . .

But I suppose you are right, Walter. Try to do it while Henry is asleep."

Henry had actually fallen asleep at his post and Walter had carried him to his bed.

"If he wakes while I'm gone, tell him the rogues ran off. And not to go near my place in case more roof should fall in."

Walter had made the barrow to his own pattern out of odds and ends and four wheels bought from the wheelwright's; its main purpose, so far, had been the carting of manure from yard to field. He dragged it out and pushed it to the place where the two stiff corpses lay and was about to load it when a flash of colour caught his eye; colour and movement on the edge of the wood, near the blackened ruin of his house. People had come to stare at the scene of catastrophe. They hadn't quite dared come along by the track that led around the house and stable; they'd slunk along the edge of the wood and stood there, staring; they'd stand all day and unchecked might even venture into the yard to get a better view. Sod the buggers! Unhurriedly Walter lifted and threw first one body and then the other into the pig sty. Unhurriedly he strolled across to the ruin and shouted, "Don't come any nearer. It could blaze up again any minute." They stood there, hoping that it would.

Sybilla said, "Walter, in all the excitement and confusion I did not say what I should have said. I am so sorry about your little house. You had made it so snug and neat. I am indeed *very* sorry. But there is room in the house. John can move in with Henry, and Margaret with me."

She attributed his lack of enthusiasm about this plan to the fear of losing his independence.

"It would be *your* room, absolutely, Walter. I know it would not be quite like the little house, but I would see that nobody disturbed you."

"Well," he said, still with some reluctance, "if what happened last night is likely to happen again, it might be as well. For the time being."

He did not mind sharing the kitchen fire with old Madge; the bedroom was comfortable enough, and when he started his next brew, Sybilla offered him the still room. But it was not like his own place, all of a piece.

As soon as spring came, as it did very quickly after that bad spell, Walter said, "With your permission, my lady, I'll sell the old sow and her litter. There's another breed I've heard of, better doers. I could make a good deal."

He was a hardy man but the idea of being a cannibal at one remove revolted him. At the end of that frost-bitten day there had been as little left in need of burial from the pigsty as from the burnt out house.

There was a little plant called periwinkle which, given half a chance, would climb and hold its bluish-mauvish open-eyed flowers to the sun; by midsummer what had been Walter's house was pretty. And time moved on.

FIFTEEN

ONE OF THE FIRST THINGS that John Barnes had said was, "Don't look at the women. Don't even *look,* lad."

"What women?"

"Whores for the use of the guards. Time they're unserviceable they earn their keep picking over. And time th'art sound enough to carry a slab, thee'll see them, in the far chamber. Don't even look."

This was indeed a highly organised community and it included a brothel. Years earlier Selim's grandfather, or great-grandfather, had decided that unmarried men made better guards and that their needs should be provided for, on the spot. Their naturally hard characters and the inhuman occupation they plied did not detract from their maleness and the alternative to an integral brothel was to have them forever capering off down to Andara; or forming homosexual relationships very prejudicial to good discipline. The ideal arrangement would have been to employ eunuch guards, but eunuchs were themselves slaves, and their state inclined them to become fat and lazy—suitable guards for women in harems but not for men in quarries. So Selim's agent in Andara was always on the lookout for healthy, youngish female slaves; not necessarily the youngest or prettiest on offer, since their price was high.

On the whole the young women led tolerable lives in a set of cave-like chambers, comfortably furnished, with hangings on the limestone walls and carpets on the limestone floors. One large, communal chamber even had glazed windows, narrow apertures cut into the outer wall of rock. They fed well and were not stinted of perfumes and unguents and pretty clothes,

168

for it was necessary to make them attractive enough to compete with the brothels of the port.

The post of Madam in this place was a covetable one, and had for many years been the perquisite of some respectable, impoverished, widowed relative of the owner. The present incumbent was an elephantine old woman named Soraya.

When the women were, as John Barnes decently expressed it, "unserviceable"—that was for roughly one week out of every four—they were employed in the "picking over," the searching of the limestone incrustations which clung to every marble slab for the nodules in which garnets were encapsulated. Somebody in the past had discovered that female eyes were quicker, female fingers nimbler at this work.

The women welcomed it, for there was a system of rewards. In a locked chest Soraya kept a mass of trinkets of no great value but all pretty, and at the end of a picking-over session the woman who had by industry or luck done best in this treasure hunt was allowed to take her choice of trinkets.

So every morning one of the lamplit passages saw a procession, moving slowly, at Soraya's pace, well-guarded, to the place where the newly ripped out slabs were sorted over. They carried a supply of delicacies, always more than even Soraya could consume in a session, the surplus of which they would enjoy. And wine also, for Soraya did not share her kinsman's strict observance to the Prophet's rules. She seated herself in a well-cushioned chair, exchanged pleasantries with the guards at the entrance, was pleased when two slaves staggered in with a new slab, pleased when one of the girls—to her they were all girls—found a garnet, or one of the other nodules, which delicately attacked with miniature chisel and hammer, yielded another, less valuable but still saleable stone, colourless, crystal clear—a diamond without a diamond's fire and sparkle.

Don't even look, John Barnes had told Sir Godfrey. An instruction easy to obey—at least so far as looking implied desiring. When he was sound enough to help carry a slab into what was called "the far chamber," though in fact it advanced just as the quarry face did, he could glance at the women, waiting to ply their small implements, and at the fat old woman who supervised them, with no feeling at all.

He was again low-spirited; for what the Greek slave had said

169

about the Pope and all Christendom driving all Moslems out of
Europe had either not happened or had failed to affect Zagelah.
The timeless time went on; the seasons' relentless march observed every other week on the day of the bathing, which was
pleasant in warm weather and so unpleasant in cold that only
the vigorous application of the canes could force shivering
bodies into the water. Sir Godfrey lost count of the seasons as
well as of the hours and the days.

He worked like an animal, a two-legged pack donkey. Because of the disablement of his hands he was judged to be unfit
for the most skilled work of all—the loosening and prying away
of the precious slabs, but he could carry them in a kind of
wickerwork basket, held to his back by bands of coarse webbing which came over his shoulders, crossed one another on his
chest and then buckled behind his waist. He carried the rough,
lime-crusted slabs to the place where the women worked, and
then on to the place where the polishing was done, and from
there to the place where they were stored. Beyond that point
no slave was allowed to go except on the biweekly outings.

At first the rough wickerwork, weighted with marble, re-
opened the wounds which the flogging had made on his back,
but they scabbed over and healed again. The webbing straps
chafed his chest raw, but there again the body's defence took
over and the skin became callused and hardened.

When did John Barnes begin to cough and grow thin and
spit blood? There was no means of knowing in this timeless
place.

John Barnes said, after a bout of coughing, "Well lad, it
seems to have got me. I hoped to see the day of liberation, but
now I doubt it; though I've stuck it out longer than most."

Even in this hopeless, subterranean, lamplit world there was
a hierarchy of a kind, and those who worked at the rock face
regarded themselves and were regarded by others as superior.

"I pray," Barnes said, "for a quick end; not to end where
you began, lad, with a lot of half-dead men."

He had his wish—or his answered prayer. He died with an
abruptness which took even the guards by surprise. One minute—or so it seemed, eye as skilled, hand as skilled . . . and
then, his load already fixed, Sir Godfrey found himself on his

170

knees, with his best friend in this infernal place saying weakly, words making bubbles in the last haemorrhage, "God keep thee. Hope on. Trust . . . in . . . God."

In a way Godfrey Tallboys had been more fortunate than many of his fellows; the lack of religious exercises had not meant much deprivation to him. And his last contact with God had been in that narrow, balconied street . . . But John Barnes had been pious . . .

What did priests say? He should remember. Only a few words could be recalled; but leaning forward, so that the marble slab in his basket slid forward and hit the base of his skull, he said into the ear of the dying man, "Go forth, Christian soul." And then a Hail Mary. Past speech now, the dying man thanked him with his eyes.

Sir Godfrey would have doubted whether he could be more wretched, but when John Barnes's body was dragged out he felt the same sense of bereavement as had followed Lord Robert's death; so why a short time afterwards he should bother about another person's plight, he could not and never would understand.

Stopped under his load and followed by his working companion, similarly loaded, he plodded into the picking-over chamber, where he lifted out the other man's slabs and was then unloaded by him. As usual two guards were on duty here. One of them said, "You, wait! There's one about ready to turn over." That was normal custom, and a not unwelcome chance to snatch a moment's rest and get back one's breath.

Ordinarily in this chamber the strictest decorum prevailed. Soraya was feared, even by the guards. The girls were allowed to talk a little as they worked, not too much and not too loudly, and not at all to the guards. This morning she had absented herself for a while and the atmosphere was different. No strict Moslem would touch a woman in an unserviceable condition, but half-joking, salacious talk was permissible at any time, and the opportunity was being snatched. Only one girl stood silent and unsmiling. Sir Godfrey had time to observe her because serious work on the slab that needed to be soon turned over would not be resumed until Soraya returned.

171

The girl was very young. About fourteen.

And she was new, he thought, judging partly by the way she held the little pick and hammer, and partly by the colour of her hair—dead black. Men liked prostitutes of exotic colouring, and even in this lost place their tastes were catered for and bleached or hennaed hair was the rule.

Sir Godfrey had acquired by this time enough basic Arabic to enable him to obey orders and so avoid trouble. He knew the names of common articles, and a few phrases of rather cringing civility which could on occasions ward off a blow; but he did not know enough of the language to know what one of the guards said to the girl or what she said in return. Whatever it was it seemed to anger him. He snarled out a term of abuse, recognisable and offensive, and she retorted with another— even worse. He lost his head and began to beat her with his cane.

She certainly *was* new. She fought back, trying to snatch the cane, failed and suffered heavier blows.

Sir Godfrey then lost his head. He sprang at the man, seized him by the collar, swung him round and dealt him a fist blow on the chin which sent him reeling back, straight into Soraya as she waddled in. She administered a push which righted him and into the deathly silence asked, "What happened here?"

Free men speak before slaves. The guard said that this man had attempted to meddle with the girl and he had gone to her aid.

"He was beating the girl," Sir Godfrey said.

To Soraya neither story had the ring of truth, both sounding so unlikely. Slaves knew that the women were not for them; and a carefully calculated diet, constant hard work, carried to the point of exhaustion, emasculated them within a month or two. Guards knew that the women were not for them to beat; any correction the girls needed was meted out by Soraya herself. Momentarily puzzled, she turned to the five other women, now all ostentatiously busy. Five false witnesses. Four said that what the guard said was true; the fifth, with an air of smug virtue, said she had been too busy to notice what was happening.

Another unlikely story!

It would have ended there, with another flogging for the man with the bad record, but for the girl.

"They lie! All are liars. *He* only is telling the truth." She ripped at her clothing, baring her shoulders and the upper part of her arms. The red welts were already rising.

That was evidence.

Soraya said, "Back to work, all of you."

In the evening Soraya sent for the new girl and gave her a little of the wine which Selim, in his folly, eschewed. Wine not only gladdened the heart, it loosened tongues.

"How old are you?"

"Fourteen."

"And where were you born?"

"In the Maghreb. In the stronghold of my father."

"Free born?"

"We were all free, until we lost the battle."

"And how many masters have you had? How many times have you changed hands? When was the battle? What happened after? Tell me. Tell me exactly what has happened to you since the battle."

"I cannot. I do not know. I fought beside my father on that day. And was wounded. You do not believe me? Look!" She parted her cloud of black hair and showed, on the crown of her head a puckered scar. Then she flung her head back and the wound was hidden. "I was insensible for many days."

"And then?"

"Then I was destined to be a present to the Grand Turk. In Constantinople. But the ship was taken; and I am here." A bitter little story told without tears.

Soraya framed her next question with cunning.

"And who took your maidenhead?"

Imagine finding in a place like this a girl who could blush. A slave who could look so proud and offended!

"It was never taken."

"Oh, come, come," Soraya protested. "You were taken prisoner—presumably by men. On a ship bound for Constantinople you were a slave, amongst sailors. Even in the slave market at Andara . . ."

"My father's enemy is a great rogue, but he is not a fool.

173

Nor a stranger; his tribe and mine have been at war for years. He knew my worth. A Nagulla of the purest blood. Do you imagine that he would himself tamper with, or allow any of his men to touch the gift he intended for the Grand Turk? On the ship I was treated like a queen. And when the ship was taken by pirates, all they thought about was to sell us and get away as fast as possible . . . If it is customary to rape slaves before selling them in Andara, then I must consider myself fortunate. Or give thanks to haste again. We were sold within minutes of our arrival."

Soraya thought: Well, virginity is a condition open to proof, and if the girl's story is true, what a present for Selim! Fourteen years old, and beautiful, and with spirit, and with just that touch of something exotic likely to appeal to a somewhat jaded taste. Soraya had always been extremely grateful to her cousin Selim for appointing her to this sinecure, which was also a place of power. Now she could repay him.

Discipline must be maintained, however. For striking one of Soraya's girls—a prerogative reserved for herself—the guard was demoted; for striking the guard Sir Godfrey was flogged. But either the hand wielding the dreaded khurbash was less powerful, or his back had hardened. Or complete hopelessness brought its compensating insensibility.

The timeless time went on; and then one morning, bowed under his load, he was aware of something different. The fat old bawd, never before seen at the quarry face or any other working area, stood there, panting a little, beside a man who bore every mark of a minor official; sober, decent clothes, serious, self-important demeanour.

Soraya raised and pointed a fat finger. "That is the man."

So what now? Another flogging? If so, may it kill me! Death and the Judgement of God would be preferable to this death-in-life, with no hope.

In fact that pointing finger had indicated if not freedom, a more tolerable life in captivity.

Over the years Sir Godfrey had acquired more Arabic than he realised. He had never set himself to learn it, repudiating it in his mind. He knew enough to get along with. But it was to his imperfect grasp of the language that he attributed the slight craziness of the conversation between Soraya, the official, and the overseer of the quarry, which, if taken literally implied that one of the ladies in the King's harem in Zagelah was discontented with that part of the gardens in which Selim's wives and concubines took air and exercise, and somebody had said that the English were very good at gardening, therefore an English slave was required to make improvements.

Sir Godfrey's sense of humour had always been simple and forthright, untinged by the sardonic or cynical—a kind that would have lasted longer in adversity. John Barnes's had been of that variety and very occasionally one of his dry, sour yet comic comments had made Sir Godfrey laugh. He had not laughed since John Barnes had died. Yet inside him now, as he listened, and was eventually convinced that he did understand aright, something very like laughter took him by the throat. The idea that a knowledge of English gardening—even if he had it—could do anything to improve a garden in Zagelah! That was almost comic. And all he knew of gardens was that they looked pretty in spring and summer, and were pleasant places to walk in at the end of the day. He recognised a rose when he saw one . . .

However, he was now well trained in the slave apathy, accustomed to standing by like a donkey, and did so now while his future was being arranged. It meant release from the hateful quarry, work in the open, a sight of the sun.

The word "garden" brought Sybilla sharply to mind. She had so loved other people's gardens, had always wanted one of her own. If she had attained one, it was not of his providing. He had ceased to visualise her at Knight's Acre now. She could not possibly have managed on those meagre rents, fixed forever by a well meaning but shortsighted old man. Sometimes he saw her back in his sister's house at Beauclaire, Henry and Richard old enough for the discipline of the master of pages. Sometimes he imagined that—giving him up for dead—she might have married again. He hoped that wherever she was, she was happy. In his mental pictures of her she was unchanged, untouched by time.

His new work was infinitely preferable to the old. The outdoor slaves, those who worked in the gardens and the stables,

175

lived in comparative comfort in a building made for the purpose and they were well fed. Those who tended the Ladies' Garden were far from overworked, often no more than two hours' rather hurried labour early in the morning, when even at midsummer the air was pleasantly cool. All their work must be done before the women's quarter was astir. The exposure of his ignorance of gardening, which Sir Godfrey had rather feared—fear being the foremost emotion in a slave world—never came; there was in fact no mention of his Englishness or of anyone's wish to improve the garden. He was simply one of three slaves, admitted, soon after sunrise, to shave and water a piece of grass about the size of a tennis court, take from every rose tree and every flowering shrub any bloom past its perfect best, see that no stray petal or leaf clogged the fountain, renew and tend flowers in the tubs which stood on the steps, and the terrace up to which they led, the garden entrance from the harem itself.

It was a very secret garden, surrounded on three sides by high walls, with no windows. One wall was broken by the gateway of iron grill work, opened to admit the workers, locked behind them, opened so that they could leave, and locked again. The fourth side of the garden was the outer wall of the women's quarters; three steps, a terrace, and another grilled doorway, hung on its inner side with Zagelah gauze, so closely gathered as to be opaque. Once, planting the tubs—they were of silver, glazed in some way so that they did not tarnish—with lilies of a kind he had never seen before, huge, pink flecked with purple and almost overpoweringly scented, Sir Godfrey spared a thought for the women who would presently enjoy them. They were slaves, too! He thought of the freedom his own countrywomen enjoyed; at every level, from the independent old women like the fishwife on Bywater quay, to the Queen whose lightest word was law to the King of England. Briefly he pitied these women, more enclosed than nuns of the strictest Order . . . But in the main his thoughts—now that food and work in the open air had restored him, and his back so long bent under the heavy marble slabs had straightened again—were of escape.

From the quarry it had been impossible; he had tried the only likely way and all that resulted had been a flogging. Here things were different. Slaves seemed to come and go almost as they pleased; they were sent on errands into the streets, into the market; and certainly the comings and goings of those who worked in the secret garden were most loosely supervised, once the two hours of rather hurried work was complete. Ermin, Sir Godfrey's new overseer, fat and lethargic—eunuch?— opened that gate, sat down, issued orders, occasionally said, "Hurry." He wielded no cane. Then he ushered them out and disappeared, to sleep, to follow his own pursuits. His underlings were free to do the same unless they were "borrowed" to work in some other part of the palace grounds, a practice Ermin did nothing to encourage, not because he feared his men would be overworked but because he was immensely proud of his own post of trust and felt that some of his importance reflected on his small staff. His usual answer when asked for the loan of his men was, "No, they must see to the tanks."

The roses and other flowers in the Ladies' Garden, like flowers everywhere, liked muck, but it was unthinkable that the eyes and noses of the ladies should be affronted by stable manure in its natural state. So it was placed in tanks filled with water, stirred three or four times a day for several days and then allowed to settle. The water then drained off and strained, and carried to the garden and applied. A faint odour of stables was perceptible for a few minutes but vanished as soon as the liquid was absorbed.

Sir Godfrey, in his free time, drifted naturally to the stable yard where beautiful horses lived in conditions far preferable to those of the quarry slaves. It took him a little time to break the habit of enforced silence acquired at Andara, where talk during working hours was frowned upon as a waste of breath and time, and where, when the gruelling day's work was over, there was no energy left for chatter. After a day or two in this easier atmosphere he found his tongue and showed himself knowledgeable about horses, thereby making himself welcome to this community within a community. One day he said to the friendliest of the stable slaves, "That horse is of different breed."

"A true word. That is a son of Shaitan. A vicious horse, taken from the Christian invaders. He killed two men and maimed several before he was turned loose. The King set high store by him and forbade the treatment that would have tamed him. And perhaps he was right. He sires good colts."

The horse they were studying had a brown hide, with a golden glimmer.

Arcol's colt?

I had three sons.

Now again, definite plans. A runaway slave must not immediately draw attention to himself by begging. Food for at least three days must be saved, and that meant bread and cheese. And perhaps by design, the clothes of a palace slave, though of finer quality than those of the quarry workers, were less adaptable for hiding things. The outfit which Sir Godfrey had been given on his arrival in Zagelah was a pair of drawers, longer and more dignified, halfway down the shin, and a jacket, short-sleeved, somewhat skimpy. Both garments were of far finer substance than those the quarry workers wore, and they were not without decoration. Around the edge of the trouser legs, the front and the sleeves of the jacket, there was a kind of braid worked in red and white.

In such a uniform with no pockets, no pouches, enough of even humble bread and cheese to keep a man for three days was difficult to conceal; he got it away from table openly, "I'll eat this later. I tend to wake, hungry, in the night." Nobody questioned, nobody suspected. It was high summer, August; he had been released from the quarry in July; under his mattress in the slave dormitory the cheese sweated and the bread dried.

He carried the food—all he owned in the world—openly, in a little linen bag, when he set out to make another bid for freedom. It had seemed to him, so recently released from the quarry, that palace slaves came and went as they liked, but even on this heavy, somnolent afternoon there was a man at the gate used by slaves and other inferior people.

"Where are you going?"

"Ermin, my master, has shoes to be mended." That explained the parcel.

He made for the market. Morning trade was over, the best of everything had been sold; this was the waiting time. Four hours after midday the muezzins would call, for the third prayer hour of the day; then business would brisken again, selling off cheaper stuff, wilting, bruised, not worth carting back home. Meanwhile, in the narrow shade of buildings or awnings, the market people rested. Sir Godfrey found a patch of shade and chose the family he would accompany. There was concealment in numbers and this was a sizeable family; an old woman, brown and wrinkled as a walnut, two men, a woman and three children, and a donkey. His mind observed, without knowing that it did so, that whereas all the family had sought shade from the afternoon's glare, the donkey had been left tethered in the full sun.

The call to prayer came, and with the rest he obeyed it, bowing towards Mecca and saying, "God help me." Then he hung about while the early evening market rush went on, and attached himself, unostentatiously, to the family he had chosen as his stalking horse. Out of the still sunlit market square and into the cool tunnel that pierced the wall, the place where Sir Stephen had lost an eye, the place where victory had seemed certain.

Useless to think back; grieve, yes, grieve for the dead, all part of a past that in retrospect seemed golden and gay, but the past was gone beyond recall. There was only the present; this moment.

And a bad moment.

There were guards on the gate.

Unchallenged the old woman, the donkey, and the children, quarrelling vociferously, had gone through; Sir Godfrey, thinking that anywhere two men could go, three could go, had attached himself to the two men, in the company of men, less noticeable . . . Out of the cool dusk of the tunnel, into the evening glow; and a harsh voice:

"Here you, where do you think you're going?"

"On an errand, for my master."

"Then you'll have a pass."

He had no pass; he carried a bag which was in itself evidence of ill intent. Over and beyond that he must be mad, for every border of every garment he wore announced that he was a palace slave.

The expression on Sir Godfrey's face when he realised that he had failed again, and been so *stupid*—how could he have overlooked so vital a thing?—justified the guard's assumption that his wits were astray. And a certain kindliness towards the mad was traditional among the Moors. Also the guard, though in public employment, did not favour the régime of King Selim and Hassan ben Hassan, it was too strict for a man who had liked his kaffe and his wine. So instead of holding this demented fellow and later taking him to the palace, there to be flogged and possibly branded as a would-be runaway, he gave him a half-rough, half-friendly push and said, "Be off with you, fool." Directing him not outwards to freedom but back to slavery.

SIXTEEN

WALTER DISLIKED living in the house. It meant that he had no privacy and that the places with which he was concerned—the kitchen where he lived and ate, the still room in which he made and kept his ale, the bedroom in which he slept—were distant from one another, and since the one staircase and the still room both opened out of the hall he must forever be crossing and recrossing that apartment. He always said, "Excuse me, my lady," or "I'm sorry to disturb you." Sybilla was usually sewing, occasionally writing, and she invariably looked up and smiled and said a few amiable words, but he always felt like an intruder, and if he had a jug in hand he felt self-conscious about it.

He had always liked his ale, but in moderation. Drunkenness he despised; since the burning of his little house he had drunk more and he spent a good deal of time arguing with himself, producing proof after proof that he was not a tosspot.

Drunkards reeled about and shouted and laughed at nothing. He was never even slightly unsteady on his feet and his behaviour did not vary.

Drunkards slugged abed in the morning, neglected their work or their business; their sight was not true, their hands grew unsteady. He was always brisk and early in the morning, did the work of two, even three men, all day, was as good an archer as he had ever been.

Drunkards craved the stuff, couldn't do without it. He could. On market days when all other men resorted to inns, he came straight home. It was just that lately, if he went to bed sober, he could not sleep. He tossed and turned and groaned inwardly as a sick man might. He had tried to discipline himself by going sober to bed for as many as three nights in succession, thinking that weariness must win and sleep come. It did not except in brief, dream-haunted snatches, just before morning, and after such nights he felt good for nothing.

Now it was October again, one year and seven months since the raid; and apart from his need for the lulling effect of ale, Walter had good cause to feel pleased with himself. Knight's Acre now had three fields under the plough and the crops had been so heavy that hired labour was needed. Walter had chosen carefully and well; one of the young Robinsons, a boy called Tom, hard-working and teachable.

Walter had also "happened upon" a good young horse to replace the old one from Beauclaire which, coddled along, had done marvellously but was now failing. The very way in which Walter had set about obtaining a new horse, cheap, was proof that he was not a drunkard; drunkards were incapable of making clever plans and carrying them through.

Walter had begun to haunt the horse market in Baildon—it was separate from the general market. His attitude was casual, he studied what was on offer, noted the prices, which were iniquitous, what with the lessened value of money and the brief but inconclusive war. However, he did at last find exactly the animal for which he was searching; a black horse, young, thickset, strong enough to pull a plough or wagon, but not too heavy to trot. Nice-natured, too; it suffered Walter's inspection with calm.

"How much?"

The dealer named his price, extortionate of course to anyone old enough to remember the old days, but by current prices fair enough.

"I'll give you half that," Walter said.

"Don't be daft."

Walter said, "You take what I offered, or I'll call the market overseer and the constable and ask if anybody has lately lost a *grey* horse." Surreptitiously—Walter never believed in calling attention to his undertakings—he held out a bit of damp, soapy cloth, black, and at the same time indicated the small pale patch on the horse's neck.

182

The dealer turned as pale as the patch—horse stealing was a capital offence.

"All right," he said.

Adding insult to injury, as he took possession of the horse, Walter said, "Next time try walnut husks, not soot."

He went home jubilant.

October produced some of its golden days. Tom Robinson could be trusted to thresh out what remained of the corn, and Henry was eager to try out his skill with the bow on some worthy target.

For deer it was known as the "grease season," full-fed through summer they were at their best.

"We'll take a day off, Harry, and go hunting."

"May I try, Walter? With my new bow?"

It was the third that Walter had made for him, but it was not full size and Walter doubted whether any shaft launched from it would be lethal. Not that it mattered. Walter would be there, just behind the boy—who was his boy now.

Layer Wood had gained its name long ago, when "lay" meant "pool." The pools, after the fine summer which had brought the good harvest, were depleted; the first two or three were mere puddles, surrounded by dried, cracked clay. But they came upon one at a lower level, its mud edge marked with hoofmarks. They hid themselves and waited and presently a deer—a lone young male—came down to drink. Henry looked at Walter, a silent question; Walter nodded. Henry loosed his arrow and missed, by that little which had given rise to the saying that a miss was as good as a mile; and as the animal raised its head, alarmed, alerted, Walter shot it dead.

Henry was momentarily depressed and apologetic, but Walter said not to mind, everybody missed a shot sometimes and after all they had the meat, which was what mattered. "We'll gut him here," he said. "Easier to carry." Bearing the carcass slung on a pole between them, they went home, happy hunters at the end of the day.

Before Walter sat down to his supper he fetched a jug of ale from the still room and offered Madge a cupful, as he often did, but she refused.

In the hall, with supper over and Henry gone yawning to bed, Sybilla sat down to write a very difficult letter, the latest of a number in what was surely a very peculiar correspondence. It had begun with a violently vituperative letter from Lady Randall. Simon, her only son had been killed at St. Albans in the first battle of the civil war; and Sybilla was entirely to blame! Had she married him and made him happy, he would have settled down at Cressacre and not gone running off to fight in a war which did not concern him at all. What was more, Sybilla had not only robbed Lady Randall of her son, but of her grandsons, too, for Simon could never bring himself to look at another woman. Lady Randall was left to face lonely old age with a broken heart—and all because of Sybilla.

Sybilla thought: Poor woman, she is distraught with grief. She wrote a brief letter of sympathy, such as one would send to any bereaved mother. That should have been the end, but was not. Gifts began to arrive, accompanied by letters which were not denunciatory, but still not quite in order; "Simon wishes you to share our plenty . . ." The letters became fond as though the lonely woman at Cressacre had transferred some of her affection from her dead son to the woman of whom he had been fond. Rather as a mother might cherish a dead child's toy.

Every letter had been answered, kindly, civilly, but without undue sentiment. The cool commonsense which the Abbess of Lamarsh had inculcated still held against all the wear and tear of the world. But Lady Randall's last letter was difficult to answer. She wrote that she was certain that Simon would wish her to adopt John. That extraordinary statement was followed by a lot of facts and figures all meant to show that Cressacre was an independent property. Nobody, no great lord, not the King himself, had any claim upon it. Between her husband's death and Simon's coming of age, she had held it, and improved it . . . "where only rabbits ran, sheep now nibble and dung the land as they nibble. Next year there will be grass, and cattle . . ." She listed the acres that comprised the estate, rents that were paid, income derived from the sale of produce; "in addition to which I have monies of my own." All this wealth would in due time pass to her adopted son.

To a mother who could just about feed and clothe a growing boy it was a tempting offer indeed and Sybilla gave it serious consideration for several days. She sought no advice from James or William, knowing what form it would take. William was unworldly, up to a point, and lavished his own money on the poor, but he had a sensible man's respect for security, and this was security indeed, a chance in ten thousand. But . . .

Sybilla had kept all Lady Randall's letters, and before beginning her own she read them through again, taking especial heed of the sentences which roused unease. Simon was often mentioned, sometimes as though Lady Randall realised that he was dead, but just as frequently as though he were still alive and were in close communication with her. Perhaps the strangest letter of all was the one which had arrived together with a blaring heifer calf. In it Lady Randall wrote: "Simon seems to think that you have lost a calf. Please accept this in its stead." The fantastic thing was that about a fortnight earlier the Knight's Acre cow had aborted.

The letter proposing the adoption only said "Simon would wish," but it ended on a disquieting note. After the facts and figures Lady Randall had written, "After all, you owe me a son."

It was just possible that the whole campaign of friendliness had been mounted by a demented woman with one end in view —retaliation. Farfetched, of course . . . But John was only seven; handed over completely to a woman who had a grudge against his mother, his life could be made a misery—it might even be short!

And there was another way of looking at it. Sybilla thought: I bore three sons; one I have lost to Walter; one to Beauclaire; must I give away the third?

She wrote, "Dear Lady Randall," and then the door to the kitchen opened and there was old Madge, making her bob and saying good night on her way to bed. Sybilla smiled and said, "Good night, Madge," and resumed writing, doing it slowly, testing each sentence in her mind before committing it to paper, trying to sound firm, and at the same time kindly. For her suspicion of the poor woman's motive could be unfounded and unworthy. And now and again she paused, wondering what the future held for John. William, when offering the whole family a home, had spoken of sending Henry to the monks' school at Baildon—perhaps he would do as much for John.

185

Such schooling did not inevitably lead to priesthood and celibacy; it could be the first step towards a secular profession. The law perhaps.

She read Lady Randall's last letter again and had a rebellious thought: The rich think that they can buy anything!

In the kitchen Walter emptied the jug, stood up and went out on his last, necessary errand—he did not acknowledge the existence of the stool room and had told Henry that such places were meant for women and sick people. He breathed deeply of the cool night air and for the hundredth time assured himself that he was not drunk, though he was now using a larger jug.

He was not drunk. Drunken men did not care where they relieved themselves; nor did they bar doors with care and see that fires were left in such a state that no log could flare, no spark fly during the night. He did these things, because he was not drunk. He doused and towelled his face, and rinsed his mouth because, while Sybilla in the hall had been making her decision, he, by the kitchen fire, had made his.

Once and for all, he would put an end to his agony, the thing that kept him awake at night, unless he dulled his senses with ale.

He came into the hall where Sybilla was making a fair copy of her letter, but he did not say either, "Excuse me, my lady," or "Good night, my lady." Instead he said, "It is cold in here," and placed a fresh log on the moribund fire, a dry log which broke instantly into a blaze which eclipsed the candle by whose light she had been working and made Walter, on the hearth, look enormous.

"I've got something to say to you."

"Just a minute, Walter, and I shall be done." She wrote her name and laid the quill aside. She was reasonably certain of what Walter was about to say. Nobody could be expected to *make* a farm out of wasteland, work it, bring it to moderate prosperity—and all for nothing. Some time ago she had offered Walter a wage and he had turned surly and said when he needed money he'd ask for it. Now he was about, she thought, to ask, not for money, but for land. She was prepared to yield. Walter could have the third field—and any other land he could clear, in return for overseeing her two remaining fields and her

186

stock. Tom Robinson, with some help from Henry, was capable of doing the actual work. It was the kind of arrangement becoming common in these shifting times.

She straightened herself, folded her hands in her lap, and because Walter for once looked so awkward and unsure of himself—he who had always been so self-confident; and was sweating, though he had remarked upon the coolness in the hall—she spoke most kindly.

"Walter, sit down. And speak freely. What is it?"

He did not accept the invitation to sit—he never had done so in her presence. Over the years—thirteen of them now—though other people's servants had called him arrogant and overbearing, and the people of Intake, she knew from talk with Father Ambrose, detested him because he treated them with contempt, towards her his manners, as his devotion and loyalty, had never once failed.

So when he said in a strange, half-strangulated voice, "I'm asking you to marry me," she could not have been more astounded had the roof fallen in. She was momentarily dumbstruck and by contrast, Walter, ordinarily so sparing with words, was now articulate and fluent.

It all poured out, from the moment at Dover, when she had played the lute and enchanted him, inspired in him the simple wish to serve. On and on. This, he thought, hearing himself, is not ale talking, it is me, the very core and centre of myself.

"Women," he said, "I never cared for. But I fell in love that night, and stayed so. I reckoned it'd be enough to serve you, help to take care of you. And time you was married, I managed . . . Time I had my own place, I managed . . . It's the nights I can't do with. Nothing but a wall between us . . ." The words came out jerkily, interspersed by hard breathing as though he had been running.

Sir Simon's declaration of love had not quickened a pulse or made her face colour; unmoved, untouched she had been in complete control of the situation. Now she was not. She attributed her hot-faced confusion, her jumpy heart to shock, to insult. She made a clutch at dignity, but she was short of breath, too.

"Walter, you know that I shall never remarry. I refused Sir . . ."

187

"A silly boy! And you were right there. You'd had one, hadn't you? Here today, just long enough to get you in pup and off again. Took the very ring off your finger to help buy that great horse. Never thought of putting a roof over your head till everybody was so sick and tired . . ."

The old Abbess had said that it was unwise to show anger; anger merely begat anger; but Sybilla was past heeding such precepts. She stood up and said:

"Stop! I will not listen to such talk. You are drunk, Walter Freeman. Go to your bed."

He was drunk, more so than she realised, or than he would admit to himself. He did not stir, he stood there, a great hulking shape between her and the fire. He said:

"Try me! You've never had a real, loving *man* yet."

Abruptly she realised the precariousness of her situation; alone in a lonely house, with children, a deaf old woman and a man, drunk and lecherous. It was as though he sensed her fear—as dogs were said to do. He moved, he took her into his arms. He said, "Don't be scared, my lovely. I'd not hurt you . . ."

She fought him and she screamed, idiotically since a scream was a call for help and here no help could be forthcoming. She screamed twice, and then Walter's mouth came down on hers and something she had never known and was never to know again overwhelmed her. Her very bones melted; she was weak, yielding, willing, eager . . . It lasted only a moment, but it taught her something not to be learned in convents or in years of placid marriage; it was a moment to be remembered with shame, but it changed her life. It lasted only a moment because Walter, holding and caressing her as though she were a kitten, suddenly collapsed and fell, bearing her down with him to the floor, and something warm and wet spouted from his neck.

Halfway down the stairs, his face as white as chalk, Henry stood, fitting another arrow . . . The one he had already launched stood quivering for a second or two in the great vein of Walter's neck, and then fell away.

Henry said, "Walter!" in a voice of utter amazement. And she tried to staunch the wound with a wadded handful of her

188

skirt. Useless. Walter died there, on the floor. And Henry cried.

He said, sobbing, "How could I know? I thought it was another raid; I heard you cry out . . . Walter! He made me the bow and the arrows; he taught me . . ." It was cry of desolation.

"Darling, it was an accident. Walter had taken too much ale, and he was angry with me . . . about . . . about something I was writing . . ." Must one thank God that one's son could not read?

All the letters lay there on the table and it was extraordinary how blood, more than any other liquid, spread itself about. The papers were all soiled.

"He'd changed his clothes," Henry said. "I thought it was another ruffian. And it was Walter . . ." In a voice of intense bitterness, he added, "I missed the deer."

"It was an accident, Henry, and I am entirely to blame. I was writing a letter, the content of which Walter did not agree. In his sober senses he would never have done such a thing, but he was drunk and tried to take the letter from me. So I screamed . . ."

"And I heard and came and killed my best friend."

"By accident, Henry, sheer accident." On one, remote fringe of her mind she noted what Henry had said about Walter's change of clothes. Yes, in order to prepare for his audacious, impossible proposal, he had clad himself in his best.

Time enough to think of that afterwards. Henry went on sobbing and accusing himself. "I didn't even know that he had a blue jerkin . . . And now they'll hang me. And I deserve it."

"Do I?"

He stopped on a gulping intake of breath and stared with wide, tear-smeared eyes.

"You? They couldn't blame you. You didn't do anything."

"I meant did I deserve to see my son hanged—because of an accident?"

She already knew what she intended to do; but she needed Henry's help—and his full consent. There must be no chance of his thinking her callous.

189

He was silent, except for a few more gulps; and she waited.

"I suppose we could . . . Could we? Bury him somewhere and say nothing?"

"I think it is the only thing to do."

"I know where . . ." The resilience of youth was already coming to his aid. "We can't dig much, and the place mustn't show . . . I could dig a little by the wall of his house, and then pull the wall and the rest of the thatch down to cover . . ." Now healing self-justification came along. "I loved Walter, but he shouldn't . . . have laid hands on you, whatever you wrote."

"He was drunk."

"I'll fetch a blanket," Henry said. She noticed that he brought one from his own bed, not Walter's. Not without difficulty, for Henry, though strong and tough, was only fourteen, and she was small, they got the heavy corpse rolled into the blanket, an enormous sausage. Henry lit the lantern—Walter's lantern—and fetched the spade—Walter's spade—and placed them both by the fire-blackened wall and the now leafless periwinkle. The lantern gave them something to steer by. Then he went back into the hall and said, "Take his feet, that's the lighter end . . ."

His voice had been in process of changing, alternating between a growl and a squeak, all his lamentations and self-accusations had been made in a shrill, childish tone. Now he used the voice that would go with him all his life, and despite all the differences of upbringing and background it was curiously like his father's. But the way in which he handled the spade to dig a shallow grave, and then from the inner side of the wall pushed it, and the remnant of thatch down, was Walter's, purposeful, sparing of effort.

He allowed himself one sentimental thought; he said, "He will feel at home here."

It was an unhallowed grave, but Sybilla felt none of the scruples which she had felt about the raiders. Walter had always sedulously avoided the Church, and would not, she felt, have desired Christian burial. But as the clod wall, brittled by fire, crumbled down and the last of the thatch rustled into

190

place, she crossed herself and murmured, "God have mercy and rest you in peace."

The best, most loyal, most devoted servant any woman ever had. But in a cold, convent room the Abbess had said: *Bear in mind that none but the very devout, and they are few, ever act without some ulterior motive.*

There was still much to do. Everything concerned with the "accident" must be disposed of; the soiled papers, the bloodied rushes on the floor, her own blood-soaked dress. The mended fire on the wide hearth consumed them all.

Deaf Madge was the first to miss Walter because, rising early, he kindled the kitchen fire and brought in enough water to last her for the rest of the day. But for his absence she gave herself and everybody else, a simple explanation.

"He never was happy or settled since his little house was burnt. I noticed. Always on the fidget, he was. He liked his house and once it was gone one place was the same to him as another. So he took off."

Outside the house interest in Walter's disappearance was minimal. Nobody in Intake had liked Walter. His fourpenny pension, when given a considerable and generous sum, but now nonsensical, had come to him by way of a complicated method of exchange tokens, through a wool chandler in Baildon, an honest man, who for weeks put the now miserable sum away and waited for the claimant who never came.

At Knight's Acre there was the farm, and the work to be done on it.

"Mother, I can manage," Henry said. "Everything I was taught, I remember, I swear. With Tom . . . But I must be master, though it is for you to tell him so."

It sounded ludicrous; a boy of fourteen, helped by another, four years older; and about to be helped by a child of seven, for Henry gave John a baleful look and said, "He can start to help. When I was his age I made myself useful." She would not commit herself, saying, "I must see. I must think." Much of her thinking was done in the dark, in the night when cheerful thoughts were rare and no prospect pleased.

191

She would wake and think: What is to become of us? The only alternative to staying at Knight's Acre and trying to manage was to seek shelter with one of the family, meekly dependent after all, and would Henry fit in anywhere now? Would he even try? And where else but in her own home would poor Margaret be so happy, free from criticism or comment?

Sleepless, in the dark, Sybilla looked back and regarded decisions that had possibly been erroneous; setting up house here; refusing to leave when Godfrey was known to be dead; refusing a perfectly honourable offer of marriage.

There was always the comfort of touching rock bottom with the thought that at least starvation was not imminent; the hens continued to lay, and to produce clutches of fluffy yellow chickens. The sow farrowed. Somehow the makeshift arrangement—I must see; I must think—took on a permanent air.

Presently the lilies bloomed again. Sybilla took an armful to the church. "How very beautiful," Father Ambrose said. "Our Lady's own flower. Any news of Sir Godfrey, my lady?" "He died in Spain." "I am sorry indeed. I will say a Mass for his soul." Going back, past the lily bed, Sybilla snapped off another and dropped it amongst the periwinkles and nettles under which Walter lay. Three men loved me, she thought; and I have outlived them all. And now I must feed the pigs . . .

SEVENTEEN

ALTHOUGH HIS LATEST ATTEMPT at escape had passed unnoticed, the failure—and more particularly the cause of it
—threw Sir Godfrey into deep depression. How could he have
been so unobservant? So witless? The answer was that slavery
unmanned a man.

So he must reman himself and plan better; obtain, by hook
or by crook, some clothes which would pass unnoticed in that
crowded gateway. Not easy, for even cast-off clothes cost
money and he had none; nor any means of obtaining it. But
he must try . . .

Then something strange happened. He, the least fanciful
man in the world, began to fancy that he was being watched.
Employed in his proper occupation, he would have understood
exactly what that slight uneasiness, a crepitation between the
shoulders and at the back of the neck, implied. An enemy,
in hiding. Here he could only relate it to his escapade; somebody knew, though nothing had been said, somebody was
watching for him to put a foot wrong again. More than once, at
work in the quiet, secret garden, he was so conscious of an
eye upon him that he had straightened up from what he was
doing and wheeled round. And there sat Ermin, half asleep
as always, having assigned jobs, knowing they would be done.
The other slaves busy. So who was watching? Not only in the
garden. It sometimes happened in the stable yard.

That summer the silver tubs on the steps and the terrace
had been planted with orange trees of a peculiar kind; they
flowered profusely, but did not fruit. They had a strong, heady

193

scent and they needed watering every morning. In early September they were still in a state which elsewhere would have been highly regarded, but Ermin ambled round and said that they were past their best and on the morrow must be replaced by hyacinths, forced into unseasonable flowering by a special method of rearing. "Water the tubs well," he said, "it will loosen the roots for tomorrow. And we shall need a lot of liquid from the tank. Be ready with it when I open the gate tomorrow morning." He lumbered away.

Next morning, a voice said, "Do not look round. Come to the tub nearest the doorway, but turn your back. And listen . . . If the answer is yes, stand still; if not walk away. You wish to be free?" He stood still. "You will take a risk? Flogging? Branding?" He stood still. The voice was very soft, hardly more than a whisper, but it had an incisive quality. "Death? Unpleasant death?" He stood still. "Tomorrow, immediately after the third prayer. The Street of the Shoemakers. The shop of the blind man. You will ask for red shoes, lined with blue."

He waited, diligently watering the little orange tree, but no more was said.

He was now in a quandary. It could be a trap. Confirmation of his suspicion of having been watched, that his attempt to get away, though unremarked upon, had not gone unnoticed.

Why should someone within the harem seem to plot with him?

One appalling answer did present itself. He was the man who had refused to train Selim's men in western methods of warfare; he had been sent to the quarry and forgotten; brought out by sheer chance. Had the King identified him, remembered a grudge and planned to destroy him in the most hideous manner. The King's women were sacrosanct—there were shocking stories whispered about concerning the fate of men who, even inadvertently, came into contact with one.

Deeply troubled Sir Godfrey went along to the stable yard where everything was in a bustle. At dawn on the day after tomorrow the King was leaving for Escalona where another attack from the Christians was expected. Horses and harness, weapons and gear were being put into a state of perfect readiness and even the garden slaves were pressed into service.

Despite an exceptionally active day, Sir Godfrey slept little. He would take the risk; he would not take the risk. It could be a trap: it could be a chance. In the end he decided to keep the rendezvous, but to go armed, so that if it were a trap, he could kill himself rather than be taken and doomed to slow death by impalement.

As in all slave communities, there was here in the palace of Zagelah a natural caution about allowing slaves to handle, for any length of time, anything that might be used as an offensive weapon. Slaves worked as armourers, as smiths, as builders, but they were always closely supervised and the tools they used carefully checked. Slaves whose work entailed a certain amount of freedom were not allowed to carry even that ordinary thing—a knife for the cutting of meat at table. Usually their meat and their bread were cut for them, but if they were served with a dish which made a knife essential, some rather blunt, round-ended knives were counted out and counted in again. Such precautions were not taken for fear of slave revolts—very rare occurrences—but as a guard against slaves fighting between themselves, or in a moment of madness turning upon an overseer who was indulging in a little persecution. Not all of them were as easygoing as Ermin, who, next morning, when Sir Godfrey said that his pruning knife was blunt, told him to take it along and get it sharpened.

After that came the problem of concealing it. He managed by tying a piece of cord high on his left arm and pushing the knife into it, as though it were a belt. After that all his movements were very careful, for he had honed the knife until it had the shape and sharpness of a sword.

He was in the market place again when the call to prayer rang out, and he prostrated himself with the others. Then, as the late market activity broke out, he turned into the Street of the Shoemakers in search of what sounded somewhat unlikely—a blind man following that trade. He was easily found, a man not particularly old, but with eyes as white as pebbles.

195

He sat on a stool near the front of a small booth whose walls were hung with shoes of many colours, and slippers richly embroidered.

"I want a pair of red shoes, lined with blue."

"Red. With blue? The custom is to match leather and lining as nearly as possible."

"It is my fancy. Red, lined with blue they must be."

"Then it will be a special order. And such things take time. Be so good as to tell me—if I give you my attention, shall I keep other customers waiting?"

"There are no other customers."

"Then follow me." He walked briskly, and with the confidence of a full-sighted man, to a door at the back of the shop. There was a long dark passage; cooking smells, women's voices. Sir Godfrey slipped his left arm free of his jacket and retrieved his knife.

"Ten steps down," the blind man said. At the foot of them he pulled aside a curtain and Sir Godfrey saw a little room, with a door and a window looking on to a street, parallel to, but at a lower level than the Street of the Shoemakers. It contained a divan upon which sat an Arab woman, a veiled, shapeless bundle.

"Is it right?" the blind man asked.

"You have done well." Her voice was harsh, rather unpleasing, a voice accustomed to making itself heard above the noises of the market. "Burn the clothes and you will have done," she said. On the divan beside her lay a pile of clothes, white, reasonably but not too conspicuously clean, the clothes of a fairly prosperous peasant, and a hat of woven straw.

"Dress," she said. "I will wait by the donkey."

She moved heavily, a fattish, middle-aged woman, he judged.

Dressed—and now with a girdle into which he could push his knife—he went out to the quiet sunny street. It was very different from the streets adjoining the market, and something about it . . . Silly to think that it was the street where Robert had died and Arcol had fought and he had been taken, but it was very like it.

"Pull the hat further down," the woman said, "and get onto the donkey." It was an animal in fair condition, but rather small, and it wore the usual panniers. "Crouch a bit, you are too tall. Don't talk unless you must, pretend to be half asleep."

The gateway again. No challenge this time. They turned right—northwards. He sat, uncomfortably hunched, eyes half closed. The woman talked sometimes, always in that grating voice, so exactly like the other women's. They had only one theme; what wickedly low prices produce taken to market fetched, and what wickedly high prices were charged by those who sold things country people must buy. Here and there people turned off from the road, taking trails and paths that led to their various villages or holdings. Every departure thinned the crowd. When only three other groups were left, the woman stopped the donkey, and said in a loud, complaining voice: "And now this misbegotten son of the one-eyed one has a stone in his shoe."

Nobody else stopped; why should they?

There was no trail or path leading off here. Groves of olives on both sides. She pulled the donkey to the left-hand side of the road and, once in the shelter of the trees, said, "Here we take to the hills. You take this." She loosened one pannier and handed it to Sir Godfrey who had thankfully dismounted. The other she shouldered herself, and set off, leading the way, and moving with a swiftness surprising in so heavy a woman.

The donkey, relieved of its triple burden, sighed with relief and began to follow. He had not had a happy life, but he had learned that those who used him—however unkindly—provided, at the end of the day, food and water.

They were now at a point slightly north of the pass between Zagelah and Escalona, where the mountains could be called mere hills. Here the ground rose steeply and the belts of vegetation succeeded one another less gradually. Olives, rough pasture, gorse, pines, bareness. At one patch of pasture, with a little stream—one of the tributaries of the Loja—running through it, the donkey decided to halt. Across this little stream the woman jumped like a mountain goat. Presently their headlong, upland flight brought them to another stream wider and deeper. Into this she plunged, not bothering to lift her skirts, and walked upstream for several yards before stepping out

197

on the farther bank. He followed. There, behind an out-jutting rock she halted, put down her pannier and said in a voice only slightly breathless, "That should defeat the hounds —if they bring them out."

It was the first time she had spoken since the helter-skelter uphill climb began. She had led the way, seemingly certain of her direction, and he had ploughed along behind, far less nimble. Now he was astonished because she spoke in a different, far more pleasant voice than she had used before.

"I am most deeply grateful to you," he said. "Who sent you to guide me?" He was dazed by the speed of it all, by the fact that he stood here in the free air, able to look down upon Zagelah, which from this height and distance looked very much as it had looked on the Count's map.

The woman shrugged off the voluminous, dusty-black peasant-woman's dress, and stood clad in a bulky sheepskin coat. It reached to her knees and accounted for her heavy look. She threw it off. "It made running hard," she said, still from behind the ugly veil. She stood, half revealed in what Sir Godfrey, though he had never been inside a harem, recognised as harem wear because amongst the slaves in the stable yards titillating little pictures had been furtively handed about. Then as he stared, the woman, with a dramatic gesture, removed the tent-like veil with its little eyepiece of coarse threadwork.

"Now you know," she said, and looked at him with a smile which expected, demanded recognition.

To the best of his knowledge he had never seen her before in his life. A mass of silky black hair, drawn back and held in a net of gold, studded with pearls; skin the colour of ivory, thin arched eyebrows over exceptionally steep eyelids and black eyes, a delicate, high-bridged nose, a sharply curved mouth, the colour of a dark red rose. And while his eyes observed, his nose breathed in the sweet odour, the product of a body which baths and unguents and perfumes had impregnated so thoroughly that even hard running inside a fleece-lined coat merely emphasised it.

Such observations of eye and nose took only seconds, but for her too long. The expectant smile faded. She said:

"You do not remember me?"

He knew that people often took non-recognition as a kind of

insult. Obviously she was from the harem, the owner of the voice which had spoken from behind the grill. Then a terrible thought struck him—somewhere a mistake had been made; he was not the man for whom escape had been planned.

She said, "I have remembered you. *For two years.*"

And even then he was not enlightened, having lost all sense of time. It was only from stray remarks in the stable yard about the length of Selim's reign—more than six years—that he had realised how long he had been in the quarry. In that lost, timeless time two years was meaningless.

Utterly at a loss he did the best thing he could have done in the circumstances. He offered her the singularly candid, blue-eyed smile which in the past had made so many people like him, even while admitting that he was stupid, or stubborn. He said:

"Madam, I am at a loss . . . My memory was never good, and six years in a quarry, trying *not* to remember, has not improved it."

"But it was in the quarry. The man was beating me . . ."

Confusion upon confusion. He remembered the day, the girl, so young, so new, his own impulsive action, the second flogging . . .

The sun sank suddenly, as it did in mountainous places, cut off by the peaks to the west.

"I remember now," he said. But he could not see the connection.

"It took me so long," she said. "It was months before Selim even looked at me. He had another favourite then . . ." Something, not a smile, though it moved her lips, changed her expression as she remembered the cunning, callous machinations which had led to the former favourite's downfall. "It takes time to establish oneself in a position of favour—and power. I had you out of the quarry as soon as I had that power."

"I never even guessed . . ."

"I think we should eat now," she said. "And then sleep, to be ready for the morning." She pulled the black, tent-like dress over the satin and silk, bent over the pannier she had carried and produced a large, double-handed, silver cup.

"If you will fill this . . ."

When he returned, in the rapidly fading light, she had laid out on a square of linen what to him seemed a feast; a fresh roasted leg of mutton, a loaf of newly baked bread, some figs, bursting with ripeness.

"I had so little time," she said apologetically. "I was ready . . . but never sure. Even after I had spoken to you, still not sure. At the last moment Selim could have demanded that I go with him . . ."

"It amazes me," he said, "how you could arrange so much."

"Money will buy anything—even loyalty, of a kind. We are not yet safe. We shall not be safe until we are in Spain, and that is to the north. I have studied maps. Selim thought I had interest in them because they were *pretty*." She laughed sardonically. "I brought a coat for you, too. In the mountains nights are cold."

"You know these mountains?"

"No. My mountains are in Africa. But mountains are much the same. In my *mind* I know this country." She dipped a finger into the water cup and drew on the rock. "This is roughly the border between Zagelah and Escalona, this the border between Escalona and Spain, and this between Zagelah and Spain." It was like a letter T with a sharply sloping cross bar. "We must somehow cross this ridge and go down to the west—when we are far north enough. Just here"—she made a dot—"is a place called Santisteban. That is in Spain."

He sat and tried to think what it would be like to be amongst Christians again; of finding some travelled friar like Father Andreas who could understand English, of borrowing money to take him home.

"I have food for a week—with care," the girl said. "Dried stuff when the fresh is eaten." She handed him a sheepskin coat, and put on her own. "We should sleep now."

"I can never thank you properly."

"There is no need. I too am escaping. You could promise me something . . . If we should be taken, kill me. Women from that place who offend are sewn into weighted sacks and flung into the river." She knew because she had seen it done.

"I promise. But we must not think about being taken."

She woke him in the first dim light, offered him water from the refilled cup, gave him a piece of bread. "We can eat as we

200

go." Again she led the way, upwards and northwards over ground that became rougher and more broken all the time. The sun came up and the red sandstone took on colour, muted pinks and purples. She halted for a second, bowed herself, touched the ground and then her veiled forehead with her right hand—not a Moslem gesture—and hurried on. He looked back and Zagelah was now hidden from view. Ahead, due north, was a peak which reared itself above its neighbours and which had weathered into a rough resemblance of a helmeted head. He took it for a landmark.

It grew hot again as the sun rose higher; they divested themselves of the coats, stuffing them into the panniers. Whenever they reached a waterfall, or a little stream, they drank. At one such halt they heard sheep and the girl said, "We must avoid people. In a place like this we should be more remarked than in a crowded street." She led the way up, up again.

A foot soldier reckoned twenty miles an ordinary day's march, though he could do more under pressure. Sir Godfrey calculated that they must have covered more than that distance by the time they halted for the night, but they had ascended, descended, veered to avoid too steep slopes or wide stretches of scree, and the landmark peak seemed as far away as ever. It took them four strenuous days to reach its base. Each of these days was much like another, except that they now ate dried food, slices of bread rebaked until it was too dry to go mouldy, a little smoked meat, flat dry figs.

Over the food they talked, desultorily, learning each other's history; Tana—that was her name—was more voluble and painted for Sir Godfrey a picture of a strange way of life, half nomadic, half pastoral. Aspects of it were sometimes reminiscent of life on the borders which he knew, raids, feuds, banditry, though her clan or tribe appeared to operate either in the mountains or in desert country which he found difficult to imagine. They were not Moslems, she said; they had come from somewhere far away to the east and were settled long before the Arabs arrived. They had once had their own language: "My grandmother still remembered it and spoke it when she was angry, which was often." Their women were not secluded or veiled and seemed to enjoy unusual power; girls chose their own husbands and if a man wished to take a sec-

201

ond wife, his first had a voice in the choosing. That, he thought, sounded civilised, but when she spoke of fighting alongside her father and brothers, and showed him, as proof, the scar on her head, his sense of chivalry was outraged. Ladies should be protected! Yet there was little about her to appeal to the protective instinct; she outran, outwalked, outclimbed him every day and that despite the fact that she, for two years, had led a most cushioned life while he had worked. She was at home in this empty, hostile terrain as he could never be; her instinct for direction was instinctive—he was always searching for landmarks, observing the position of the sun. She never failed to find water, sometimes making a diversion in order to do so. When he offered to carry both panniers she said, "Why should you? It would make you slower."

They talked about horses—it had been agony, she said, never to see a horse, except through a window: her father had owned the best horses in the world. Hounds, too. She had had two of her own. "Trained to fight. They were both killed."

In exchange he told her about Arcol, also trained to fight—but he cut that story short, it evoked painful memories, and told her instead of Arcol's wilfulness and how it took an old donkey to get him aboard. That amused her and she laughed like a boy. It was, on the whole, rather like travelling with a tough, ingenious young squire, incongruously disguised as a Moorish woman.

She told him that Selim, because he had taken the crown of Zagelah by a trick, was deeply suspicious of treachery and had built up not only the best spy system, but the most efficient courier service in the world . . . "That is why," she said, "we must avoid even a shepherd. By now Selim knows that he has lost a concubine and a slave. Everybody in Zagelah and Escalona will know too. When we come down it must be in Spain."

He asked idly, stupidly, "If we manage it, will you go home?"

"Home? I have none. We were wiped out. Do you imagine that if one of my tribe had been alive and could crawl and had strength to cut my throat, I should have been left alive to become a slave? No, in future your home will be mine."

"Of course," he said, "of course." Honesty compelled him to

202

add, "I may no longer have a house of my own. But I have family, and friends."

More and more as day followed day and they made slow, though steady progress, he had considered what a man might find after an absence so long that death must be presumed.

Tana said, "We could buy a house; many houses, I think. Do you think I came away emptyhanded? From the stronghold of an enemy? Look!"

She loosened the ugly black dress. And the rose-coloured, heavily embroidered satin jacket which she wore under it. Between the base of her long neck and the jut of breasts, small but firm, there were three strings of pearls; around her slim waist was a band from which two pouches were suspended. She pulled them out with an apparently unself-conscious gesture and tipped out their contents. Gold coins, a tangled mass of jewelled ornaments, sapphires, rubies, diamonds which even in this dimming light glittered. He had never seen, he thought few men had ever seen, such a collection of wealth.

Tana said, "Spoil! I took everything I could lay my hand upon. I thought that if I ended in a sack, in the river, it should be for some act of which my tribe would have approved."

Innocent then, he was able to contemplate her future in England. Young—he knew her age, sixteen, so two years ago, in the quarry, he had been right in thinking her very young—rich. But in England she would, for a time, be a stranger. He determined that whatever he found—Knight's Acre sold, Sybilla remarried—he would take care of Tana, see that nobody took advantage of her, find her a decent husband; in short behave to her as though she were his sister.

"I must eat less," she said, on the fifth or sixth evening, snapping her slice of the brittle bread in two. "I think maps are liars, we should have been out of the mountains by now." She scowled fiercely.

"I will eat less, too," he said, and put his whole piece back into the pannier and took the half she had returned.

They were not only not out of the mountains, but trapped in them, with peaks to the east as well as the west. Even had

203

they been sure that they were far enough north to have Spain, not Escalona to the west of them, they could not have reached it; and never would unless they found a gap.

They had retained both panniers because they were a convenient means of carrying the sheepskin coats during the heat of the day. What food remained, wrapped in the linen cloth, lay at the bottom of one pannier when they settled themselves for the night. The idea of guarding it had not occurred to them; they had climbed into heights where they were the only things living. Yet something came in the night and robbed them . . .

"We might as well have eaten it all," Tana said bitterly, but not without humour. "I heard something snuffling and gobbling. I *hit* it."

"What was it?"

"How could I tell in the dark? It was hairy."

Wolf? Wild goat? Mountain hare? It had left no footprints on the bare rock.

"You should have called me," he said. Women wakened in the night by a mouse's activity behind the wainscot, or an owl hooting, or a roll of thunder, ordinarily turned to the nearest person.

"You could have done no more than I did. I hit it, and it was hairy and slipped away." She must have hit it hard whatever it was. The side of her hand and the little finger were swollen and bruised. She had exceptionally narrow, fragile hands.

She said, "So today or tomorrow we must find food. I once hungered for three days, but my horse carried me."

"I once hungered for five, but then we were besieged and could not move."

Inaction lessened hunger.

Their experiences of going without food, different as they were, interlinked. Hold on and you survive. So they survived that day. And part of the next. By that time the shape of the country had changed, the corridor between two impenetrable ranges, a path littered with boulders, with scree, always descending. The last thing that Sir Godfrey saw at the end of that hungry day was a glimpse of green. Pasture? Tree tops? But far away, deep down, and for their purpose on the wrong side of the brutally rugged range.

204

Abruptly, on the third day of hunger—although towards the north peaks still towered, shaped as one decided, a castle, a church steeple, a mushroom, a tree—underfoot the land sloped down and neither of them, fully in control of the mind, followed it. Sudden. Bare rock, gorse and pine, beeches. And somewhere the plaintive cry of sheep.

Tana said, "I think we should still be careful . . ."

So they were careful, and hiding behind the grey boles of the beeches in a way of which Walter would have approved, they watched. A Moorish shepherd, leading his flock to lower pastures, stalking along as though sheep did not concern him; a woman, clad exactly as Tana was, and two children acted as sheepdogs did in countries where both women and dogs had more worth.

This was still Moorish territory, and they must be glad that the shepherd had a wife, not a dog which might have scented them. They must also be glad that amongst the surplus or the diseased fruits of their branches, the beeches had shed a few early and edible nuts. Enough perhaps to keep a man alive, not enough to stay hunger or give strength.

Cautiously they crossed the sheep trail, left the trees and grass behind and below, and re-entered the hostile land of rock. And there, after a day in which they had eaten nothing at all, Tana broke down.

He had heard the expressions, beating one's breast, tearing one's hair, but he had never seen anyone actually performing such actions. Now he did, for Tana's self-recrimination was as thorough and wholehearted as everything else about her.

"I have doomed you to death," she cried. "I overestimated myself . . . In the garden you were not overworked and you always had food . . . Now you will die, and I shall have killed you!"

She beat her breast, she tore her hair, she banged her head against the rock.

"We are not dead yet," he said, appalled by the sight of such distress. "And if we do die . . . at least we shall die free." It was all he could think of to say; fasting had not improved his mental processes or made him handy with words. He could, he thought, prevent her from hurting herself, and with this

205

in mind he took her hands and pulled her away from the rock. He said, "My dear . . . You are not to blame. I came of my own free will. I . . . I encouraged you . . . Perhaps I should curse myself . . ."

Then the incredible thing happened, and with incredible speed. At the touch of his hands she changed from a woman wild with misery and self-reproach to one wild with desire, something only a dead man could have resisted. He was idiotically surprised by the violence of his own response.

He had always brought to the matter of sex the straightforward simplicity he had brought to life. As a young, unmarried man he had made occasional visits to brothels because not to have done so would have seemed eccentric. But the traffic of flesh without genuine feeling had always repulsed him slightly. Until he met and fell in love with Sybilla, he had never experienced a genuine feeling towards any woman, and once married had been contentedly faithful. Opportunities to be otherwise had not been lacking. There were many ladies, beautiful ladies of very high rank, disposed to favour a handsome young knight who had distinguished himself in the lists. But intrigue had never appealed to him; at its best it involved furtiveness, at its worst, scandal. More than one angry lady had decided that he was too stupid to take a hint.

He loved Sybilla, Sybilla loved him and their lovemaking had been placid and pleasant, entirely satisfactory to two people not passionate by nature, but loving, considerate, and kind. The years of enforced celibacy had bothered him little— if he couldn't bed with his loved one, he was content to bed with nobody.

As for this girl, the thought had never once occurred to him though they had been alone together, living in close intimacy for so many days. She was so young, he was forty-three—and felt far older. Also, absurd, perhaps, but true, he was not merely a one-woman man, he was a one-type-of-woman man. Sybilla was his ideal and Tana was about as different from Sybilla as a female could be . . .

However, there it was, it had happened, and it was a stunning experience.

Afterwards, depleted, completely drained, just before he fell into a sleep of exhaustion, he found himself hoping that what

206

she had said—about loving him from that moment in the quarry and similar things—was the result of hunger-light-headedness. But what had *he* said? Lightheaded from hunger, taken out of himself by joy he had not even imagined, *he* had said, "I would die now, content."

But death, which would have solved everything, was not to be theirs. Stumbling along next morning, now taking the easiest way, they heard sheep again; sheep first and then market-place voices and, rounding a bluff in which a peak was rooted, they found themselves on the verge of what seemed a busy town.

Santisteban?

Hope receded as they saw that this was not the place they were seeking; no streets, no houses, no church.

Centuries ago shepherds had realised that sheep from the uplands were hardier, longer of leg, and thicker of fleeces. Those from the lowlands were fatter and more docile, less likely to go back to the wild. So they had met and made exchanges, a ram for three ewes. Then people who owned no sheep realised that men making the exchanges were hungry and thirsty, and then came with food and drink; and then other people, who owned nothing, had realised that people craved entertainment.

Here, in a most unlikely place, a market had established itself, step by step over the years. Boundaries, never very certain in such rugged country, and the rule of kings, of popes and prelates, had affected the gathering place hardly at all. It was an international, multilingual market where one could buy almost anything and the money changers were busy at their benches. One day to be called banks.

Tana said, "I think we should not go down together. It is not Santisteban. Selim's rule might even extend . . ." She gave him one of the solid gold coins and said, "Buy what you can, and ask the way. I will do the same."

"Perhaps," he said, "we should not be seen to leave together, either. Whichever of us first learns the way will go in that direction and wait." It was necessary to ask, for apart from the way by which they had made their entry, which

207

was not a real trail at all, better trodden ways led off in all directions.

The place reeked of food cooking. Moorish women were grilling mutton and boiling rice and frying doughcakes and rolling them in powdered sugar. A woman who looked like a Spaniard was stirring a great pot of something he did not recognise; it looked like white worms; as she stirred she talked and he decided that her speech did not sound like Spanish, so he passed on to a table where a man was slicing ham. Ham! Something he had not tasted for six years—the pig being regarded by the Arabs as an inedible beast. He indicated his wish for a slice and stood and devoured it. Nothing had ever tasted so good! He ate three slices while he listened. The man was undoubtedly Spanish. So he ventured to put his question. Santisteban?

He had never seen the word written, had only heard it said, by Tana, in Arabic, and now pronounced it as she had done, but in his English voice. The ham-seller looked blank, shrugged his shoulders, spread his hands, answered in Spanish that he had never heard of such a place. Sir Godfrey pointed towards what seemed to him the westerly of the trails, and the man understood. "Escalona," he said.

But this was a friendly place. Wars might be waged on either side of the mountains, but in this old upland market place there were only buyers and sellers, so the man was disposed to be helpful and, turning away from his table, inquired of his neighbour who sold knives, saying the word as Sir Godfrey had said it. He also looked puzzled for a moment and then said, "Ah! *Santi*steban?" He gave the word the correct stress. Sir Godfrey nodded and then pointed vaguely, regretting very much that he had learned no Spanish at all; he could not even say "Thank you," or "How far?" He simply had not bothered. He had a sharp, self-reproachful memory of Sir Ralph Overton, who had practised so assiduously, acquiring as many as ten words or phrases in a day. He had no means of knowing that Sir Ralph, with all that he knew, his taste for gossip, his keen sense of self-preservation, lay at the bottom of a gully, not far from the city of Escalona, a mass of greening bones.

But, the right trail—it seemed to lead to the northwest—

indicated to him he smiled and held up his fingers. One, two, up to ten miles. The gesture was not understood. No matter, he thought, we shall find out.

Then he had a bad moment. He had bought three slices of ham, and now bought more; a whole heap of pink and white, succulent meat slapped into a fig leaf. He was uncertain about how Tana felt towards ham. In their talks she had always emphasised her tribe's difference from their Arab neighbours. Some pretence at being converted had been necessary, but her tribe still worshipped the sun, giver of all. He thought: Well if she will not eat ham, she can eat what she has chosen; and he placed the big, folded fig leaf in his pannier and proffered the gold coin. The ham-seller looked at it, not entirely with suspicion, but with curiosity, turning it this way and that. The three slices of ham, eaten too hastily and gulped down into an empty stomach, threatened for a moment to rebound. For a moment he thought he was going to be sick, and in the same moment he contemplated the wisdom of turning away, vanishing into the crowd without waiting for change. Common-sense alone kept him still. Such extravagance would be remarkable—and he had already indicated his destination. So he stood, with the stolidity that had so often been mistaken for stupidity and waited while the ham-seller placed the coin between his teeth and bit it and then dropped it on the table. It was gold! And here gold in any form was acceptable, just as any harmless man was acceptable. Sir Godfrey took his change and, sauntering deliberately, bought bread, apples, figs, and then, ignoring the invitations to enter enclosures inside which bears danced and dogs fought, and all the booths that sold trivialities, even amber from the far north, made his way towards the trail, slightly north of west. He looked about as he went, but Tana, covered from the crown of her head to her ankles, was not to be distinguished from any of the other Moorish women in the milling market place. So he went along, sat down on a boulder and waited. Food had restored him and now that he had time to think he realised the folly of his be-haviour on the previous evening. It had been, in a way, an act of despair, death seeming so likely as to make what one did or did not do of small importance. It had been a failure of self-control, a violation of his marriage vows, a contradiction of his principles. And would colour the whole of his relationship with the girl in future. Armoured in innocence he had been able to visualise himself presenting Tana to Sybilla, to James, to William as his deliverer, expecting nobody to think evil because none had existed. It would be different now; he felt that guilt was written all over him.

It must never happen again.

Having decided that, he began to be uneasy because she had not yet joined him. Had she not seen him leave? Had she misunderstood the direction, or been misdirected? Or—his heart gave a lurch—had the worst happened? He remembered the curiosity which his gold coin had evoked, suppose hers . . . and suppose Selim's spy system operated even in this distant, Tower of Babel place.

The thought brought him to his feet and set him running back towards the noise and the stench when a moment's cool consideration would have sent him galloping towards Santisteban, for if she had been taken there was nothing he could do; he could only doom himself as well. But he ran marketwards, and at a turn in the trail met her, hurrying too, and heavily laden. For a second the breathlessness of haste and agitation prevented speech; they could only lean against each other in a way which any Arab onlooker would have found highly suspicious. Finally he said, "I was afraid that something had happened . . ."

"It almost did . . ." Behind the veil she laughed, but shakily. "I almost died of fright . . . The woman selling doughcakes did not like the look of my money . . . She took it to the money-changer, and Godfrey, I could not move. I knew I should . . . melt into the crowd . . . but I was paralysed. I did not know that one could be so frightened . . ."

However the money-changer had declared the coin good and fear had unlocked its hold. She had bought bread, fruit, cheese, smoked mutton and two portions of the fresh meat which he had seen an Arab woman grilling; cubes of mutton not much bigger than a dice, threaded onto a piece of wire, the meat cubes interspersed with onion and some other vegetable, green.

"One for you," she said, "and one for me," she said. "I am *so* hungry."

"Have you not eaten?"

"Oh no! I thought we should break our long fast together."

His hastily gobbled slices of ham were uneasy again, spurred this time not by fear but by self-reproach. But he took the proffered handy meal and learned, as they walked and munched, that Tana had been more successful than he had in extracting information.

Santisteban was four days' easy walking away. "And that delayed me too," she said. "First I said the name wrongly and must be corrected. Then I was warned that it was in Spain and Moors were not welcome there. I said that it was a place I wished to avoid, and that was why I asked. And I took a roundabout way to this path. Just in case . . . but I do not think we are being followed."

She ate her portion of meat on the skewer, two slices of ham, half a loaf, three of the doughcakes. She seemed to be insatiable—but she had waited to take the first mouthful with him.

And whoever had told her that only four days of easy walking would lead into Santisteban had never followed this trail which led upwards, to the last summer pasture, and a little hut in which some shepherd had sheltered. After that the land fell away in a series of steep declines, more difficult to descend than to ascend since in climbing upwards handholds offered some momentum. The journey took a full five days, but they knew on the fourth day that they were in Spain, because on that day they reached sheep country again, and this time the flock was led by a bellwether, an experienced old ewe who knew which way to go.

"All Arabs are terrified of bells," Tana said. "We are in Spain. Beloved, we are free!" She lifted the ugly veil from her head and threw it down, and then turned and embraced him.

It was the moment for which he had passionately longed and hopelessly hoped; but it was marred for him by what had taken place immediately before. The thing he had vowed should never happen again, had happened, and the statements which he had hoped were the product of hunger-lightheadedness had been repeated many times. It still seemed incredible to him that one so brief encounter with a man old enough to

211

be her father should have kindled such intense and lasting devotion, but there it was!

She had hidden nothing from him; the scheming and plotting—a horrifying harem intrigue by which she had attained the position of favourite and the title—Light of the King's Eyes; her dangerous contacts with Soraya in order to find out his name, his nationality. "She is a relative of Selim's and could have betrayed me. To think about another man is a crime . . ." He had simply saved her from a few strokes of a cane, and she, in return, had risked her life many times. "I made up the story that being English you would know about gardens; had you been German or Italian I should have said the same. It was necessary to have you in the garden. Heart of my heart, I used to watch you, wondering when the moment would come when I could act . . ."

He did not love her—he assured himself of that whenever he thought about the situation in which he found himself. He was deeply and everlastingly in her debt, he admired her wholeheartedly, but he did not love her, or at least only with his body, formerly so disciplined and now out of control. Sometimes he wondered whether it were possible for a man to be in love with two women at once, in two very differing ways. It was a question with which his simple, single-minded nature was not equipped to deal. And now as sheep country became cultivated country and their longed-for destination, a huddle of red-roofed tiles and white walls, became visible, became near, his happiness was diluted with guilt and foreboding.

He said, as they approached the little town, "Tana, we must now be careful. We need help from the Church, and if they knew the . . . the truth about us, help might not be forthcoming."

"Why do we need help from the Church or anybody. We are free, we have plenty of money." She sounded defensive.

He needed to make contact with the one international body that he knew of. After all, William was a Bishop, able to read and write the Latin which was the Church's common tongue. William, he thought, would not have accepted his complete disappearance without some inquiry, and where a question could penetrate, so could information. He was not so stupid as to imagine that anyone, friar or priest, in this little country

212

town on Spain's border, would have information of what had been happening at Knight's Acre in his absence, but it was possible that they could put him into touch with someone who had.

His natural delicacy—remembering last night and all the other nights—prevented him from explaining honestly; so he said that what he craved was some news of what had been happening in England during the past years.

Tana, prey to no such scruples, said:

"You mean your wife!"

She had known of Sybilla's existence—and of the four children—from one of the first of their suppertime talks. He had offered the information then with no thought of being defensive. She spoke of her past, he spoke of his. Nor since the flight of innocence, had he in any way deceived her, careful to point out that in England a man could have only one wife. Nor had he been free with endearments; nothing more than "my dear," never, even in his most abandoned moments, using any of the terms which were Sybilla's: "Darling," "Sweeting."

If Tana sensed any reticence in him, she gave no sign; her own endearments were fervent, picturesque—had he known it, Oriental in flavour.

She now asked, "What do you mean by being careful?"

"Sleeping apart."

"It will take the heart out of my breast. But if it is your wish . . ."

And so they entered Santisteban.

EIGHTEEN

AT FIRST THEIR WELCOME was not very warm; their shoes were in tatters, their clothes in rags and much soiled; they looked like beggars, and foreign at that. But they had money, and by chance the first inn they saw was the best in a town that boasted four. Tana proved herself capable of communicating by mime; they needed food, they needed wine, hot water for washing; after that she needed more hot water in order to wash her hair; they both needed clothes, and sleeping places—she folded her hands together and laid her head on them in sleep's posture. She gave Sir Godfrey a look that he could not interpret, and held up two fingers. Two rooms.

Life in Santisteban except on market days was dull; a small crowd gathered to peep through open doorways or windows to view this couple who had come from nowhere, looked so poor, yet acted as though they were rich. Somebody ran for the priest.

He was a fairly young man and intelligent; he had more Latin than many of his kind, who knew just enough to stumble through a ritual. Sir Godfrey had never known more Latin than was needed to make the correct responses, and even those phrases, through long disuse, were rusty; also his Latin was English-Latin, Father Pedro's was Spanish-Latin and the two things were different; but Sir Godfrey crossed himself and said a "Hail Mary," quickly and badly, but just well enough to establish himself as a Christian. Then Tana mimed again; on the white scrubbed table she drew a Crescent, enemy of the Cross; she pointed to the mountain range, and then ripped from Sir Godfrey's shoulders what remained of his Moorish

214

peasant robe and exposed the scars which the scalding khur-bash lashes had made.

And the priest, understanding the mime, asked, "Where is Fernando?"

He was easily found. An old man now, crooked and crip-pled, willing—if he could be caught sober—to undertake any job which a one-armed man could do. But, like Sir Ralph Overton and many another man, he had once, until he was disabled, worked his way about the world. He was a profes-sional mercenary.

Partly to compensate himself for his now humble status, and partly to lure an absorbed audience into paying for an-other cup of wine, Fernando told long, boastful stories about his adventures and the priest sensibly decided that if there was one person in Santisteban capable of understanding these strange tongues, Fernando was the man. He knew less than he claimed to do, but wine emboldened him to bridge any gaps with guesses. He informed his hearers that Sir Godfrey was English and a Christian and a martyr; he had been a pris-oner with the Moors and beaten very often for refusing to give up his faith; he confused numbers, thus increasing Sir Godfrey's captivity by some years, and, failing to understand Tana's role in the story, explained that she was Sir Godfrey's daughter.

To his audience—few of whom had ever been more than twenty miles from Santisteban—Fernando's cleverness was im-pressive, and Sir Godfrey's story so moving that tears were shed, generous and pious resolves taken on impulse. There must be a feast to welcome back this man from the dead; two feasts, in fact, one given by the civil authorities and one by the members of the Hermandad, that ancient, self-elected body of men who were responsible for the keeping of law and order. Kind ladies ransacked their wardrobes in order to pro-vide Tana with an outfit and the tailor's two most respected customers managed to convince him that it was nothing less than his duty to enlarge the suit of clothes upon which he was currently at work to make it fit Sir Godfrey, too tall for bor-rowed clothes, and to do so fast and without charge.

Father Pedro also knew a generous impulse. A prisoner with the Moors, this good Christian must certainly have neglected

215

his religious obligations and probably committed sins as well; but he had suffered for his faith and was entitled to leniency, an over-all absolution and a Mass of thanksgiving. Never an ostentatiously pious man, and for years a stranger to God, Sir Godfrey was greatly touched by this consideration for his soul; and although he knew that the priest would not understand, he confessed that he had committed adultery, many times. He also knew that absolution always included the adjuration to avoid the *occasion* for sin. This, in his mind, he was determined to do; and he asked, as he had not formerly done, God's help in resisting temptation.

Tana, miming sleep, had indicated a wish for two rooms, but that was because Godfrey had said they must be careful; she had every intention of waiting until the house was asleep and then creeping along to his bed. In this she was thwarted, because the innkeeper's wife, though sharing the charitable impulse and saying that she would not charge for accommodation, was thrifty too and did not prepare extra rooms. Tana was to share the bed of her own daughter—what more could anyone ask? Sir Godfrey had a bed in a room which held four, one occupied by the son of the house and one by a permanent guest, a childless widower who found living at the inn more convenient than keeping house on his own.

So they slept apart; and the civic feast and the Hermandad feast were both strictly male gatherings. "I did not think it would be like this," Tana said, looking more miserable than she had done during the hungry days. The wives of the leading citizens of Santisteban were kind to her but she was not grateful. "It is like being back in the harem again. With dumb women! They give me things—which I could buy—and they *pat* me. Like a pet monkey."

He felt sorry for her, the more so because he was beginning to enjoy himself. He was back in a world which, though strange, was not completely alien to him; he could talk only to one person, Fernando, and that imperfectly, but then he had never been much of a talker, and when men lifted winecups and smiled in his direction, he understood. And smiled back, growing, minute by minute, more into the shape that he had once known, a man among men. There were even moments

216

when he dared to think hopefully of Knight's Acre; James and Emma only five miles away; William at Bywater, Walter close at hand . . . All his family and many of his friends had thought at one time or another that he was feckless, and now that quality in him which had made him buy Arcol and thus run into debt, and build a house a bit bigger than he could really afford, took over. He had a naturally happy nature and all his training had been directed at a certain *insouciance*. A man of forethought—what if my horse stumbles, or riding at the ring I do not withdraw my arm soon enough and break my shoulder?—such a man could never have become the knight he had been, reckless, feckless.

As he was restored, Tana dwindled. She had her moment, astride a horse again. Fernando had understood the word horse, the two uplifted fingers and the word "good." He was also capable of understanding that though clothes, accommodation and feasts might be free, horses must be paid for and he had provided the best that Santisteban offered.

Tana could not get away from this disappointing place quickly enough and she rode as Sir Godfrey had never seen a woman ride before, crouched low, her hair—what had happened to the net?—mingling with the horse's black-blown mane. Wicked, absolutely wicked to think that she brought to horse-riding the same violence and skill as she brought to lovemaking, and to remember, and yearn . . .

They now carried with them what was virtually a passport, written by Father Pedro, warmly commending to anyone who could read Latin this Englishman who had come back, as from the dead. The letter repeated Fernando's errors about how long the imprisonment had lasted, and about the relationship between the man and the girl. It also mentioned something very near to Father Pedro's heart. He judged it unlikely that a man regularly beaten for adhering to his faith would have been able to have his child baptised; since the baptism of those of mature years demanded some collaboration from the subject, and since he himself could not communicate with the girl, Father Pedro could only hope that should this letter fall into the hands of some English-speaking priest, he would take action . . .

For the first four days of their journey the letter was very helpful—even in one small village where the priest could not read it completely. He recognised Latin when he saw it, however, and gave the missive due respect. The village inn being so poor and squalid, he invited Sir Godfrey to sleep in his own house and arranged for Tana to be accommodated in the home of a parishioner. Tana said, with some justification, "You are using the Church as a shield against me." She hoped very much that soon they would be forced to halt for the night in the open; or in some village with an inn and no priest, both hopes doomed to disappointment, for they were riding through a countryside relatively highly populated, and Spain, though its civil life was falling into chaos, was still the most ardently religious country in Christendom; every village had a priest.

On the evening of the fifth day they reached a town which had what Sir Godfrey had been hoping for—a Dominican Priory in which lived a friar who understood English, who had in fact spent some time in London. For Sir Godfrey to be able to communicate was like being freed from another form of captivity. But the interview took an embarrassing turn. He had already handed in his letter and there were discrepancies. Sir Godfrey said six years, the letter said sixteen.

"That was a mistake, Father. I was in captivity for *six* years." He tried to explain about the man in Santisteban who knew a very little English; he mentioned being in Escalona in early 1453, in the attack upon Zagelah in the February of that year. His congenital inability to narrate and explain did little to allay the ever-ready Dominican suspicion. Nor did it account for the young woman, described in the letter as his daughter. Unless English knights had begun to take girls with them when they went into battle. Even that Father Ignatius could almost believe, having lived in England . . . At the same time, Zagelah, six years ago, had made a mark on the collective Dominican consciousness. Father Ignatius switched his impersonal, celibate gaze from the young woman, admitted to the only room in the Priory in which women were allowed to set foot, and said:

"There was a report that the Count of Escalona took certain members of my Order with him."

218

Sir Godfrey did not regard this as a test of his genuineness, but he gave the right answer.

"Oh yes. There was Father Andreas and six others, younger men."

"Of their fate nothing was known; death was assumed. Any detail would, of course, be welcome."

"I cannot say what happened; only what was arranged . . ." his clear, candid gaze clouded. "In a battle one does the part assigned . . . There is no time . . . The Count of Escalona had his son . . . It was arranged that he and the religious should follow when we had made an entry—and cleared the streets . . ." Impossible now not to remember Robert, roasting inside his armour. "It was a disaster. The Moor, Abdullah, was betrayed, and so were we in our turn. I never heard of any other prisoner. I think *my* death has been assumed." That brought him back to his real reason for seeking out an English-speaking member of the loosely knit but widespread Church. "My brother is Bishop of Bywater . . . I rather hoped, or wondered if inquiries . . . or news from England."

"Inquiries would hardly have reached us, here, Sir Godfrey. In Seville, possibly. Some news seeps through from time to time. Civil war, I understand, brief and ending in a compromise."

This news did not affect Sir Godfrey much. War was still something that involved only fighting men; his sons were too young, James was too old, and William had never been a militant cleric. He had himself once fought in a battle on a field flanked by two others; in one a peasant was ploughing, and in the other a boy was flying his hawk.

Then Father Ignatius said, "And the young woman? *Is* she your daughter?"

"Does the letter say that? In Santisteban there was this one man . . . an old soldier who knew a few English words. No indeed. This lady was also a prisoner. In Zagelah, I owe my freedom to her. But for her I should still be there . . ." Suddenly the weight of his debt to her settled on his mind as heavily as the marble slabs had pressed on his shoulders. But for her . . .

Tana sat there, upright, immobile, scowling, so obviously

219

aloof from it all, and yet disapproving, that only someone with a rightful regard for her immortal soul would have ventured on the next question:

"Is she a Christian?"

"No, Father."

"A Moor? A Moslem?"

"No. She . . . she has a faith of her own. But I do not understand it. The lady speaks only Arabic—and my knowledge of that language is limited."

"There are Moors in Seville. Converts," Father Ignatius said, not sorry to defer the matter, but adding that Sir Godfrey must be mindful of his duty and his responsibility. He then changed the subject by inquiring whether they needed financial assistance and seemed relieved to learn that this was not so. He recommended a certain inn.

That night he woke, and in the dark, in the haze of being aroused from a deep sleep, found her in bed beside him. For a moment he thought that he had only dreamed the awakening and was now dreaming this, for like all cautious travellers in unfamiliar places he had bolted his door. But she was real enough—and importunate.

Once, so hotly and openly pursued by a lady intent upon dalliance he had felt ridiculous, so much so that he had cancelled his name from the lists of remaining events in the week-long tournament and simply fled, feeling even more ridiculous. But for that lady he had had no feeling at all; with Tana his flesh at least was in love. And although he had vowed to God, what could God do, short of striking one of them dead, or him impotent, which was far, far from being the case . . .

Afterwards she snuggled against him, soft and content as a cat. He asked how she got into his room, and she said, through the window. That should perhaps have sounded ludicrous, too, and would have done with any other woman, but with Tana it was simply further proof of devotion, unintentionally inspired and completely undeserved.

"Now that I belong to you again, I shall enjoy this country," she said.

With another woman it would have been possible, even easy,

to think an uncouth thought—a bitch on heat—but not with this woman who had been willing to die for him, and with him.

And a fall from grace was a fall from grace; depending only upon his own will, he had made a resolution and failed; asking the help of God he had made a vow and broken it; repetition of the offence could hardly worsen it.

So there followed some days and nights over which, in memory, an enchanted air seemed to hang. They were free, and for the first time since they had attained freedom, Tana was happy. It was still fine weather, and away from the hills warm, even at night. They now avoided villages and towns, or paused in them only long enough to buy food. Money knew no language, coins in a palm, a finger pointing obtained them all they wanted.

They made no further contact with the Church. News, if there was any, would be in Seville—where this happy gypsy journey must end.

He had occasional bad moments, realising that when there was no sexual traffic between them—as in their first days in the mountains, and in their first days in Spain—he had been able to see himself taking Tana to England, of somehow fitting her into his life. So long as she was his saviour, the thing was possible, while she was his lover, it was not. That must be thought about—not today, tomorrow. Some obscure instinct told him to make the best of *now*. And now was travel through country where the first-harvested grapes had already been crushed and made into wine, unmatured, something one drank like water and within a short time felt the effects of; where the later-harvested grapes were being gathered and carted, in donkey panniers, on low carts, on the backs of women; where, because the wine harvest was a season of plenty, meat was available. And Tana could cook, in two ways. She could make a tripod of green branches over a fire and from it suspend a joint, much in the manner of somebody using a spit, or she would dig a hole, line it with stones, light a fire in it and then put meat and onions, wrapped in leaves, into the red hot cavity and close it down with clods.

Once or twice he had a demented thought: We could live like this forever. A thought to be dismissed instantly.

Insulated as they were, by language and by their way of life, they had received no warnings of the perils of the road. All roads, everywhere, were infested with robbers, but those of Spain were worse than most because, although in some remote, backward places like Santisteban the Hermandad might be active and respected still, in more central regions it had become completely ineffectual. In many towns the chief magistrates were either in league with the bandits, or intimidated by them and so reluctant to pass sentence.

Outwardly Sir Godfrey and Tana did not appear to be likely prey for thieves; the clothes they had been given were plain and simple, they wore no jewels, carried no goods. But they had horses, and every evening before settling upon a suitable place to camp, Sir Godfrey made a sharp reconnoitre. He then unsaddled and tethered the horses, and fed them—grass was wilted and yellow at this season—and Tana cooked.

One evening, with a fine leg of lamb suspended, hissing over the flames, thcy were surprised to find that they had company. They were camped on open heathland and Sir Godfrey had made sure that there were no other nomads in the vicinity, no likely hiding places; but there the two men were, looming up silently, grunting out greeting in Spanish and eyeing the meat hungrily. Both carried bludgeons, both wore knives, far larger than Sir Godfrey's ground-down pruning knife. Tana said, "Be amiable!" She returned the greeting, in Arabic, and indicated, by gesture that the intruders were welcome to share the meat. As a token of good will she broke the long crusty loaf into four and gave them each a portion, instantly devoured.

Sir Godfrey watched uneasily, cursing himself for not having provided himself with a sword. Thcy might be simply two hungry men, attracted by the scent of cooking meat, they might, having eaten, go away, but there was something about their manner, both furtive and arrogant, which made him suspicious. One of them pointed to the joint and then to his mouth—an order to Tana to serve. She looked very amiable indeed, and acted sensibly. She tested the meat by running a sliver of wood into it, and the blood ran red. She shook her head and held up her ten fingers; wait ten minutes. The men laughed and then spoke together. That in itself was not sinister, not necessarily secretive, Spanish was their tongue, but it made him uneasy. They were both a good deal younger than he was. He was acutely aware not only of the wealth Tana had concealed about her, but of the fact that she was female. Even in England, sturdy beggars were dreaded; men divorced from home, from womenfolk, had been known to hunger for other things than food, and to snatch when they could.

Tana appeared as unperturbed as though she were cooking in her own kitchen. Smiling again she held up five fingers and as earnest of this promise, fed the fire more sticks. That done, and the flames leaping wildly, she said, "Godfrey. Leave this to me, *please*. Do not come near." There would be no trouble, he thought, until after they had eaten . . . She served the meat as she always did, pushing over the tripod that composed the makeshift spit so that it fell away from the flames, and then lifting it complete, the meat being too hot to handle. With a gesture that was even pretty in its wholehearted hospitality, she laid the meat before them, and they took out their knives. Their bludgeons lay close to their sides; could he grab one while they concentrated upon the food? A bludgeon in his right hand, his knife in his left, he could hold them, long enough at least for Tana to loose a horse, mount and ride. Then it happened so swiftly that he, as well as they, were taken completely unawares. She turned back to the fire, snatched a blazing brand in either hand . . . Straight to the eyes . . . Through the howls of pain her voice carried. "Get the horses! These may have friends . . ."

In the course of a lifetime not lacking in action he had never seen a movement so swift, so callous, so effectual.

It was no distance to where the horses were tethered and as he threw over the saddles and tightened the girths he could see the men, blinded, screaming, eyebrows and beards aflame, and Tana backing away towards him, the still-blazing brands ready to strike again. At exactly the right moment—horses being terrified of fire—she flung them down and flames began to snake through the dry heather and the gorse. She got herself into the saddle in the way that she had sometimes displayed for his amusement, a cat's leap, ignoring the stirrup.

He had been suspicious, on guard, working out a plan of defence; now he suffered a bout of the inborn English disease—sympathy for the defeated enemy. When, easing from a headlong gallop, Tana said with unimaginable viciousness, "I hope they enjoy their meat—if they can find it!" he knew a pang. The men had been potential, but not declared enemies . . . and now they were blind.

And this infinitely crafty and resourceful, callous wild girl was somebody whom he must take back to England; introduce to a way of life where ladies played lutes and did embroidery, busied themselves in sweet-scented still rooms.

But—and it was a fact to be faced—she had again saved him, if not from death, from injury; for had he succeeded in snatching the bludgeon from one man, the other would have been alerted. And the result debatable.

After that they slept in inns, sharing a bed, and so they came to Seville, one of the busiest ports and, for all but people with parochial prejudices, the most beautiful city in Christendom. And in its harbour the most beautiful sight in the world—an English ship, loading oranges, not yet fully ripe, and hides, and wine. Her name was *The Mermaid,* and Sir Godfrey remembered the ancient story of the Bywater man who had caught a mermaid in his fishing net and taken her home and been unhappy ever after . . . He could hardly believe that this vessel was out of Bywater, that would be too good to be true, but so it was; here amidst all this foreign shipping, in the meaningless chatter of foreign tongues was a link not only with England, but with Suffolk; and the name Tallboys meant something. The brother of the good old Bishop, given up for dead, years ago!

In Santisteban his welcome had been warm, once Tana had explained, but it had been impersonal; he was a Christian, delivered from Moorish captivity; this was different, a great welcome, but tinged with respect for his rank. And the news, when he could bring himself to ask the most vital question, was overwhelming.

"Lady Tallboys, God love you, Sir Godfrey, alive and well, and at Intake. Or so it was when I last heard."

All the colour and noise of the harbour, the sunlight flaked and dancing on the river water went into blackness. He, Godfrey Tallboys, proven knight, was about to faint like a green girl! From a great distance his voice, but not his voice, said:

224

"When?"

"Three months since. July. We made landfalls at Amsterdam and Lisbon." The captain of *The Mermaid,* Captain Fletcher, himself a family man, obliged by his calling to absent himself from home for long periods, but never, naturally, anything like six years, did not wait for the next question but volunteered the answer. "I know, sir, because my old grandmother sells fish. Intake is on her round. I've heard her say more than once that Lady Tallboys was a good customer—and pleasant with it . . . Sir, may I fill your cup?"

NINETEEN

A GOOD CUSTOMER—and pleasant with it—Sybilla went to the door, for Madge could not hear the loudest knock, and said to the old fishwife, "I am glad to see you." True enough. Tom Robinson did not sleep in the house because he was expected to go home and do his share in the work of keeping his bed-ridden grandfather comfortable and fairly clean, but he ate his midday meal in the kitchen with Madge. Henry ate in the hall, often impatiently. They were both boys doing the work of full-grown men; John had the hearty appetite of a healthy growing boy, even old Madge enjoyed her food, so a visit from the fishwife was welcome.

"I hope I see you in good health," Sybilla added. The old woman prided herself upon being so active at the age of— she guessed—well over seventy. However, on this sultry September morning she did not respond as usual, saying that she was as hale and hearty as ever she was, due to a fish diet and life in the open: instead she said sadly, "I don't know, my lady. I'm beginning to feel my years."

"It may be the weather—so hot for the time of year." She gave her order, and Madge came forward with a dish while Sybilla went upstairs to fetch the money.

All that year the weather had been so unseasonable that pessimistic people had talked about the world coming to an end; in early spring, when rain was needed, not a drop had fallen for two months; April and May had been very wet, and in late June the hay had been cut and gathered between thunderstorms of great violence, some accompanied by hail. July and much of August had been cold and sunless, so that corn was still green when harvest should have begun. Then, halfway through August, intensely hot weather had set in and continued. Everywhere the harvesting which should have been almost finished was in full swing.

"If you'll pluck me some rosemary and a bit of thyme, my lady, I'll stuff the fresh fish. And if the plums are ready I could make a bag pudding. That should stick to their ribs," Madge said.

Sybilla went into the garden, accompanied by Margaret whom Henry, backed by John, refused absolutely to have in the corn field; "She's more trouble than help," he said. In the garden she was equally useless, didn't know rosemary from lavender, a rose from a marigold, went into one of her rigid fits at the sight of a wasp. She did not even, poor child, offer company; to be with her was to be virtually alone.

So many of the things which now flourished had come from Cressacre that it was impossible not to remember Lady Randall, who had ceased all friendly overtures when Sybilla refused to allow John to be adopted. Walter haunted the garden, too—he had planted the roses. And Godfrey had died without ever knowing that she had her own garden . . .

Think quickly of other things! Attend to what you are doing!

She cut the rosemary, gathered the thyme and the plums; assured Margaret for the hundredth time that wasps were not dangerous. Margaret had never been stung so far as Sybilla knew, it was the sight of the insect that upset her. On the way back into the house she tested the lavender; it, like the corn, had ripened during these last sunny days and was ready to be gathered.

In the kitchen Madge had gutted the fresh herrings and begun to get together what she needed for the bag pudding— so-called because it was boiled in a cloth.

She was, Sybilla reflected, very fortunate in having Madge, so willing and co-operative. They exchanged smiles as Sybilla laid the herbs and the fruit on the table.

Outside again, cutting the lavender and noting that the roses which in June had never produced a proper flower, the sodden buds rotted before they could open, were now coming into full flower, she thought again about potpourri, as she had thought every summer since she wrote to Lady Randall that next year she hoped to make her own. This year? It was a pity she thought that sweet lavender, scented roses, bright, aromatic marigolds should—by way of potpourri—lead to sordid thoughts about money. But there it was, in order to make proper, long-lasting potpourri one needed not only things one could grow but others which must be bought, and were costly.

Despite the fact that Henry and Tom had managed unbelievably well, Knight's Acre was still, though self-supporting in most respects, very poor. Money, or so it seemed, lost value every day.

Once, realising how her Intake rents had become ludicrous, she had mentioned to James the desirability of raising them a little. He had listened with apparent sympathy and promised to consult again the document to which he had referred when she asked about deer-shooting. The answer was displeasing; the rents had been fixed, "in perpetuity." No such clause governed what he had inherited; he had raised the rent of all his free tenants, and inaugurated a vigorous campaign to encourage his serfs to buy themselves free. He said he was sorry, but there it was, "in perpetuity" meant what it said. He did not offer financial aid to his brother's widow who, had she had a grain of sense, would now have been comfortably installed at Cressacre. And the sight of Henry did nothing to endear the Knight's Acre family to the father of a boy whose weakness of mind and body seemed to increase with his age. Irrevocable as the gout. Gout encroached: one day, Sir James knew, it would reach his heart, and he would die, and leave Moyidan in his son's incapable hands . . .

We all have our own troubles!

On this unusually warm September day, having gathered the lavender, Sybilla went through to the kitchen where nothing had been done. The silvery herring lay there, gutted but unstuffed; the plums, the suet, the flour, the cloth for the bag pudding, unrelated entities on the table and the fire almost out. Madge sat, her arms on the table, and her head on her arms.

Dead? Everyone must die, and like the woman who sold fish, Madge was old, but unsure of her age. Sybilla approached tentatively and gently touched Madge on the shoulder. Perhaps asleep.

Madge said, "I feel ill all over." She raised her head a little and then let it sag again.

The terrible thing was that with a woman so deaf one could not expect an answer to a question: In what way do you feel ill? Nor apply a word of consolation: You will feel better soon. At Lamarsh bed rest was esteemed a palliative for most things, but to get Madge upstairs, without help, without Madge's co-operation, would be impossible. Sybilla touched her again and Madge responded by raising her head, but a gesture towards the upper floor, the offer of a supporting arm brought nothing but a moan and a violent shudder.

Fever? Yes. Oh, pray God, not the sweating sickness, so dangerously contagious, so often fatal.

Margaret stood staring and Sybilla thought: Oh, for a daughter who could help, could be trusted to fetch a blanket and a pillow! Margaret would go willingly enough but she would have forgotten the errand before it was completed. Sybilla herself brought a pillow and a blanket and lowered Madge to the floor.

The midday dinner hour was close at hand and the boys would be coming in hungry. Give them the bread and bacon which they would have had had the fish woman not called? But in this weather the fish, called fresh to distinguish it from the smoked kind, would stink by evening; it was always at least three days old by the time it reached Intake. So mend the fire, stuff and cook the herrings, and at the same time heat two bricks, one for Madge's feet, one for the small of her back.

When she heard them in the yard she called through the open door; "Stay outside. Madge is ailing . . ." She handed the food out to them, as though to beggars. Eating out-of-doors in such weather was no hardship and not knowing about the bag pudding they did not miss it, they ate the plums raw and hurried back to the field. Now, given time, she could think about febrifuges, marigold buds, lime leaves, marjoram—all steeped in hot water.

Madge, still hot to the touch but shivering still, was a good patient. She drank what she was given and, halfway through the hot afternoon, said that she felt better. "I'll get to my bed," she said. "Johnny is waiting for me. We promised to wait." It was fever talk, Sybilla knew, but even delirium was a step forward from inertia, and Madge, clutching at the stair rail, at the wall on the other side, heaved herself towards her own bed. And lay down, with a sigh almost of contentment. "It'll all come right in the end," she said.

Since no word of cheer or comfort could penetrate, Sybilla touched the hot dry hand, which turned under hers and clutched with sudden strength. Apparently the lime infusion was working, for when Madge spoke after a long silence, what she said was sensible. "I'm being a sore bother to you, my lady." Sybilla gave the hand some reassuring pats and presently the old woman seemed to fall asleep. Standing back from the bed, Sybilla thought: Not the way sufferers from the sweating sickness behaved; they tossed and raved wildly, sweated profusely and were insatiable in their demands for water. Just a touch of summer fever.

Downstairs, tidying the kitchen and making an onion and bacon dumpling for supper, Sybilla remembered that at Lamarsh the first thing patients were offered after any fever was chicken broth, the liquid in which a fowl had been boiled so gently that the pot hardly bubbled. She'd get Tom to kill a fowl for her before he went home. But this evening he did not, as he usually did, come into the yard, hopeful for a handful of something to munch as he made his way across the common to the village.

"He went straight home," Henry said in answer to her question.

"Oh dear, I wanted him to kill a chicken."

"I can kill a chicken," Henry said confidently. He then reflected for a moment and said, "There's a knack to wringing a fowl's neck. I never learned it . . . I think I'd better cut its head off. Which one, Mother?"

"It can wait till morning, darling," she said and went up to administer another dose to Madge, should she be awake.

In such a short time, a change for the worse: Madge was breathing as though through some thick, gluey substance, each breath a battle. "Please . . . the priest. Dying . . ."

230

Supper must wait. Sybilla ran down, out by the front door and into the long-shadowed evening.

"He ain't here, my lady," Father Ambrose's housekeeper said, surliness thinly veneered by civility. The lady had been a great disappointment. While the big house was a-building the priest had confided to his housekeeper his hopes about the improvement which the arrival of a better kind of parishioner would bring. And a few flowers was all. Father Ambrose understood Sybilla's position, his housekeeper did not and attributed all the lady's failings to sheer bad management. She couldn't even rule her own household. Look what had happened to Bessie Wade! And that Walter, for whom the lady had stuck up so stoutly, running off like a thief in the night.

"Where is he?"

"He was sent for. Down in the village. Ah, they know where to come when there's trouble. Most times he ain't welcome. And horses' work to get them to church, 'cept Chrismuss and Easter. Give they will not!" (And that goes for you, too!) "And him so pious with the money the good lady left. Better a leak in my roof than in God's, he says. And his very bed swamped every . . ."

"*Where* in the village?"

"Martin's. Leastway it was one of them redheaded lot . . ."

She had lost her audience. Sybilla was running towards the Common.

She saw the old priest shuffling towards her, carrying his little lidded basket. When she was near enough, she saw that he was crying, slow gummy tears oozing and dispersing themselves in the many furrows of his face. From the lid of his basket a fold of his stole protruded. He had been to one deathbed and now she must call him to another.

As soon as he saw and recognised her he stopped and held up one hand. "Do not come close, my lady. I am straight from a deathbed. Plague!"

For all its familiarity, a heart-stopping word.

"You are sure?"

With uncharacteristic testiness he said, "Of course I am sure. I've lived through it twice—both kinds. And this is the worst. I asked you . . ."

231

"I'm safe enough. I also have lived through it, Father."

It was so long ago, when she was so young, that she had no real memory of it; only of the nuns saying jokingly, "You'll die of old age; even the plague couldn't kill you." And everyone knew that you couldn't have the plague twice.

Falling into step beside him she said, "My old Madge is asking for you . . ."

"What ails her?"

"A sudden fever. And her breathing . . ."

"That is the worst." He wiped his face on his sleeve and quickened his step a little. "With the other kind . . . carefully nursed . . . once the buboes break, there is hope. But this is deadly."

Attempting to fend off what she did not wish to believe, Sybilla said, "But she was quite well this morning."

"Robin Martin was scything his corn." Thus reminded of the swiftness of this enemy, he broke into a shambling trot. But Madge was dead before they reached her bedside.

Father Ambrose shed a few more of the difficult tears of old age. Sybilla stood dry-eyed, the knot which tears might have melted hard and painful in her throat. The dead woman, he said, in an attempt to comfort himself as well as Sybilla, had been a faithful Christian, a regular attendant at Mass; only last Sunday . . . But in a way that made it all the greater pity that the last rites, the formal phrase that sped the Christian soul on its journey should have been denied her, while Robin Martin . . .

However, such matters were best left to God. Man must deal with what he could deal with.

"In such times," he said, "burial is a problem. I know from the past. Anybody can dig a grave, it is the handling. A man needs to be very drunk . . ." That was the terrible thing about plague; only the most devoted family—or the most devoutly religious—would nurse the stricken, only reeling drunkards carry them to their graves.

"I am sorry," Sybilla said, "I have nothing . . ." The last of the Cressacre wine, the last of Walter's ale, had been drunk long ago.

"I can manage that," Father Ambrose said firmly. "I shall

232

use the sacramental wine. It is but wine, until the moment of consecration."

He hurried off to fix the red-painted wands at the village entry, a warning that this was an afflicted place.

Eating heartily of the dumpling, Henry said, "I thought it was just an expression—running about like a hen with its head off. But it did."

"Halfway round the yard," John said. "Very comical."

Margaret laughed because the boys laughed. The candlelight shone on their faces, young, lustrous-eyed, healthy looking. The thought of the peril looming over them moved her to an unusual display of emotion: "My darlings," she said and embraced them all. Henry shrugged free and went into the yard, disapproving, she thought, of being treated like a child.

When he had been gone long enough for any natural purpose she went to the kitchen door, ravaged by fear. Robin Martin had been scything his corn! She was about to call when she heard Henry retching. He knelt, bowed over, supporting himself by the lower rail of the pigpen. He said, "Go away!" but she went and knelt beside him, her left hand supporting his forehead—no fever yet!—her right arm steadying his heaving body. Spasm after spasm. Could it start this way?

Finally it was over and he leant against her for a moment, exhausted, grateful for support. Then he braced himself, stood up, essayed a shaky joke. "I bolted my supper and it wasn't hasty pudding!"

"How do you feel?"

"Empty. I shall be hungry in a minute."

Inside the lighted kitchen she examined him covertly; slightly pale, slightly watery eyed. Not flushed. Could it be that beheading the fowl had been more of a strain than he would admit? John looked up from the simple game which he was—a concession now—playing with Margaret, boring because he invariably won, and asked:

"What happened to you?"

"I threw up, if you must know. Mother, I am hungry now."

She made him a bowl of bread and milk, salted, not

sweetened, the way he preferred. Immediately John was hungry, too, and Margaret. She made more bread and milk.

"Two suppers," John said gloatingly. "I wish you'd throw up every evening, Henry."

In their extremely dull lives supper in the kitchen, after the excitement of seeing a cockerel, headless, run about the yard, and then an extra meal, made an occasion. They went noisily to bed and Sybilla did not hush them, as she should perhaps have done, with a dead woman in the house.

She kept a candle burning and hardly slept at all, prowling about as though vigilance could protect. She thought about Madge's burial. On his way out Father Ambrose had said that in time of plague there was no time for coffins; the dead must be buried quickly: "And after all, Our Lord had only a shroud."

She had a blue dress, her best, once carefully kept for occasions, then even more carefully kept against Godfrey's return. Useless now. Madge, who had lived in homespun, should go to her last bed wrapped in silk.

In the morning they were all still well and lively, thank God.

Too youngish men whom she did not recognise, not direct tenants, both happily drunk, took Madge away and laid her in the ground not beside Johnny, whoever he was, but by Robin Martin, a real sinner, reclaimed at the last.

With the corpse removed, Sybilla went through the house with the purifying shovel, heads of lavender smouldering on a few hot embers, scooped from the kitchen hearth. It was not a guaranteed guard but it was a ritual.

Father Ambrose said, "Three days, my lady, and no fresh case. It is early for hope, this thing obeys no rules—except that it is always *carried*. In this case by the herring-seller, God rest her."

"How do you know?"

"Because when I went out to plant the wands at the village boundary, she lay dead in the lane."

Sybilla thought: I made them eat in the yard because Madge lay ill in the kitchen, but what they ate was fish the

234

old woman had handled! That was too piercing a thought, so she said:

"She was old; she told me that morning that she was feeling her years. And if she carried it, why only to two households? She visited others."

"It strikes where it will," he said. The crisis appeared to have cleared his mind and concentrated it upon the present; now it clouded and slid back again. "In the confusion, my lady, I have been forgetful. I forgot to ask you. Any news of Sir Godfrey?"

"He died in Spain, Father."

"I am very sorry. I will say a Mass for his soul."

On the fifth day—dare one hope now?—she was kneading bread dough in the kitchen when she heard sounds from the yard and ran out to see Henry and John awkwardly supporting and moving Tom. Henry had drawn Tom's left arm around his own neck and held it there with his left hand, while his right was as far about the bigger boy's waist as it would go. John had his shoulder under Tom's right elbow.

"He fell down," Henry gasped. "Heat stroke, I thought, and we dragged him into the shade, but he got worse."

She had a thought of which she was ashamed: Oh, *why* did he come to work this morning? Then she thought: Where? Not the kitchen in which we cook and eat, nor the hall through which we have to pass. The solar. She took John's place on Tom's right hand and said to the child, "Take the cushions from the settle and put them in the solar."

Tom, groaning and moaning, was hardly prone before Henry said:

"Come on, John. There's only us now."

It was immediately evident that Tom Robinson would be less easily handled than poor Madge had been. He was younger and stronger and put up more fight against both the discomfort he was suffering and any efforts to relieve it. He seemed lucid. He wanted no brews, he said, repudiating the lime infusion; he'd seen what brews could do.

Sybilla spoke sternly: "Tom, if I am to nurse you, you *must* do what I tell you. Otherwise I shall send for your family to come and take you away."

"They wouldn't come." That might be true. He struggled weakly against the blanket that she snatched from her own bed, and against the hot brick. "I'm roasted enough. I'm on the rack."

"Just try to lie still. You will be better soon."

He threw himself about and moaned. "I'm in Hell. Satan and all his imps. With red-hot pitchforks."

The three cushions from the settle slithered about. He needed a more solid mattress.

In accordance with custom she had hauled down and burned the one on which Madge had died, with the pillow, the covers, and the old woman's scanty clothing. The one on the bed she had once shared with Godfrey and now shared with Margaret, was double size, so was the one in the boys' room. It must be Walter's . . .

Respecting his privacy, she had never entered his room during his occupancy and since his death she had avoided it. Probably Madge, industrious and conscientious, had gone in from time to time to wipe off the worst of the dust, or to air the room. It was with a definite effort of will that she now opened the door.

And it was not because the room was scattered with his belongings that he seemed still to be in possession. On the night of the fire he had lost everything except his bow, his arrows, and the clothes he was wearing. The bow, unstrung, and the arrows stood propped in a corner. The few fresh clothes with which he had provided himself hung limp from a peg. She remembered Henry saying that he did not know that Walter had a *blue* tunic—perhaps he had been wearing it for the first time when . . . This was no time for such a thought . . .

There was nothing else in the room that said—Walter! For he had never tried to make this place his own as he had that other room. Yet he still seemed to be here, a just-not-visible or palpable presence.

She moved to the bed which Madge must have stripped and made tidy. Madge's mattress—too hastily disposed of— had been easily handled. Walter's, though not much larger, was not; it was a trifle thicker and stuffed with horsehair,

236

resilient, bouncy. But she must get it down because—the thought flashed—if Tom's fever increased and affected his mind, and lent his body a spurious, brief strength, he could be dangerous; firmly tied down to this mattress . . . Where did that thought come from? or the strength which suddenly enabled her to deal with the recalcitrant thing? Almost as though stronger hands had come to her aid; and, at the stairhead, a more resourceful mind. Let it slide . . . It slid, impelled by its own weight and bounciness to the turn in the stairs which Master Hobson had regretted, but which had been unavoidable, and then a mere push landed it into the hall, a few jerks took it into the solar and Tom was installed.

In the kitchen, Margaret, unsupervised during this commotion, had pummelled the bread dough, dropped it on the floor, recovered it in pieces, slightly soiled. On the whole insensible to admonition or rebuke she seemed on this day to take Sybilla's mild, "Oh dear!" seriously, and allowed her head to droop sideways. Contrition?

Later, at table. Sybilla said, "Margaret, sit up and eat your dinner."

"Margaret's neck hurts."

John said, "So do my legs . . ."

So the nightmare began.

The one glimmer of hope, the old priest's words about good nursing; the one miracle that Henry, dearest of all, was not stricken. "I think," he said, "that maybe being sick saved me." And who could argue with that, the whole thing so mysterious, taking such varying forms. Tom Robinson in the solar raving about devils and poisonous brews and toads, which he abhorred, crawling over his bed; upstairs, Margaret wailing, tracking every pain, her head, her neck, her arms, legs, teeth all hurt. John did not complain or demand attention, but his torpor was frightening and he was the first to have the difficulty in breathing, once so much so that Sybilla resorted to an action which she had seen performed on a man who had fallen into the moat at Beauclaire and taken out, seemingly dead. She worked John's skinny little rib cage between her hands, press, release, press . . .

Henry said, "It would be easier for us if they were all up *or*

237

down. I doubt if I could carry Tom up. The others I can bring down." He carried John down, and then the bed, fetched Margaret, and her bed.

"Now we," he said, "can take turns at sleeping on the settle."

"That I cannot allow, Henry. Not while you work as you do."

For doggedly, singlehanded, he was proceeding with his harvesting. "I'm sorry, Mother, not to help you more, but somebody must get the corn in."

He forbade her to cook. "Bread and cheese will do for me."

He was there, fortunately, when Tom, having suffered all the torments that the Devil could inflict, refused to be strangled by him, and with fever strength threw himself about the solar, howling, trying to dislodge the enemy by dashing him against the wall. Henry hit him, knocked him down and hauled him back on to the mattress. He had rejected Sybilla's idea of tying Tom down to the bed. "It would just make him more difficult to deal with. I'll tie his feet and his hands together."

The timeless time went on. Father Ambrose called once to tell her that every household in the village was stricken; "And those who are not are sitting about, waiting . . . Nobody works, my lady. I have often thought that for one the plague kills, fear kills four." He was justified in this harsh judgement, for unlike Sybilla he had never suffered the plague, he had merely outlived two outbreaks and now, with less certainty of immunity than she could claim, went fearlessly about, not only administering to the dying but tending the sick. In a village which barely tolerated him. After that one visit to Knight's Acre he came no more. The sick there were in good hands.

She had in reserve a small quantity of a dark, viscid liquid, a specific for toothache. A few drops, slow-dripping as Father Ambrose's tears, ensured, even for a sufferer from toothache, release from pain and then sleep.

In the short interval that Henry allowed himself from the field at midday—not to eat, one could eat bread and cheese anywhere, but to see that in the house things had not got beyond his mother's control—he saw her measuring drops.

"It seems to ease Tom's delusions. It certainly eases Margaret's pains."

"Couldn't they *all* have a dose? Tonight? So that you and I could sleep?"

There was no real reason why he should not sleep, but despite her determination to be in charge on the ground floor, resting her bones on the settle, Henry always seemed to know, to hear when Tom yelled, or Margaret said, "Mother," or when she rose to make certain that in the night John was still breathing.

She said, "I have so little of it. It must be kept for pain, or waking nightmares."

"I see," Henry said.

He went out, she thought to the field.

Momentarily relieved from delusions and from pain, Tom and Margaret seemed to sleep. Sybilla worked on John, again in difficulty with breathing; press, release, press again. He gave a cough and ejected some sticky, grey and yellow-streaked, blood-streaked matter.

"I can breathe now," John said, and turned on his side and slept.

Despite all her care the pest-house stench had crept about. It followed her into the kitchen and mingled unpleasantly with the sweet smell of baking bread.

She went to the kitchen door for a breath of fresh air and felt the unseasonal heat of the afternoon. She was so weary that she felt ill. She realised now the price that must be paid for independence and pride. In bigger households people fared better at such times; there would be someone not yet stricken, someone who shared Father Ambrose's immunity, somebody like herself who had survived. Isolated here she was fighting almost singlehanded against death, and at the same time doing ordinary, essential things like cooking, since Henry must be fed.

Lack of proper sleep, constant anxiety, had reduced her to something near self-pity; though she knew she had only herself to blame for her plight. And she must not stand here wasting time; she must go and hunt for eggs if Henry were to have the supper she planned for him.

Days were drawing in now, and Henry always left the field in order to milk the cow while the light lasted. This evening he was late—then very late. She remembered how Tom had fallen down in the stubble and had to be helped indoors. In panic she ran out, across the yard, through the space between the stable and the burned-out house and across the rough track which served as a side entrance. It was bounded on its farther side by a bank, from the top of which she had a view of the field. Nothing moved in the dusky light. The stooks of cut corn, each made of four sheaves, stood on end and leaning slightly towards one another, stood in even rows like small tents. The cut stubble lay in even rows, alternating, like velvet stroked this way and that. The still uncut wheat stood straight and tall, stretching away in this half light, to an immeasurable distance. Henry could have fallen at its verge, his scythe beside him; or, feeling unwell, sat down against a stook . . .

The final blow! She moved to descend the bank on the field side; she must find Henry, bring him in; but her legs failed her, wilted like candles in an overheated room and she fell, not into the field, but back, onto the track.

"Christ in Glory!" Henry said, "I could have killed you . . . Are you hurt?" The grey horse stood puffing and blowing within inches of where she lay.

"No. Not hurt. I stumbled . . . Looking for you . . ." She took his outstretched hands and pulled herself up. "No, not hurt," she said, though pain stabbed at her hip. "Where have you been?"

"Moyidan. For what we needed. It took so long because . . . Let's get in. I'll tell you all about it." She tried not to hobble, thankful for his proffered arm.

The cow lowed plaintively.

"I'll just milk her," Henry said. "Could you take these? There'll be no need to cook for days . . ."

The grey horse was saddled with a sack, wore only a halter, but carried, slung over the sack, two well-stuffed bags.

"They've barricaded themselves in," Henry said. "With guards. I had to shout, who I was and what I wanted. And the barrier is at least a mile from the house . . . Two gates, about four yards apart, and the space between filled in with brambles and branches. All this"—he indicated what he had brought

240

—"was handed out to me at the end of a long pole." He laughed.

Emma had always been a good housekeeper and now for once she had been generous, mindful of the needs of the healthy as well as of the sick. She had sent a huge flask of the brown, poppy medicine, which was all Henry had asked her for, and another flask, labelled "For cooling fever," as well as a cheese, a brawn, a joint of spiced beef and a game pie. And a pomander ball, an orange stuck all over with cloves and dried as hard as iron.

"Now," Henry said, eating voraciously, "they can all have a dose. And we can sleep. I'll tell you another thing, too . . . Maybe at Moyidan they're harvesting, I couldn't get near enough to see. But down there . . ." he jerked his head towards the village, "and all along the road I didn't see one single man at work."

It confirmed something that Father Ambrose had said: "At such times people simply sit about, waiting for death. I have often thought that for one killed by pestilence, four die of fear."

"It looks to me," Henry said, "as though corn will be scarce and dear this winter. And we shall have some to sell."

Perhaps Emma's medicine for cooling fever contained some powerful ingredient; or perhaps the plague, like other ailments, mounted to a crisis and then receded. For whatever reason, gradually but surely all three invalids began to improve.

TWENTY

"YOU WISH TO BE rid of me," Tana said.

"I want you to be happy."

"Without you?"

He said miserably, "My dear, wherever you are, it must be without me."

He thought that parting would hurt them both, but his wound would cut deeper and be slower to heal because he was older and bore a burden of guilt, but that was the kind of thought which he could never put into words.

"And all behind my back," she said. "You trade me away like an old horse."

No statement could have been more unjust. He had been most meticulous.

In the house of the Dominicans, to an English-speaking friar who remembered Father Andreas, painstakingly explaining and asking help; in the mansion of the rich merchant, a second generation Converso Moor with two lively daughters, one about Tana's age, one a year younger, and a mother who spoke Arabic. "Absolutely to be trusted," the friar had explained; "he is a good Christian. Too rich to be interested in whatever wealth the young woman may have; and, like all Conversos, much in awe of the Church. If *we* commit her to his care, she will be safe."

The idea of making some such arrangement had occurred to Sir Godfrey when, elated by news from home, slightly flown with wine, he had left *The Mermaid* and stepped back into the polyglot streets. He heard Arabic being spoken by unveiled women, caught glimpses of inner courtyards of Moorish-style houses, felt the warm sun of the autumn day. *If* Tana could be persuaded, *if* proper safeguards could be found, would she not be happier here than in England where he would be the only person who understood a word she said, and where he would have his family. So he had turned to the Dominicans and found just the aid he sought.

He was aware that he was not being honest, either with himself or anybody else; he had given Tana her due—the girl who had liberated him—but he had not said that she had been his mistress, and before that a member of the royal harem; he had not explained by what savage means she had gained the position of first favourite, or that her wealth was the result of robbery. He had allowed it to be assumed that she was a Moor. He had shied away from the truth which Tana now put into words: "You wish to be rid of me."

He did so wish. He had in the past months foreseen a difficult situation, but only vaguely; now, with the news that Sybilla was still his legal wife, still at Knight's Acre, his mental sight cleared. If Tana would only understand and consent, his happiness would be unclouded—and yet . . .

Even as he blundered on, and saw on her face the expression of scorn which it so readily assumed, he was bound to admire her anew; for what other woman in the world would not have rounded on him, accused him of ingratitude, said, "After all I have done for you . . ." She was too proud for that.

He had wanted to be near the shipping area, and on arrival in Seville had sought accommodation there, though inns in that district were not of the best. "So long as there is a bed to lie upon, and some hot water so that I can wash my hair, I ask no more," Tana had said. And she had not protested when he had indicated that two sleeping chambers were required. Asked for how long, he made a helpless gesture, not understanding; but here foreigners were no rarity and attracted small attention. He had then gone straight out to look for an English ship and had found *The Mermaid,* conceived his idea and spent the afternoon in putting it into effect. Tana meanwhile had washed her hair, her first act after a gypsyish period; she had washed it in Santisteban after their sojourn in the mountains, she had washed

243

it in Seville, after their long ride. And now, dead straight, black as night, shining and silky, it hung about her as she listened, rejected and accused.

The room which she had been assigned faced the river and had a little balcony, no great advantage now with the dockside so busy; it was a soiled river which now, at its lowest, just before the winter rains, ran just below the outjutting stone ledge with its crumbling rail. In the time that it took him to explain that far from trading her away, he had made most careful arrangements, refuse from ships and from houses, including a broom and the grossly inflated body of a dead dog, drifted past.

Tana said, "And this is what you wish?"

"What I think might be best."

Swift and sudden as her action against the putative robbers, she flung herself over the rail and into the sullied water.

Swift and sudden as anything he had ever done in his life, he followed and the Great River engulfed them both.

In Andara he had taught himself to swim, ineptly, but well enough to keep himself afloat. The body, like the mind, had a memory and he swam now. He snatched at the nearest thing which said, "Tana," a great hank of floating hair; he made some clumsy strokes, only his legs—booted and heavy—and one arm operative, and by great good luck managed to snatch at a pole, solidly planted at the foot of some steps for the convenience of a boat delivering goods. He clutched at it, heaved himself and his dripping burden out of the sullied water and sprawled for a moment, physically and emotionally exhausted.

Tana said, "So you do love me . . ."

With that she became content and amenable. Aboard *The Mermaid* she made no demands, no complaints. In fact, with that last violent, would-be self-destructive gesture, she seemed to have turned in upon herself, to have become resigned. Sad, in a way, like a wild creature caged. But she now understood; this bucking rearing ship was part of England, where he belonged; its captain and most of its crew were from Bywater, where his brother was part of the Church which she hated and feared; the most discreet behaviour was called for.

244

Bywater, its roofs and trees just rimed by a light night frost, loomed up out of the sea. Presently, amidst all the shouting and manoeuvring needed to bring *The Mermaid* alongside the jetty, her captain found time to speak to his distinguished passenger. "Here we are, sir, and I can just imagine how you're feeling."

Sir Godfrey had no idea of how he felt. People spoke, he thought, too lightly about the movements of their hearts, saying over trivial things that their hearts rose, or sank. His seemed to be doing both in such rapid succession that rise and fall were simultaneous. This was not the homecoming he had envisaged.

It was not the homecoming any of them had envisaged. Captain Fletcher had imagined himself at the Welcome to Mariners, the centre of awed attention, the man who had brought Sir Godfrey Tallboys back to England; the crew would also share this glory, see their families, present the gifts expected of returned sailors, make love to or quarrel with their wives, get married, see a child for the first time.

The harbour master and the customs official—wines being dutiable—came aboard and one of them said, "Well, you missed the plague!" The word spread as rapidly as the thing it stood for. It shattered all homecoming dreams.

Sir Godfrey had intended to go straight to the inn, hire two horses and ride to Intake. Now he must see William, because William would know . . . Sybilla, alive and well in July. How now? He had one terrible thought: A judgement on me! He could not speak. He could only seize Tana by the wrist and charge up the slight rise which only in flat East Anglia would be called a hill, at the top of which the Bishop's residence stood.

She seemed to move reluctantly, dragging him back, she who had always gone ahead, so lithe and nimble. Suspicious, poor girl, because she did not understand. He forced himself to master his breath, his tongue. "My brother . . ." he gasped, and pointed. "Bad news!"

He should have been warned. William had no use for formality, he had always been accessible to anyone. Now the outer door was barred and Sir Godfrey, trembling with impatience,

245

had to tug the bell twice, three times before it opened, narrowly, cautiously.

"The Bishop . . . I must see him. I'm his brother."

"His Grace is not yet in residence."

But William had always been there. The good shepherd tending his flock. He ignored conferences and convocations . . . And now, through the narrow space of the guarded doorway, Sir Godfrey could see what had been William's hall, with rich dark hangings on the walls, the glitter of silver on cupboard and table.

William was dead! How many others?

"Go and fetch somebody who was here—before. Chaplain, groom, secretary. Move yourself, man."

It was the recognisable voice of authority though used by a shabby fellow.

William had never maintained an adequate entourage, and dying suddenly had left his affairs in a muddle, made worse by the fact that there had been other deaths; but one man seemed to have survived both the plague and the new Bishop's ruthless clean sweep; he had been retained because he had a good memory, knew where to find anything which was there to be found, and wrote a good clear hand. He was brought, blinking to the door. He stared, with disbelief and then with recognition.

"Sir Godfrey! Wh . . . wh . . ."

"Never mind that. Do you know anything—recent—about my wife?"

There had been weeks of complete confusion, of genuine grief for a good old master, of trepidation, wondering about his own job, of being asked to find this, refer to that, of trying to accommodate himself to the new and very different régime; but the good memory served. He produced the required information as a well-trained dog would offer a retrieved thing.

"Lady Tallboys and her children suffered from the plague, Sir Godfrey—but they all survived."

He said, "Thank God!" and broke into such a sweat as might have marked the end of a fever, or the onset of the sweating sickness.

"How do you know?"

"Lady Tallboys wrote a letter . . . It arrived . . . It was too late."

246

Sybilla had written; pride, independence, joy in her own house all brought low by the commonsense which informed her that to manage was impossible.

Doggedly, growing haggard and old, Henry had proceeded with cutting and carrying the corn. But who would thresh it? Tom Robinson had survived, but as a shaky, feeble wreck of himself. He tried, pathetically grateful for the nursing he had been given, but he fainted the first time he ventured into the field and Henry had shown a disquieting callousness. "Let him potter about the yard, Mother. I have enough to do without swoons."

Father Ambrose, so valiant, not only doing his duty by the dying and the dead but caring for the very old and the sick, had undertaken to tell her that nobody, nobody in Intake, could pay rent for at least a year; the village was ruined, most of the breadwinners dead or so weakened as to be useless.

"I have always tried," he said mournfully, "to use what the lady willed for God's use, for the purpose she intended. It is no longer possible. Rain may drip on the very altar. The living must be fed; the holdings restocked."

Restocked? All that was left now of her poultry was a wary old cock who seemed to have observed the fate that had overtaken his trusting fellows.

What added to her feeling of weak despair was her own lameness. Such a slight fall. She had limped about, tending the sick in the final hopeful stages of their illness, and then, when the voracious hunger of post-fever set in, cooking and cooking, ignoring the pain, thinking always that it must be better tomorrow. But it was not.

So she had capitulated and written to William, sending the letter by the first person who entered the village after Father Ambrose, counting days, had thought it safe to pluck out the wands. A pedlar.

Of the three refuges offered to her she had chosen Bywater because in William's house there was no woman except his bad-tempered, slovenly housekeeper, who might by gradual stages be ousted; because William was kind and had power, could get John into the monks' school at Baildon, and poor Margaret, perhaps, into some kind of religious house; the only safe future for a half-wit.

247

She made her decision and dispatched her letter without consulting Henry.

When she told him he was angry in the worst way; not hot and argumentative, as she had feared—and was prepared to deal with—but cold, polite, relentless.

"Yes," he said. "For you and the children, that might be best. But I shall stay here. In my own place."

"Darling, that is impossible . . . One of my reasons . . . I can no longer stand by and watch you work yourself to death."

He ignored that. "What would you do with the house? The fields?"

"We might," she said, careful to include him, "find a buyer."

"Now? With land going back to the waste wherever you look? And is it yours to sell?"

A little flurried, she said, "Why yes. Yes, of course. Your father being dead . . ."

"I am my father's heir, Mother. If he had left an estate of more value, it would have been taken into custody, to be kept for me until I was of age. I should have been somebody's ward."

Over a few of the words, estate, custody, ward, he hesitated slightly, unfamiliar words, learned by rote.

"If my father had left three hundred fields, that would have been the law."

Walter! Walter, who knew a great deal about many things and a little about most, had implanted this unlikely piece of information, these strange words into Henry's mind as soon as Godfrey was deemed to be dead.

"Apart from which," Henry said, "the land is mine because I have toiled and sweated. I helped to *make* this farm. And nobody is going to take it away from me."

"Darling, nobody wishes to. Henry, one must be sensible. It will be a year before Tom is useful—if he ever is. You cannot manage what it once . . . once took three of you to do. And when I spoke of selling I had no intention of defrauding you. I thought . . . Some kind of businesss, in Bywater . . ." Brooding over the letter, chewing the quill, she had realised that Henry was too old now for schooling, too old to be left idle. "Timber," she said diffidently, "or wine." Both very respectable trades.

248

"Or a well-fitted pedlar's pack!"

She was sharply reminded of the Abbess of Lamarsh, so skilled in the dealing of verbal wounds—and Henry's aunt, after all.

"It must be faced," she said. "I have tried to do the best for us all. It is not as though I can help much, now. So lame . . . And I look at all the corn you have hauled in. Who'll thresh it, winnow it, sack it up?"

"I shall. It will take time, but time is on our side now. The later to market the better, this year. You go to Bywater, Mother, and rest and live like a lady. I stay here." He gave a little snort of unmirthful laughter. "Before you go, show Tom how to bake a loaf. It's about all he's good for now. But I can manage."

She could just imagine how they would live. Who'd wash and mend for them, change bed linen, have a hot nourishing meal ready?

"You haven't really considered it."

"I could consider till my beard grew down to my knees, and still think the same."

"Very well, since you are so set. I will write again. Try again."

The old boyish grin brightened his face.

"That's more like my mother!" He lifted one of her work-roughened hands and kissed it. "You shan't regret it. I don't intend to be poor all my life."

"Yes, Lady Tallboys wrote," the little clerk said. "His Grace had expired on the previous day. I took it upon myself, since there was no one else to do so, to send her the sad news."

"I see. Thank you." Sir Godfrey had been fond of his brother, was sorry that he was dead, but at the moment the good news outweighed the bad and he had a practical thought. Whatever else William had spared upon, he had kept good horses.

The horses, willingly, even eagerly provided once the clerk's recognition had established his identity, were good, but Tana who on an inferior animal had ridden like the wind, now rode

249

like an old market woman carrying eggs. Plainly she was unwilling to arrive.

"There is nothing to fear," he said, forced for the tenth time to rein in and wait for her to catch up. "If we hold to our bargain . . ." A bargain made on a rotting balcony overlooking the Guadalquivir, by two people emotionally exhausted, prepared to settle on almost any terms. She should stay with him, have his protection, his brotherly love, his companionship in an alien land; she was to forget, make no claim, do, say nothing that would cause Sybilla a moment's unease. The unusual thing about this bargain was that the terms were on both sides volunteered, not exacted. Neither of them was at that moment in a reasonable state of mind. He was shaken by the latest proof of devotion—she would sooner drown than be parted from him; she was so elated by the fact that he had not, in fact, wished to be rid of her—as he could so easily have been, simply by doing nothing—that they were both prepared to build, upon an illicit love, some plan for the future. A post that happened to be handy had saved them both from death; they were enjoying what was almost a sense of resurrection.

The brief winter day was just ending when they reached Intake. "That is my house," Sir Godfrey said. Knight's Acre presented to Tana the same bleak, unlighted face as it had turned to Sybilla. Sybilla had thought it large, Tana found it disappointingly small. She had never lived in an ordinary house; her father's strong mountain fortress, tents, or, sometimes, on the extreme borders of his domain, grass-roofed huts; the quarry, and then the palace at Zagelah; after that sometimes no roof but the sky, and then inns.

Passing the turn-off to Moyidan, Sir Godfrey, without slackening pace, had turned his head and said, "That is where my other brother lives. Where I was born." And the old castle, reared long ago by a man who, if he could have written his name, would have spelt it Taillebois, just showed above the trees. Tana also understood, from the behaviour of everyone who understood English, Captain Fletcher and the crew of the ship, the people in the rich-seeming place at the top of the hill, that Godfrey, in his own country, was a kind of chieftain. So

250

the plain stolid house that Master Hobson had built and his son-in-law had plastered and decorated did not strike her as impressive; a house unworthy of him; and too small to contain two women.

Lady Randall's rose trees, grown to good height, still held a few frost-pinched leaves on their branches. He was glad momentarily that Sybilla had attained some kind of garden. He said, "This way," and took the track to the yard. It had changed somewhat during his absence, more outbuildings, Walter's house gone. But the well was there, and a woman was drawing water. She was bareheaded and the wind teased her white hair. With a slow, weary, old-woman's action, she unhooked the bucket and steadied it on the rim of the well with one hand while with the other she pushed back her hair with a gesture of careless impatience. She did not look towards them, the time when the sound of a hoof alerted her was long past. Any movement at the yard's entry meant that Henry and Tom and the grey horse were back from the field.

As she brushed back her hair he recognised her, but with an almost stunning incredibility. Old, bowed over, doing a serving-boy's job! His Sybilla.

He spoke her name. Then she looked, stared and gave a cry that could be heard down in the village. The bucket tilted and fell into the well as she ran towards him, arms outstretched. He had slipped from the saddle and run to meet her, lifting her, holding her, as in the old days, as in his dreams . . .

Tana, still mounted, unnoticed, sat and watched. The sun, just before plunging down behind the woods to the south of the river, sent one last gleam, cruelly revealing. The feminine eye, turned in assessment upon another woman, missed nothing, the white hair, the thin, slightly crooked body, the heavy clumped shoes that dangled from the edge of the shabby skirt, even the red coarse hands which clutched and clung.

With cold hostility, with hot jealousy, with hope, with fear, Tana watched that long embrace and listened to the broken, incoherent exchanges of endearment in a language she did not understand.

On the broken balcony in Seville he had said, "Sybilla must

251

never know." But Sybilla would presently know, without a word being spoken. The children of love always resembled their fathers.

The embrace ended. Sybilla said, "Darling, set me down. But hold me, still. I am so weak with joy."

So with one arm around his wife, Sir Godfrey—the least likely man to be in such a situation and the least competent to deal with it—reached out his hand to his mistress. He said, in Arabic, "Welcome to our home," and in English, "Darling, this is Tana who set me free. But for her I should not be here."

Somewhere along the journey Tana had discarded the rough sheepskin coat and acquired a hooded cloak of mulberry-coloured cloth. She had worn it throughout the voyage, huddling, he thought, against the cold. Now, without assistance from the offered hand, she dismounted and at the same loosed the loop at the neck of the garment, so that the hood fell back and the front gaped.

Another instant feminine assessment. Beautiful in a strange way, shining with youth, black hair as sleek as satin caught back in a pearl-studded net.

Of course! Of course!

Be sensible. No man could be expected to live like a monk for seven years. But more than sense was at work—the memory of the night when she herself had felt the brush of sheer, unthinking, physical passion. Walter, living, had always tried to make life easy for her, and now, rotting in his shallow, unhallowed grave, he made this easy.

She said, "I thank you from my heart."

"She knows no English."

An embrace then.

The face she pressed to Tana's was damp, from the mingled tears of joy, from the long kisses. Tana turned her face away. The old woman smelt like a peasant, of onions, of woodsmoke, of cooking.

Released, Tana stepped back, bowed, put her hand to the soil of an English farmyard and then to her forehead.

"A gesture of the utmost respect," Sir Godfrey explained.

Sybilla matched it. She made to Godfrey's deliverer the deep curtsey due to one's social superiors. The injured hip screamed its protest but she ignored it, and standing again, as straight as she would ever be, she said, "My love, tell her how grateful I am, how welcome she is."

The gleam faded; twilight flooded the yard as Sybilla thought: And the child—his child—shall be welcome, too.